Shakespeare and Young Adult Literature

Shakespeare and Young Adult Literature

Pairing and Teaching

Edited by
Victor Malo-Juvera
Paula Greathouse
Brooke Eisenbach

ROWMAN & LITTLEFIELD
Lanham • Boulder • New York • London

Published by Rowman & Littlefield
An imprint of The Rowman & Littlefield Publishing Group, Inc.
4501 Forbes Boulevard, Suite 200, Lanham, Maryland 20706
www.rowman.com

6 Tinworth Street, London SE11 5AL, United Kingdom

British Library Cataloguing in Publication Information Available

Library of Congress Cataloging-in-Publication Data

Names: Malo-Juvera, Victor, editor. | Greathouse, Paula, editor. |
    Eisenbach, Brooke, editor.
Title: Shakespeare and young adult literature : pairing and teaching /
    edited by Victor Malo-Juvera, Paula Greathouse, Brooke Eisenbach.
Description: Lanham : Rowman & Littlefield Publishing Group, 2021. |
    Includes bibliographical references and index. | Summary: "This is the first book that
    offers educators suggested approaches for teaching young adult literature in tandem
    with the most commonly taught works of Shakespeare"—Provided by publisher.
Identifiers: LCCN 2020047781 (print) | LCCN 2020047782 (ebook) |
    ISBN 9781475859560 (paperback) | ISBN 9781475859577 (epub)
Subjects: LCSH: Shakespeare, William, 1564-1616—Study and teaching (Secondary)
Classification: LCC PR2987 .S463 2021 (print) | LCC PR2987 (ebook) |
    DDC 822.3/3—dc23
LC record available at https://lccn.loc.gov/2020047781
LC ebook record available at https://lccn.loc.gov/2020047782

∞™ The paper used in this publication meets the minimum requirements of American National Standard for Information Sciences—Permanence of Paper for Printed Library Materials, ANSI/NISO Z39.48-1992.

Contents

Introduction

Pairing and Teaching Shakespeare with Young Adult Literature

Victor Malo-Juvera and Paula Greathouse

The works of William Shakespeare are a staple in secondary schools. In surveys of teachers in the United States, the Bard's plays have been found to be the most or among the most frequently taught texts from 1907, where *Julius Caesar* occupied the top spot (Tanner, 1907), to 2010, where *Romeo and Juliet* was the most taught—in the intervening century *Julius Caesar* had only dropped to fourth place (Stotsky, Traffas, & Woodworth, 2010). Other popular plays such as *Macbeth* and *Hamlet* have also regularly appeared on lists of the most frequently taught texts throughout the last 100 years (Hill & Malo-Juvera, 2018). Shakespeare is also a mainstay of the Advanced Placement Language and Literature test, with *King Lear* being referenced seventeen times on the test since 1971, along with many of his other plays, the next most frequently being *Othello* (ten), *The Tempest* (nine), and *The Merchant of Venice* (seven) (Albert Team, 2020). Beyond being taught ubiquitously, Shakespeare's plays are performed around the world from high school drama clubs to New York City's Shakespeare in the Park to the Globe Theater in London, as well as a myriad of cinematic adaptations. The influence of Shakespeare on American culture is unequivocal.

Compared to Shakespeare, the genre of young adult literature is still in its infancy, yet despite its youth, it has grown into a literary force majeure. Since the publishing of *The Outsiders*, which is often credited as being the seminal young adult novel (Malo-Juvera & Hill, 2019), the genre has exploded into a global economic powerhouse as young adult texts continue to grow in sales (Association of American Publishers, 2018) and have been turned into blockbuster movies, Broadway plays, and even theme parks. Beyond the commercial success, its educational value has not been overlooked; in fact, young adult novels are being taught so frequently that *The Outsiders* and *Speak* were found to be in the top ten of all titles taught in high schools (Stotsky, Traffas, & Woodworth, 2010).

Despite the many young adult titles that have found their way into classrooms, others have endured roadblocks as they are often the targets of censorship. In the 1970s, books such as *Go Ask Alice* and *A Hero Ain't Nothin But a Sandwich* were removed from school libraries by the Island Trees School Board (Campbell, 1981) and *The Chocolate War* has been subject to censorship attempts since its publication in 1974 (American Library Association, 2020). Fifty years later, young adult books are still frequent targets of censorship and many of the most popular young adult books, such as *Harry Potter, Perks of Being a Wallflower, The Absolutely True Diary of a Part Time Indian*, and *Looking for Alaska*, have been among the most challenged in schools and school libraries across the country (American Library Association, 2020).

Beyond issues of censorship, some educators feel that young adult literature is inferior in literary quality when compared to canonical texts; however, Miller and Slifkin (2010) rebutted those beliefs and argued for the inclusion of young adult literature in AP-level courses. Their position is echoed by the National Council of Teachers of English/Council for the Accreditation of Educator Preparation standards for teacher preparation who require that teacher candidates be knowledgeable with young adult literature (National Council of Teachers of English, 2018). Thus, despite the challenges that young adult literature faces, its inclusion in classrooms continues to grow.

Considering the widespread popularity of both Shakespeare and young adult literature, their pairing can offer teachers and students a wide array of instructional possibilities. Shakespeare addressed many topics that are still relevant today, such as same-sex relationships (*Twelfth Night*), interracial relationships (*Othello*), domestic abuse (*Taming of the Shrew*), suicide (*Romeo and Juliet*), adultery (*The Winter's Tale*), and alcohol abuse (*Macbeth*); however, young adult texts have addressed issues that either did not exist in seventeenth-century England or that are viewed much differently by modern society. Consider that recent titles have tackled topics such as police violence (*The Hate U Give*), immigration issues (*American Street*), and the life of teens after gender reassignment surgery (*If I Was Your Girl*). Furthermore, young adult literature provides a more diverse array of narrative voices that extend beyond the White male gaze that dominated Shakespeare's time and his works. Young adult texts have been written that detail rape from the victim's point of view (*Speak*), how children experience war (*Tree Girl*), how queer teens handle religious issues when coming out (*The God Box*) and that chronicle racial issues with protagonists from almost every cultural group such as African Americans (*Monster*), Hispanics (*Mexican White Boy*), Asian Americans (*American Born Chinese*), and Native Americans (*Absolutely*

True Diary of a Part Time Indian). There is also hope that as the publishing industry produces more diverse books, that the voices, themes, conflicts, and settings represented in young adult literature will continue to expand. Pairing Shakespeare and young adult literature can allow teachers to combine some of the best the Bard has to offer while at the same time increasing relevance and engagement for their teen readers, and in many cases, for themselves.

THE COLLECTION—PURPOSE AND ORGANIZATION

The purpose of our collection is to offer teachers engaging ideas and approaches for pairing Shakespeare's most frequently taught plays alongside young adult novels, which often provide a unique examination of a topic that teaching a single text could not afford. The pairings offered in each chapter allow for comparisons in some cases, for extensions in others, and for critique in some. Throughout this collection, authors use the term "secondary" as opposed to high school; this is intentional as although Shakespeare is often associated with that level, we have known many teachers who have used texts such as *Romeo and Juliet*, *Julius Caesar*, and *Hamlet*, among others, in both middle and junior high schools. We also refrain from specifying specific reading levels for any of the texts discussed as we have found assigning Lexile and grade levels to be restrictive without adding any benefits. We intentionally leave those types of decisions to our teacher readers who know their students best. Similarly, although the pedagogical approaches offered within chapters align with current English language arts and literacy standards, we eschewed referencing any specific ones as lists of standards can become unwieldy in texts and because teachers can easily determine how activities meet their local requirements.

Each of the chapters is organized correspondingly, with an introductory section, a summary of texts, and then instructional activities for before, during, and after reading; furthermore, each chapter has extension activities that move beyond the texts. In many cases, activities build on each other, and in other cases, they exist independently, allowing teachers to pick and choose which fits their students best. Because our collection is geared toward secondary teachers, we have organized it in the order of the most frequently taught Shakespeare texts determined by using a combination of multiple national surveys of teachers (Hill & Malo-Juvera, 2018) and appearance on AP Language and Literature tests (Albert Team, 2020).

Our collection opens with Susan Groenke's pairing of Jacqueline Woodson's *If You Come Softly* with Shakespeare's *Romeo and Juliet*. Framed as culturally relevant pedagogy that aims to reshape traditional English language arts curriculum toward student relevance and sociopolitical consciousness, her chapter examines the timeless and universal theme of forbidden love and provides opportunities for students to consider the connections that exist between prejudice, hatred, and violence. Lessons for analyzing micro-aggressive language in both texts, understanding marriage laws and customs throughout time, and writing about nonviolent solutions to conflict are provided.

Melanie Hundley and Sarah Burriss's chapter examines issues of power and authority using *Julius Caesar* and Robert Cormier's *The Chocolate War* by focusing on how language can be weaponized to manipulate others. Caesar's Rome and Trinity High School are both battlegrounds for power, where themes betrayal and belonging play out with grave consequences. Their chapter centers on how rhetorical techniques are used to manipulate and betray, on how power is derived from rhetoric, and on how portrayals of masculinity limit characters' full participation in the texts.

Revenge and suicide are examined in Joseph Haughey's paring of *Hamlet* and Matthew Quick's young adult novel *Forgive Me, Leonard Peacock*, which provides a compelling illustration of Shakespeare's text through a character who both idolizes Hamlet, quoting freely from his soliloquies, and shares many of his characteristics. The protagonists of both texts are melancholic young men bent on revenge, but both are also intellectual and philosophical, each of their stories offering insights into the other's, and by pairing their respective texts, secondary teachers can highlight how contemporary *Hamlet* remains today.

The Prince of Denmark remains center stage in our next chapter by Amy Connelly Banks and Chris Crowe, which matches *Hamlet* with Walter Dean Myers's *Monster* to examine personal identity. Their chapter suggests ways teachers can use selected poems and a short animated video, "Hair Love," as pre-reading strategies; how students can examine the use of monologues or have a discussion about justice as during-reading strategies; and how to engage students in discussions about identity formation as post-reading. It concludes with suggestions for using other texts and activities to extend student understanding of identity and identity formation.

"I might have to kill somebody tonight" begins Jen McConnel's chapter that mixes *Macbeth* with Angie Thomas's young adult novel *On the Come Up*. The words are not uttered by Macbeth in planning for regicide; they are spoken by Thomas's protagonist Brianna Jackson as she prepares to do combat in rap battles. McConnel's pairing draws on the multiple thematic connections between the texts such as ambition, claiming power without waiting for an external authority to recognize them, and a willingness to fight for personal beliefs even in the face of opposition and hostility.

The Moor of Venice attracts the focus of our next chapter, which pairs *Othello* with *All American Boys* to engage students in examining issues of alterity or otherness both in the texts and in the world around them. Authors Jennifer S. Dail and Michelle B. Goodsite share approaches for connecting specific passages of the texts with each other as well as for connecting the texts to contemporary issues in the world such as racial issues related to Black Lives Matter and systemic discrimination.

Othello is joined by serial killer Jeffrey Dahmer in Lisa Scherff's compelling pairing of *Othello* with Derf Backderf's graphic novel, *My Friend Dahmer*. Using the broad concept of the beast or monster within, Scherff provides unique opportunities for teachers and students to critically examine Othello, Iago, and Jeffrey Dahmer, in an exploration of possible antecedents to people transforming into "monsters." Her chapter also provides starting points for introducing students to the graphic novel form.

The rage of beasts climaxes in monstrosity in Laura Bolf-Beliveau's chapter "Monsters Matter: Reimagining Caliban Using Monster Theory." Bolf-Beliveau pairs *The Tempest* and Akwaeke Emezi's *Pet* to explore how monsters are an integral part of cultures because they often reflect society's fears, needs, and behaviors. Her chapter uses Jeffery Cohen's *monster theory* to provide a theoretical heuristic to better understand how these creatures inform our perspectives on literary monsters like Caliban from *The Tempest* and urban legends like Slender Man. Emezi's *Pet* helps readers see how marginalization of others leads to oppressive and dangerous realities for those who do not embody mainstream beliefs. Using engaging supplemental texts and activities, this chapter shows why monsters matter.

Pauline Skowron Schmidt and Matthew Kruger-Ross provide strategies to teach a thematic unit focused on gender identity using *A Midsummer Night's Dream* and Becky Albertalli's *Simon vs. The Homosapien Agenda*. Pre-reading strategies include introducing vocabulary terms associated with sexual and gender identity, as well as a contextualization of these issues by looking at recent U.S. Supreme Court cases. During-reading strategies include mapping characters, prompts for discussion, and guidelines for film analysis. After-reading strategies include creating infographics and generating artifacts that represent aural literacy. Extension activities include exploring gender identity at the school and community level.

Megan Lynn Isaac takes us into the dark world of secrecy and spying in her pairing of *Much Ado about Nothing* and E. Lockhart's *The Disreputable History of Frankie Landau-Banks*. Elizabethan spy networks, panoptic surveillance practices, verbal codes, and high school secret societies may seem like a diverse set of topics, but as readers consider the ways each of these structures shapes human relationships, parallels between the events of the play and the novel emerge. Students are also invited to map their own surveillance footprint, chart how characters spy on each other, and research membership policies in extracurricular groups, among other activities.

In our final chapter, "To Write or Not to Write—That's the Question," Bryan Ripley Crandall outlines National Writing Project practices by pairing young adult literature with *Hamlet, As You Like It,* and *Romeo & Juliet* to teach OpEds, scriptwriting, and poetry. His chapter places Shakespeare's works in conversation with writers such as Kwame Alexander, Jason Reynolds, and Nic Stone, and his chapter offers multiple paths to guide adolescent writers to explore and improve their writing.

REFERENCES

Albert Team. (2020, July 23). *The ultimate AP English literature reading list.* Albert. https://www.albert.io/blog/ultimate-ap-english-literature-reading-list/.

American Library Association. (2020). *Banned and challenged books.* http://www.ala.org/advocacy/bbooks.

Association of American Publishers. (2018, July 20). *Book publisher revenue estimated at more than $26 billion in 2017.* https://newsroom.publishers.org/bookpublisher-revenue-estimated-at-more-than-26-billion-in-2017.

Campbell, C. (1981, December 20). Book banning in America. *The New York Times.* https://www.nytimes.com/1981/12/20/books/book-banning-in-america.html.

Hill, C., & Malo-Juvera, V. (2018). Introduction: The center of the canon: The high school classroom. In C. Hill & V. Malo-Juvera (Eds.), *Critical approaches to teaching the high school novel* (pp. 1–17). Routledge.

Malo-Juvera, V., & Hill, C. (2019). The young adult canon: A literary solar system. In V. Malo-Juvera & C. Hill & (Eds.), *Critical explorations of young adult literature: Identifying and critiquing the canon* (pp. 1–16). Routledge.

Miller, sj., & Slifkin, J. M. (2010). "Similar literary quality": Demystifying the AP English literature and composition open question. *The ALAN Review, 37*(2), 6–16.

National Council of Teachers of English. (2018). *NCTE/NCATE standards for initial preparation of teachers of secondary English language arts, grades 7-12.* https://ncte.org/app/uploads/2018/07/ApprovedStandards_111212.pdf.

Stotsky, S., Traffas, J., & Woodworth, J. (2010). Literary study in grades 9, 10, and 11: A national survey. *Association of Literary Scholars, Critics, and Writers.* Retrieved from http://alscw.org/wp-content/uploads/2017/04/forum_4.pdf.

Tanner, G. W. (1907). Report of the committee appointed by the English Conference to inquire into the teaching of English in the high schools of the middle west. *The School Review, 15*(1), 32–45.

Chapter 1

Engaging the Classics through Culturally Relevant Pedagogy

Reading Jacqueline Woodson's If You Come Softly *as Complement to* Romeo and Juliet

Susan Groenke

Culture plays a central role in learning, as it can determine how we communicate; receive and understand information; and shape our values and beliefs and, thus, our thinking processes. A pedagogy that acknowledges and responds to the influence of culture on learning offers full, equitable access to education for students. Culturally Responsive Pedagogy (CRP) is a pedagogy that recognizes the importance of understanding students' cultural experiences in all aspects of learning. Gloria Ladson-Billings (1994) defined CRP as one "that empowers students intellectually, socially, emotionally, and politically using cultural referents to impart knowledge, skills, and attitudes" (pp. 16–17). Ladson-Billings (1995a) explained that CRP is a "pedagogy of opposition not unlike critical pedagogy but specifically committed to collective, not merely individual, empowerment" (p. 160).

Ladson-Billings (1995a, 1995b) described a framework for CRP encompassing multiple components, including that culturally relevant pedagogues seek to develop sociopolitical consciousness, which includes a teacher's obligation to find ways for "students to recognize, understand, and critique current and social inequalities" (Ladson-Billings, 1995b, p. 476). Sociopolitical consciousness begins with teachers recognizing sociopolitical issues of race, class, and gender in themselves and incorporating these issues into their teaching.

Pairing young adult literature with canonical works like Shakespeare's plays can be a powerful way to reshape traditional English/Language Arts (ELA) curriculum toward student relevance and develop students' sociopolitical consciousness at the same time. In this chapter, a CRP approach toward teaching Jacqueline Woodson's (1998/2018) young adult (YA) novel *If You Come Softly* in tandem with Shakespeare's *Romeo and Juliet* is explored. Both stories take up the timeless and universal theme of forbidden love, and also provide opportunities for students to consider the connections that exist between prejudice, hatred, and violence.

Through a CRP approach, students can explore power—how it operates through language and actions, through our societal institutions (e.g., marriage laws and customs), and in our own families and communities. Ultimately, students can learn ways to speak truth to power—a powerful tool adolescents can take far beyond the ELA classroom.

Romeo and Juliet by William Shakespeare

Romeo and Juliet is one of the greatest examples of the theme of forbidden love in Western literature. Romeo Montague and Juliet Capulet should be sworn enemies—their families have hated each other for as long as Romeo and Juliet can remember, for reasons Shakespeare does not disclose. But when they meet at a masked ball, they fall in love and choose to defy their families' prejudices and expectations, setting in motion a chain of events that ultimately leads to tragedy.

If You Come Softly by Jacqueline Woodson

Like *Romeo and Juliet*, *If You Come Softly* is ultimately a tragic love story where the two main characters—Jeremiah, a Black boy, and Ellie, a White, Jewish girl—fall in love. The story is told from the alternating perspectives of Jeremiah and Ellie, who are both fifteen, both upper middle class, and both students at a mostly White private New York City high school. While Jeremiah and Ellie live in the same city and attend the same school, their cultural and familial life experiences differ greatly. The young couple's willingness to enter into and explore these differences leads them to fall in love and to stand up on behalf of their love when society and even their families try to keep them apart.

BEFORE READING

Exploring the Theme of Forbidden Love

Forbidden love can be described as romantic love that is not allowed due to social or religious restrictions (age difference, cultural beliefs/differences, etc.). In *Romeo and Juliet*, when Count Paris asks Lord Capulet, Juliet's father, for permission to wed Juliet, Capulet wards off Paris's advances, explaining Juliet, only fourteen, is "yet a stranger in the world" (I.ii.8). He tells Paris, "Let two more summers wither in their pride,/Ere we may think her ripe to be a bride" (10–11).

Age, then, would stand in the way of Juliet's love life (if she loved Paris, which she does not), but so, too, does the fact that the person she *does* love— Romeo—is a Montague. This love is forbidden because Juliet is a Capulet, and the Capulets and Montagues, like the Hatfields and McCoys, are sworn enemies.

Similarly, in *If You Come Softly*, Ellie, a Jewish White girl and high school sophomore, is told by her mother, "You're too young for boys" (p. 24). When Ellie responds that her mother was married and pregnant at eighteen, her mother responds, "Things were different then." Ellie's mother fears that, like her, Ellie will rush into a relationship and lose out on other life experiences. Ellie's father, too, says that she can "be friends" with a boy who is nice and smart (and Ellie's mother suggests that he should also be Jewish and rich), but "we don't want our baby leaving the nest just yet. It makes us feel old" (p. 95).

What Ellie's parents don't know is that she has already fallen head over heels for Jeremiah, a Black boy, who is hesitant to date Ellie at first because she is White. When they do start dating, both Ellie and Jeremiah are afraid to tell their parents about each other.

To prepare students to analyze the theme of forbidden love in depth when they begin reading the play and Woodson's novel, first read with students "The Story of Pyramus and Thisbe" from Ovid's *Metamorphoses*. Before reading, teach (or remind) students how to annotate, or add notes, to the poem to aid understanding while reading. Harvey Daniels (2011) has good suggestions for "text codes" he teaches students, which include, but are not limited to, a check mark for matched predictions, a question mark for areas of confusion, and a star for something that seems vital, important, or memorable. Students might also circle unknown words. Teachers can "think aloud" as they read the poem with students to model their own annotation of the text.

Also, the poem is quite long, so teachers might want to "chunk" the text, or break the text down into smaller parts. Teachers can ask students to share their "text codes" for the first couple of "chunks" of the text and discuss possible meanings, and then have students work in pairs or larger groups to work through the rest of the poem and share out with the rest of the class. Some guiding questions for students might include the following:

- What is personified in the first stanza of the poem?
- What plan do Pyramus and Thisbe concoct in the second stanza? What is your opinion of their plan?
- Near the end of the poem, Thisbe blames the parents for their untimely death. Do you agree with her? Why? If not, who is to blame? Explain.

- According to this story, for what reason does the mulberry fruit redden at its ripeness?
- Of what other stories does this poem remind you? How does it relate to what you know or might have heard about Shakespeare's famous play, *Romeo and Juliet?*

As a final activity with the poem, ask students to consider the "wall" and the "chink in the wall" that are symbolic elements in the poem. Explain to students that a motif in stories of forbidden love is an obstacle (or "wall") that stands in the way of the lovers, and an opportunity (or "chink in the wall") that the lovers seize to maintain their relationship despite the obstacles they face. Ask students to consider how this motif plays out in popular movies, songs, or other media that young people are familiar with (e.g., the *Hunger Games* trilogy, *Twilight, Titanic, Jungle Fever, Beyond the Lights, Cinderella, Shrek, Beauty and the Beast, The Notebook, Edward Scissorhands, Like Water for Chocolate, Boys Don't Cry*), and also have students consider why so many writers use the theme of forbidden love in their stories and films. Teachers might also want to show the YouTube clip of "Pyramus and Thisbe in *The Simpsons*" and ask students to compare and contrast the poem to the animated clip.

In the "During Reading" section of this chapter, an activity is described that has students consider more deeply the "walls" (obstacles) that stand between the doomed lovers, and the "chinks in the wall" (or opportunities they seize to keep their relationships alive despite the obstacles they face).

Exploring Microaggressions

To prepare students for a more in-depth, during-reading activity where they explore microaggressive language in both *Romeo and Juliet* and *If You Come Softly*, teach students to recognize how different audiences can interpret language and microaggressions. This can be a powerful activity to help students understand the implications of their own speech, and most importantly, how they might modify questions and comments in ways that are less likely to reflect biased/stereotypic assumptions and beliefs.

To begin, define microaggressions and provide examples of how they operate. As the "Teaching Tolerance" website suggests, microaggressions are "coded messages of disapproval that are based in identity: comments and actions that echo larger, structural bigotry, telling marginalized people they don't belong, that they are less than" (n.p.). Racial microaggressions, more specifically, are defined as "brief and commonplace daily verbal, behavioral, or environmental indignities, whether intentional or unintentional, that communicate hostile, derogatory, or negative racial slights and insults toward people of color" (Sue et al., 2007). Sue et al. (2007) defined several forms of racial microaggressions, including the *microassualt* (e.g., referring to someone as "colored" or "Oriental," using racial epithets, deliberately serving a White patron before someone of color); the *microinsult* (e.g., when an employee of color is asked *How did you get this job?*); and *microinvalidation* (e.g., telling a Person of Color he/she/they speaks good English; colorblindness).

Then, pass out the graphic organizer presented in figure 1.1. Read the first couple of statements in column A aloud to students, asking students to consider how a person could interpret the statement as a "put down." Ask students: *What is the possible intent and possible impact/interpretation of these statements?* Have students then draw lines from column A to column B, matching what they think the best possible interpretation is.

Then, ask students to finish the graphic organizer, drawing a line connecting the statements in column A to what they believe is the best possible interpretation from column B (several statements in column B apply more than once in column A). Ask students to be ready to explain their choices. After students have finished matching the statements with the interpretations, discuss the following question with students: *Does the intent change the impact of the statement for the person who experiences the microaggressions?*

Next, ask students to rewrite the statements so that they do not contain a hidden or negative message. For example, the statement "No, where are you really from?" might be sincerely intended as "I'm interested in you and

Column A Statements	Column B Statements
"You throw like a girl."	Black people are criminals.
"You are a credit to your race."	People with disabilities are less important, likeable, or competent.
"You speak good English."	Feminine traits are undesirable.
"That's so gay" or "No homo."	All Muslims are terrorists.
[To an Asian student] "Can you help me with my math homework?"	People of your background are unintelligent.
"No, where are you really from?"	How you feel about your gender identity is irrelevant to me.
"You're not a typical gay guy."	I assume everyone is straight (heterosexual).
[To a girl] "Math is hard, isn't it?"	Being gay is wrong and unacceptable.
[To a boy] "Do you have a girlfriend?"	Your appearance dictates your skills or knowledge.
"Don't be a sissy."	Everyone from your group acts the same.
[Store manager to employees] "Keep an eye on the Black shoppers."	You are not American.
[To a woman with a headscarf] "What are you hiding in there?"	Your experience as a member of a minoritized group is not important to me.
"She looks like a she-male."	
"That's retarded."	
"You don't even seem Black."	Girls and women have inferior abilities.
"I don't see color (or race). We are all equal."	

Figure 1.1 Microaggressions pre-reading activity. *Note: Modified from Togans, Robinson, & Meredith, 2014.*

would like to know more about you." But the impact/interpretation might be, "People like you are not real Americans/are not my equal." A neutral wording of the statement might be "Where did you grow up?" or "How long have you lived in this town?" Have students share their revised statements.

After students have completed the activity, discuss the following questions:

- When people discuss microaggressions, a common response is that they are "innocent acts" and that the person who experiences them should "let go of the incident" and "not make a big deal out of it." Do you agree or disagree with this point of view? Explain your reasoning.
- If a person pointed out to you that one of your comments was a microaggression, how would you respond at the time? Would it change the likelihood of your making a similar comment in the future? Why or why not? (Kite, 2014)

DURING READING

Making Connections

Pairing young adult literature with classic works requires that teachers know how to help students make intertextual, or text-to-text connections. Bright (2011) offered the idea of mapping "vertical and horizontal" intertextual connections that students can make across classic texts and their complementary YA counterparts. Vertical connections are those "focused on theme, character, and plot," while horizontal connections are those made "across the texts, from past to present" (p. 38). Ideas for helping students make vertical connections across texts are provided below. Ideas for helping students make horizontal connections are shared in the "After Reading" section of this chapter.

Mapping Vertical Connections. Bright (2011) explained that vertical connections are those focused on theme, character, and plot. If you've helped students consider the theme of forbidden love—and its motif of "wall"/"chink in the wall" through the pre-reading activities in this chapter, students are ready to look more closely at selected passages and consider the obstacles that stand between both couples in *Romeo and Juliet* and *If You Come Softly*. More specifically, students can zero in on analysis of Juliet and Ellie in both texts as they compare their thoughts and the actions they take to overcome obstacles to their relationships. Lewis (1972) called Juliet "Shakespeare's most remarkable female" (p. 488), and this focus can help students begin to consider why. To get students started, provide them the "Character Comparison Activity" (see figure 1.2).

Figure 1.2 presents several tasks and passages for students to consider across both texts. Task 1 asks students to apply the motifs of the "wall" and

Task 1	Passages
A motif in stories of forbidden love is an obstacle (or wall) that stands in the way of the lovers, and an opportunity (or "chink in the wall") that the lovers seize to maintain their relationship despite the obstacles they face. What is the wall that stands between Romeo and Juliet? Jeremiah and Ellie? How do Juliet and Ellie describe these obstacles? Read the passages from each text and then define in your own words.	*Romeo and Juliet:* 'Tis but they name that is my enemy; Thou art thyself, though not a Montague. What's Montague? It is nor hand, nor foot, Nor arm, nor face, nor any other part Belonging to a man. O, be some other name! What's in a name? that which we call a rose By any other name would smell as sweet; So Romeo would, were he not Romeo call'd, Retain that dear perfection which he owes Without the title. Romeo, doff thy name, And for that name which is no part of thee Take all myself (II.ii.38-49)
Next, compare how Juliet and Ellie react to/consider these obstacles and try to create "chinks in the wall" to continue in/maintain their relationships.	*If You Come Softly:* "All people," Marion [Ellie's mother] was often saying. "All people have suffered. So why should any of us feel like we're better or less than another?" But where were they then — these black people who were just like us — who were equal to us? Why weren't they coming over for dinner? Why weren't they playing golf with Daddy on Saturdays or quilting with Marion on Thursday nights? Why weren't they in our world, around us, a part of us? (p. 70). "The world was like that a long time ago. But it wasn't like that anymore, was it? No. My stupid sister might be like that. And maybe my family sometimes. But not the rest of the world. Please not the rest of the world." (p. 76)

Task 2	Passage
Why doesn't Juliet tell her father she has married Romeo? And why doesn't Ellie tell her parents about Jeremiah? Compare passages in the text to consider possible rationales.	*Romeo and Juliet:* When Juliet asks to be freed from the arranged marriage to Count Paris, her father responds: But fettle your fine joints 'gainst Thursday next, To go with Paris to Saint Peter's Church, Or I will drag thee on a hurdle thither. (III.v.154-156) I tell thee what: get thee to church o' Thursday, Or never after look me in the face: Speak not, reply not, do not answer me; My fingers itch (162-165)
	If You Come Softly: "Tell me about him," Marion said, a small smile at the corners of her lips. "Tell me about this boy." I shook my head… "No." "Does he go to temple?" "Is this boy's daddy rich?" "Maybe in your junior year, there'll be a boy" (p. 31). "All people," Marion [Ellie's mother] was often saying. "All people have suffered. So why should any of us feel like we're better or less than another?" But where were they then — these black people who were just like us — who were equal to us? Why weren't they coming over for dinner? Why weren't they playing golf with Daddy on Saturdays or quilting with Marion on Thursday nights? Why weren't they in our world, around us, a part of us? (p. 70). I didn't want this — to have to explain…who would understand? He was Miah. Jeremiah Roselind. And when we walked out of Central Park that afternoon, he had taken my hand in his and held it. Who would understand that in this stupid family — the way our hands looked together — dark and light at once. The way his hair felt so different from my own. Who in this family of people who married people who looked just like them would ever *get it*? (p. 138).

Figure 1.2   **Character comparison activity.** *Author created.*

the "chink in the wall" and define, in their own terms, what the obstacles are between Romeo and Juliet and Jeremiah and Ellie. This task also asks students to compare how Juliet and Ellie react to/consider these obstacles. Task 2 asks students to consider why Juliet doesn't tell her father she has married Romeo and why Ellie doesn't tell her parents about Jeremiah. A third task could be posed that asks students to consider how Juliet and Ellie respond to their family's and society's beliefs about the people they love. Teachers might ask students to consider: *How do Juliet and Ellie attempt to create "chinks in the wall"?* Other guiding questions for facilitating these tasks might include the following:

- How do Romeo and Juliet feel about their family's hatred of each other? How do Jeremiah and Ellie feel about their families' beliefs on race? How do you know?

- Can Romeo and Juliet love each other without fear of social repercussions? Can Jeremiah and Ellie?
- How are Romeo and Juliet and Jeremiah and Ellie "star-crossed lovers? How is their love "doomed" from the beginning?
- What options do you have if you don't agree with, can't fully be yourself, or love who you want to love due to your family's prejudices/beliefs?

Finally, present a final task asking students to consider: *Can love overcome society's prejudices and labels?* Students can compare the two endings of *Romeo and Juliet* and *If You Come Softly*, using textual evidence to support their interpretations, and then debate their answers. Philosophical Chairs is a good activity to facilitate classroom debate. Give students time to take a position on the question (yes, no undecided). Then divide the classroom into one side for "Yes," one side for "No," and "Undecided" in the middle of the room. Students take turns between providing "Yes" and "No" arguments for —ten to fifteen minutes. Students then write a reflection that includes the comment that most challenged their thinking, whether they changed their mind or not, and their answer to the question and rationale (with textual evidence).

Exploring Microaggressions

Insults abound in many of Shakespeare's plays, and *Romeo and Juliet* is no exception. One of the first insults in the play is a simple gesture, rather than a verbal taunt, when the Capulet servant Sampson "bites his thumb" in the direction of the Montague servants. Verbal insults, however, appear throughout the play. In Act I, Scene I, Tybalt calls Benvolio a coward for drawing his sword among servants. After breaking up the street brawl in that same scene, Prince Escalus refers to the Montagues and Capulets as "beasts." In Act II, Scene IV, the Nurse refers to Mercutio as a "scurvy knave." (Teachers can find whole books dedicated to Shakespeare's insults: see Hill & Ottchen's [1995] *Shakespeare's Insults: Educating Your Wit* and Kraft's [2014] *Shakespeare Insult Generator* to name just a few.)

But when does an insult become a microaggression? Focusing on this question in both *Romeo and Juliet* and the YA novel *If You Come Softly* can provide a prime, culturally relevant pedagogical opportunity to help students "recognize, understand, and critique current and social inequalities" (Ladson-Billings, 1995b, p. 476).

An integral component of CRP can include helping students understand microaggressions, or small, subtle, sometimes-unintended acts of discriminatory language. Microaggressions are more than just insults, insensitive comments, or generalized jerky behavior. Microaggressions have to do with a person's membership in a group that is discriminated against or subject to stereotypes. As students might have learned in the pre-reading activity that introduces them to microaggressions, microaggressions can take many forms and be racial, heterosexist, and gendered (among others, and sometimes all at the same time!).

Readers can learn a lot about how language reveals power dynamics and societal prejudices/beliefs through a focus on microaggressions. Such a focus can help students become aware of the heteronormative and misogynistic language in *Romeo and Juliet* (e.g., Ressler, 2005), as well as contemporary examples of racial microaggressions in *If You Come Softly*.

For this activity, first provide students a list of key passages from *Romeo and Juliet* as shown in figure 1.3. Work through the first one to two passages with students, reading the passages out loud and "thinking out loud" together about what the passages mean. Teachers may need to clarify vocabulary words and help students understand much of the double word play in the play. Then work through the other columns, reminding students that a microaggression has to do with a person's membership in a group that is discriminated against or subject

Passage	Description/Interpretation	Who/what is the group being discriminated against or stereotyped?	Underlying Attitudes/Beliefs (Interpretation/Impact)	What does this tell us about the power dynamics in Verona society?
Act 1, scene 1, 64-65	Possible answer: Tybalt is asking Benvolio why he has drawn his sword and intervened in a quarrel among the servants of the Capulets and Montagues, who are fighting each other because the families are sworn enemies.	Possible answer: Tybalt calls the servants "heartless hinds" which shows he considers them to be mere, lowly servants. A "hind" is a female deer so he is also saying the servants are womanly—so women as a group are disparaged here, too. Tybalt tells Benvolio—if you want to fight a real man-- fight me.	Possible answer: Servants are compared to animals (female deer) who are not worth bothering with. Women are weak and feeble. Women hold no power. It is an insult to be compared to a woman.	Possible answer: Differences exist between social classes. Tybalt must be upper class and he snubs his nose at members of the servant or working-class; he considers them less than human. Women in Verona society are not respected or seen as having any power. TERMS TO KNOW: Misogyny: dislike of, contempt for, or ingrained prejudice against women Patriarchy: a system of society or government in which men hold the power and women are largely excluded from it.
Act 2, scene 4 106-120	Bawd=a madam of a brothel. "Bawd" can also mean *hare*, which is meant to sound a bit like "whore" and *hoar* (meaning old, stale, mouldy) sounds exactly like whore. A *lenten pie* shouldn't contain any meat; the joke here is that even an *old* whore is acceptable if no fresh meat is available.	Mercutio is calling the Nurse not just a *bawd* but an old whore, unattractive.	Women are prostitutes, valued only for their sexual labor ("whore" is a derogatory term for "prostitute"). Old women are unattractive.	Misogyny RULES! Mercutio has no respect for elders (may also be a class thing).
Act 3, scene 5	Lord Capulet has arranged a marriage between Juliet and Count Paris, but Juliet refuses to marry Count Paris. Lord Capulet calls Juliet a "minion" (or someone with no power), and tells her he will drag her to the church to marry if he has to. "Fettle your fine joints" has a sexual undercurrent. "Green-sickness" was a form of anemia thought to afflict young unmarried women, the cure for which was marriage: "carrion," and "tallow-face" also suggest pallor.	Girls/Women	A woman's disobedience and defiance will not be tolerated. Women have no say in defining/participating in the rules/laws of marriage. It is unacceptable to be unmarried (and a virgin) (you are considered sickly if you are either).	Marriage customs decided by father/head of household usually to benefit family's economic or social status, with no say from women involved. Example of how a patriarchal society works, with marriage one of its supporting institutions

Figure 1.3 Analyzing microaggressive language in *Romeo and Juliet*. *Author created.*

to stereotypes. Help students determine what groups are targeted in the selected passages; what underlying beliefs/stereotypes are conveyed; and what we can infer more broadly about the society's power structures and prejudices/beliefs from our close readings. Students can be encouraged to continue looking for and adding passages from the play that exhibit microaggressive language. Then do the same with passages from *If You Come Softly* (see figure 1.4).

Take this opportunity to talk to students about what societal beliefs about Black people exist in the book, and how those beliefs get transmitted through racial microaggressive actions. Also, take the opportunity to talk about the effects of racial microaggressions on Jeremiah's relationship with Ellie, and ultimately, on Jeremiah. You might have students consider how Jeremiah (separately) and Jeremiah and Ellie (together) choose to respond to microaggressions communicated about their interracial relationship. Some guiding questions for students might include the following:

Passage	Description/Interpretation/ Connection	Who/what is the group being discriminated against or stereotyped?	Underlying Attitudes/Beliefs (Interpretation/Impact)	What does this tell us about the power dynamics in American society?
"Once Anne and I were walking through Central Park ....Would Anne have reacted that way if the guy had been white?" (p. 69).	Possible answer: Ellie is thinking about how her sister, Anne, has acted around Black people in the past now that she is interested in Jeremiah. Anne didn't see a human being, she saw a criminal—someone to fear. This is how police see Black people, too, and don't give them the benefit of the doubt. Ellie knows that Anne would not have reacted the same way if it were a White guy. Ellie is starting to think about race maybe for the first time. It reminds me of the Central Park birding incident where Amy Cooper (White) called the cops on Christian Cooper (Black) and said he was threatening her when he was just asking her to restrain her dog in the bird park.	Possible answer: Black people	Possible answer: Black people are thugs and criminals. Black people should be feared. They are a threat. All Black people are the same.	Possible answer: Racism exists and is shown through our everyday actions. White people have a deep fear and mistrust of Black people, based on the media and pervasive anti-Blackness (implicit bias). Racism hurts Black people, too, because they have to deal with White people's fears all the time rather than just get on with their lives.
ELLIE "Why'd you get transferred out of that other class?" I whispered.... JEREMIAH "Or the melanin thing?" (p. 76).	When Jeremiah started at Percy Academy, he was automatically placed in a remedial class, even though he was never tested. He is transferred out of the remedial class and into more advanced classes when the teacher realizes he is in the wrong class. Ellie tries to play it off, but Jeremiah corrects her and suggests it happens disproportionately more times to Black students than White students. That can't be just a coincidence.	Black people	Black people have limited intellectual capabilities. Black people are not smart. Your skin color dictates your skills or knowledge. All Black people are the same.	Scientific racism—scientists (and Thomas Jefferson!) over time have actually tried to prove that Black people are intellectually inferior to White people. When it can't be proven, the belief persists anyway. When Black people prove this wrong, they are considered individually exceptional (or a credit) to their race.
"You're too young for boys" (p. 24)	Ellie's mom thinks it will be more appropriate for Ellie to date when she is a junior (she is only a sophomore). Maybe the assumption is that with age comes maturity, but Ellie's mom was married and pregnant at age 18.	Teenagers	Ageism: prejudice or discrimination on the grounds of a person's age. Young people are often stereotyped as moody, hormonal, going through an "identity crisis" and thus not mature enough or adult enough to make good decisions. Young people aren't taken seriously.	Teenagers are caught between this "you're not a child" anymore, and "you're not old enough" stage that can limit their capabilities, dreams, etc. It keeps teenagers in this kind of holding pattern, reliant on adults and affected by their whims/decisions.

Figure 1.4 **Analyzing microaggressions in *If You Come Softly*.** *Author created.*

- Where do the beliefs that inform/influence microaggressions come from? Who benefits?
- What are possible ways to respond to/disrupt microaggressions? How does Jeremiah respond? Jeremiah and Ellie?
- How do the microaggressions make Jeremiah and Ellie feel?
- *If You Come Softly* was written twenty years ago. Do you think the reactions would be the same today? Why or why not?

AFTER READING

Who Can Tell My Story?

A major component of CRP centers on reshaping traditional curriculum to be accessible, relevant to students' backgrounds and cultures, and empowering (Nieto, 1996; Villegas, 1991).

Teachers can help make canonical works relevant by engaging students in conversations about the canon, "Standard English," and why young adult authors like Jacqueline Woodson would choose to retell the story of *Romeo and Juliet.*

For this activity, students will read Woodson's (1998) essay "Who Can Tell My Story?," which describes how Woodson's perspective as an African American woman in a relationship with a Jewish woman influenced Woodson's retelling of the classic play. Prior to reading the essay, ask students to journal on the following questions:

- What are all of the languages you speak? Think about the language(s) (words, phrases, nicknames, mediums like texting, etc.) that you use at home with your family, with your friends, at church, and at school. How are they different? Does the language change depending on the context? Why do you think this is?
- Has anyone (including teachers, parents) ever made you feel bad for the way you talk, or tried to correct your speech? If yes, describe the situation and how you responded. Why do you think this person tried to correct or shame you?
- What is "Standard English"? Whose standard? How does learning how to speak and write "Standard English" in school make you feel?

Ask for volunteers to share their reflections and note similarities and differences that exist across students' stories. Opening classroom space for conversations about language can help students consider how they navigate and negotiate their linguistic and racial identities across multiple contexts

(Baker-Bell, 2020). Another important way to reshape ELA curriculum is to consider approaches to language education that do not cause emotional harm or internalized linguistic racism, or lead to other negative consequences on students' sense of self and identity.

Next, lead students through a close reading of the essay, "chunking" the essay into smaller sections. Guiding questions might include the following:

- What do you think Woodson means by "language spoken on the outside" and language "used to procure scholarships, employment, promotions"? Woodson compares "Standard English" to a "nice suit." How does Woodson view "Standard English"? How does this compare to your view?
- What is Woodson saying about the language her family uses versus "Standard English"? What does Woodson mean by "filter my own experience through them" and "create something that is mine"? How did Woodson do this with her retelling of *Romeo and Juliet*?
- Why does Woodson get offended when asked if White people can write about People of Color? What do you think about this question? How have Woodson's feelings changed about being asked the question? Why did they change?
- How have Black characters been stereotyped in literature over time?
- What do you think about Woodson's statement: "no one but me *can* tell my story"?
- What reasons does Woodson give for writing *If You Come Softly*? How is Woodson like all of the characters in her story?
- What do you think of the questions Woodson asks of herself before writing about other people?
- What does Woodson mean when she says, "As a black person, it is easy to tell who has and who has not been inside 'my house' "?
- What do you make of Woodson's final statement in the essay?

Rewriting the Violence in Our Lives

At the time of this writing, one of the largest protest movements declaring "Black Lives Matter" is happening all over the world. The movement communicates that Black citizens are "fed up" with long-standing police violence and brutality, most recently demonstrated in the murders of Breonna Taylor, George Floyd, Ahmaud Arbery, and Rayshard Brooks.

There is a long history of violence against Black bodies in the United States (Goff, Eberhardt, Williams, & Jackson, 2008). This more recent history led to the formation of the Black Lives Matter (BLM) movement in 2013 after the murder of Trayvon Martin, an expression of frustration, rage, and protest regarding the failure of systems of the state to protect and value the lives of Black people. The main impetus of the BLM movement is to humanize Black people and make evident the physical and psychological suffering Black people have faced over time.

Romeo and Juliet is certainly a violent play. Tybalt kills Mercutio; Romeo kills Tybalt and Count Paris; and hatred between the Capulets and Montagues leads to the tragic suicides of Romeo and Juliet. Similarly, *If You Come Softly* ends with the tragic death of Jeremiah, who is shot by a police officer who assumes he is a criminal. In the Preface to the twentieth anniversary edition of *If You Come Softly*, published in 2018, Woodson writes, "I didn't know . . . that a book I was writing in the mid-nineties would not only continue to resonate with many but would become relevant to more and more people . . . as the cases of police brutality skyrocketed" (n.p.).

Through a focus on the violence in the play and the YA novel, teachers can encourage students to think about the connections that exist between hate, violence, and death, and imagine alternative ways to resolve conflicts that don't resort to violence.

After reading both texts, outline the decisions that were made by various key characters in the play (e.g., Prince Escalus, Lord Capulet, Friar Lawrence, Nurse) and the YA novel that deepened the conflicts between the couples. Then ask students to consider decisions that could have been made to resolve the conflicts. Ask students: *Given your perspective, what would you have done differently and how would that have affected the story?*

Next, ask students to write a story that parallels *Romeo and Juliet* but that takes place in their own cultural context. Students can choose a conflict between two rival families or groups of people that relates to their lives and communities today. The story must maintain fidelity to the plotline and characters. However, the story must imagine an alternate ending that allows for a different resolution of the conflict.

To begin, have students write in their journals about how the theme of violence and conflict might resonate in their own lives. Bring up current and past news events that highlight how attitudes and beliefs can result in violence. Ask for volunteers to share other examples and/or reflections from their journals.

Next, ask students to decide on a rivalry that will become the focus of their parallel story. Help students flesh out the root causes of the conflict and brainstorm with the class possible peaceful alternatives that can end conflict and bring about needed change in the community. As needed, students can use storyboards or flowcharts to help plot their story. Finally, help students think about ways to make their stories public, either through public service announcements (PSAs), letters to local newspapers, community theatre/ poetry slams, or school productions.

BLM activists have called on teachers to educate students about the BLM movement's central beliefs and practices and have created BLM-inspired curriculum for students in elementary grades through college levels (e.g., Coleman-King & Groenke, 2019; Pitts, 2017). The aim of much of this curriculum is not just to teach about racism but also to "point to solutions and methods of action so our students don't become disillusioned. . . . Bringing this movement to the classroom can open the door to larger conversations about truth, justice, activism, healing and reconciliation" (Pitts, 2017).

EXTENSION ACTIVITIES

Exploring Marriage Laws and Customs over Time

One of the conflicts in *Romeo and Juliet* centers on Lord Capulet's arranged marriage between Juliet and Count Paris, because Juliet doesn't want to marry Paris, and oops! she has already married Romeo in a secret ceremony performed by Friar Lawrence. Several wedding/marriage customs of Shakespeare's time become apparent in the play: marriages are arranged by the father, or head of household, often to improve economic/social status; daughters have no say in the matter; heterosexist relationships are normalized; marriage is forever; and at least one wedding custom includes hosting a fancy dinner or reception after the ceremony for invited guests. Also, as part of the wedding ceremony (officially sanctioned by the church), vows are exchanged, and once married, a couple's sexual relationship is officially sanctioned by the state (as the Nurse's willingness to help place a ladder for Romeo to access Juliet's window on their wedding night suggests).

Also, in *If You Come Softly*, Ellie's older sister Anne, a lesbian, asks Ellie to attend her commitment ceremony with her partner, Stacey. In describing the ceremony to Ellie, Anne explains, "We're committing to each other." When Ellie says, "You've been together for years. Isn't that kind of obvious?" Anne responds, "It's obvious to me and Stacey, but we want the rest of the world to know too. You know—like a wedding but not with all that 'honor thy husband/protect they wife' stuff" (p. 52). At this, Ellie starts thinking maybe one day she and Jeremiah could have a commitment ceremony.

As both books highlight, marriage is a culturally recognized union between people that establishes rights and obligations between them. But it is also a political and social institution that belies power dynamics. Juliet is told by her father that she will marry Paris or be exiled (and possibly beaten), which leads to the tragic consequences of the play. Anne and Stacey, in *If You Come*

Softly, have a commitment ceremony because they cannot legally get married (at the time the book was first published in 1998). A marriage is legally binding—a commitment ceremony is not.

In this activity, students will explore the concept of marriage and marriage laws/customs over time. To begin, ask the students the following questions: "Why do people get married?" "What are the legal, economic, and social benefits of marriage?" Through discussion, create a list on the board with the students answering the question. Be prepared to share the following reasons: legal decision-making benefits; grants next of kin status; inheritance benefits (can inherit without tax consequences); joint parenting; joint adoption; marital tax deduction; filing taxes jointly; social security benefits; longer life expectancy; less chance of developing depression.

Next, give students the descriptions of "Marriage Laws and Customs through Time" below (*Note:* Modified from Graff, E.J. [1999]). Inherent in each law or custom is a set of attitudes or beliefs about the purposes of marriage in that time and place. For each law/custom, ask students to list as many underlying beliefs as they can identify.

- In many societies, members were forbidden to marry outside the tribe, clan, culture, or religion, while marriage within the family was considered acceptable. The ancient Hebrews, for example, enforced strict rules against marrying foreigners, but had only the barest of rules against marrying within the family. The Romans allowed first cousins to marry, and early Germanic clans gave the nod to uncle/niece marriages.
- For centuries, and in many different parts of the world, marriage could not take place without a dowry—the money, goods, or estate that a woman brought to her husband in marriage, or a gift of money or property by a man to or for his bride.
- For centuries, the most enduring slave systems—including the Greeks, Romans, Hebrews, medieval Germans, and Americans—denied legal recognition to slave marriages.
- For most of human history (until around the eighteenth century), long-term partnerships were arranged. Marriages arranged by friends, family, and professionals ensured a match that benefitted the family name, budget, and community stability. Some sources report more than half of the world's marriages today are arranged.
- In the 1700s and 1800s, many laws extended the biblical idea that a husband and wife become "one flesh." In British law, a 1765 statement by Lord Blackstone read, "In law husband and wife are one person, and the husband is that person." This meant that a wife could own no personal property, make no personal contracts, and bring no lawsuits. The husband took

over her legal identity—a concept called "coverture," because his identity "covered" hers.

• Before the twentieth century, contraception (deliberate prevention of conception or impregnation) was widely viewed as immoral within the institution of marriage (especially in the West and among Christians). The 1876 book *Conjugal Sins* insisted that contraceptive attempts "degrades to bestiality the true feelings of manhood and the holy state of matrimony." During a period of escalated anti-contraception feelings and backlash laws in the nineteenth century, more than half of the states in the United States enacted laws that criminalized and prevented any sex acts that "made love without making babies."

• In 1850, Indiana's State Legislature passed the most open divorce law the United States had ever known. It stated that judges could grant divorce for any reason at all—not just under conditions of adultery, attempted murder, or other extreme circumstances. Though scandalous at the time, divorce has become a common and acceptable practice within mainstream American society.

• In 1948, the California Supreme Court led the way in challenging racial discrimination in marriage and became the first state high court to declare unconstitutional an anti-miscegenation law (miscegenation means a mixture of races, especially marriage or cohabitation between a White person and a member of another race). In 1967, the U.S. Supreme Court struck down the remaining interracial marriage laws across the country, and declared that the "freedom to marry" belongs to all Americans.

• In 1976, the West German Civil Code was revised to eliminate traditional matrimonial phrases requiring "husbands to support wives" and "wives to obey husbands." It now reads, "The spouses are mutually obliged to adequately maintain the family by their work and property."

• In 1987, the U.S. Supreme Court struck down a Missouri prison's refusal to allow its inmates—convicted felons, "people who couldn't vote much less support their wives or future children"—to marry, since "inmate marriages, like others, are expressions of emotional support and public commitment . . . having spiritual significance."

• In 2000, same-sex marriage was legalized in the Netherlands. In 2004, same-sex marriage was legalized in Massachusetts. In 2014, the United States legalized same-sex marriage in all fifty states.

Read through each of the descriptions of marriage laws and customs and after each one, direct students in considering what the underlying beliefs and values are for each description. Power dynamics will certainly come to light, as students consider the rights bestowed to married couples, unequal gender roles, the economics of marriage, and groups that have been discriminated against and denied the right to marry.

Another activity alternative is to encourage students to consider marriage equality today. Have students draw parallels between the 1967 court ruling in *Loving vs. Virginia*, the U.S. Supreme Court case that legalized mixed-race marriages, and the 2015 marriage equality case *Obergefell v. Hodges*, which had a 5-4 ruling in favor of same-sex marriage nationwide. Read the excerpts from the Supreme Court's full decision (which can be found online) as well as dissents. While *Loving vs. Virginia* was a unanimous decision, the *Obergefell v. Hodges* decision was a split court. Discuss what it means to be given equal dignity under the law and how civil rights issues continue today.

Finally, as an extension to any of the above activities, ask students to select someone they know who is (or was) in a long-term relationship/marriage and interview them, using the guiding questions below. Be sure to tell students they can choose whether or not to share interview data with the class, but they do need to be prepared to share what this assignment taught them.

Guiding Questions for Interviews:

- How old were you when you met your partner or spouse? Was it love at first sight, like with Romeo and Juliet?
- What was your relationship like in the beginning?
- How/why did you decide to enter into a long-term relationship?
- How involved was your family in the decision? Did your family approve? (If yes, why? If not, why not and how did you negotiate this with your family?)
- Have members of your cultural group ever been denied the right to marry? How does this affect your views/beliefs about marriage?
- How is your relationship different from when it began? How is your relationship the same as when it began?
- If you are married, what customs, rituals, and traditions were a part of your wedding? If you are planning to marry, what customs, rituals, and traditions will be a part of your wedding? If you do not plan to marry, why not?
- In true "Romeo and Juliet" fashion—what would you be willing to give up to be with the one you love? Can love overcome obstacles?
- Does true love exist?
- What advice would you give teens today about marriage/long-term relationships?

CONCLUSION

A significant part of CRP is a connection to students' lives and an obligation to aid in the empowerment of students. Several studies have revealed how using culturally relevant materials engages students in the ELA classroom (e.g., Feger, 2006; Morrison, 2002). Pairing young adult literature to mandated canonical works is certainly one way to reshape traditional curriculum that can disempower students and inspire sociopolitical consciousness. More specifically, pairing Jacqueline Woodson's *If You Come Softly* with Shakespeare's classic play *Romeo and Juliet* offer culturally relevant opportunities to engage students in literature that speaks to all of us, help students see how power works through language, and encourage students to speak up and speak out against oppressive societal prejudices and traditions. If these things are possible in the secondary ELA classroom, why would we teach any other way?

REFERENCES

Baker-Bell, A. (2020). *Linguistic justice: Black language, literacy, identity, and pedagogy.* New York, NY: Routledge.

Bright, A. (2011). Writing Homer, reading Riordan: Intertextual study in contemporary adolescent literature. *Journal of Children's Literature, 37*(1), 38–47.

Coleman-King, C., & Groenke, S. L. (2019). Teaching #BlackLivesMatter and #SayHerName: Interrogating historical violence against Black women in *Copper Sun*. In W. J. Glenn & R. Ginsberg (Eds.), *Engaging with multicultural YA literature in the secondary classroom: Critical approaches for critical educators* (pp. 122–131). New York, NY: Routledge.

Daniels, H., & Steineke, N. (2011). *Texts and lessons for content-area reading.* Portsmouth, NH: Heinemann.

Feger, M. (2006). "I want to read": How culturally relevant texts increase student engagement in reading. *Multicultural Education, 13*(3), 18–19. Retrieved from http://files.eric.ed.gov/fulltext/EJ759630.pdf.

Goff, P. A., Eberhardt, J. L., Williams, M. J., & Jackson, M. C. (2008). Not yet human: Implicit knowledge, historical dehumanization, and contemporary consequences. *Journal of Personality and Social Psychology, 94*(2), 292–306.

Graff, E. J. (1999). *What is marriage for?* Boston, MA: Beacon Press.

Hill, W. F., & Ottchen, C. J. (1995). *Shakespeare's insults: Educating your wit.* New York, NY: Three Rivers Press.

Kraft, B. (2014). *The Shakespeare insult generator: Mix and match more than 150,000 insults in the bard's own words.* San Franscisco, CA: Chronicle Books.

Ladson-Billings, G. (1994). *The dreamkeepers: Successful teachers of African American children.* San Francisco, CA: Jossey-Bass.

Ladson-Billings, G. (1995a). But that's just good teaching! The case for culturally relevant pedagogy. *Theory into Practice, 43,* 159–165.

Ladson-Billings, G. (1995b). Toward a theory of culturally relevant pedagogy. *American Educational Research Journal, 32*, 465–491.

Lewis, A. J. (1972). Response to prejudice in *Romeo and Juliet, The Merchant of Venice,* and *King Lear. English Journal,* 488–494.

Morrison, J. D. (2002). Using student-generated film to create a culturally relevant community. *English Journal, 92*(1), 47–52. Retrieved from http://www.jstor.org/stable/821946.

Nieto, S. (1996). *Affirming diversity: The sociopolitical context of multicultural education* (2nd ed.). White Plains, NY: Longman.

Pitts, J. (2017, Summer). *Bringing Black Lives Matter into the classroom—Part II.* Retrieved from www.tolerance.org/magazine/summer-2017/bringing-black-lives- matter-into-the-classroom-part-ii.

Ressler, P. (2005). Challenging normative sexual and gender identity beliefs through *Romeo and Juliet. English Journal, 95*(1), 52–57.

Sue, D. W., Capodilupo, C. M., Torino, G. C., Bucceri, J. M., Holder, A. M. B., Nadal, K. L., & Esquilin, M. (2007). Racial microaggressions in everyday Life: Implications for clinical practice. *American Psychologist, 62*(4), 271–286.

Togans, L., Robinson, L., & Meredith, K. L. (2014). Breaking the prejudice habit: Microaggressions activity. Retrieved from http://breakingprejudice.org/teaching/group-activities/microaggression-activity/.

Villegas, A. M. (1991). *Culturally responsive pedagogy for the 1990's and beyond.* Washington, DC: ERIC Clearinghouse on Teacher Education.

Woodson, J. (1998). Who can tell my story? Downloaded from https://www.hbook.com/?detailStory=who-can-tell-my-story.

Woodson, J. (1998/2018). *If you come softly.* New York, NY: Penguin Books.

Chapter 2

Betrayal, Brotherhood, and Belonging

Language and Power in Julius Caesar *and* The Chocolate War

Melanie Hundley and Sarah K. Burriss

Adolescence is a time of change and self-discovery. Discovering who you are and what you stand for often happens at a time of emotional, social, or intellectual turmoil. In conversation with a high school student, they described school as "hell . . . and every day is a battle of some kind." While this comment may seem pessimistic, the idea that school is comparable to a war zone is not uncommon. Issues of power and authority thread through the experiences of many high school students. The metaphor of high school as a battlefield occurs frequently in the literature that our students encounter in school. Classical texts such as Shakespeare's *Julius Caesar* and Cormier's *The Chocolate War* make visible the lengths to which people will go to gain and maintain that power and authority. These texts build on questions that adolescents ask: *What is power? Who has power? Who has authority? Who can take it away? What will people do to get power or authority?* Many of the answers to these questions are wrapped up in the language that adolescents, their peers, their teachers, and their families use. Words become tools and weapons wielded in the battles that are part of their lives.

Both adolescence and war provide a setting in which there are battles, trenches, enemies, heroes, generals, soldiers, and betrayal. Shakespeare's *Julius Caesar* and Cormier's *The Chocolate War* demonstrate how the streets of Rome and halls of Trinity (a private, male, high school in New England) are battlegrounds where the themes of power, betrayal, and belonging play out with grave consequences for the participants. Caesar's Rome provides a window into the ways in which greed and power go hand in hand with manipulation and betrayal. Jerry's high school provides a view of the power games that teens play when jockeying for control and status. Rome and Trinity, as microcosms of the world, provide stages for the epic battles between good and evil, heroes and cowards, brothers and betrayers, and leaders and followers. Both provide painful portrayals of the misuse of power and authority perpetrated by those who are supposed to be loyal to, or protective of, the people in these texts.

Language is an instrument of power used to manipulate, control, and demean the characters in *Julius Caesar* and *The Chocolate War*. In both texts, we are privy to the machinations of the characters and we, as readers, see the thoughts and motives that shape the language used to gain political or social power. The focus on language as a rhetorical tool provides us a lens with which to examine themes of power, betrayal, and belonging. Both Rome and Trinity are locations in which the battle over social and political power rage—who has power and authority over the actions of the populace of Rome and the student body of Trinity? We discover that those who gain and use power are also those who can exert control over the words they use.

Julius Caesar by William Shakespeare

Julius Caesar, written by William Shakespeare and first performed around 1599, is a dramatized telling of the events surrounding the infamous murder of the titular character. The play opens with a street scene where Roman citizens are celebrating Caesar's triumphant return from battle, only to be chastised by a passing group of senators. This scene establishes the power struggle among the senators, Caesar, and citizens that threads through the play. Additionally, the characters engage language play that highlights their social class and the differences among them. Worried about Caesar's accrual of power as a threat to republican rule, a group of senators schemes to murder Caesar, which they accomplish in a dramatic scene that ends with the famous line, "And you, Brutus," as Caesar learns of his erstwhile friend's betrayal. Following Caesar's murder, the senators scramble to determine who will lead in a series of speeches. Brutus claims that he loved Rome more than he loved Caesar, so the murder was justified. Antony, on the other hand, defends Caesar's commitment to the people of Rome and is convinced to read Caesar's will, where Caesar left a sum of money to each citizen. Swayed by Antony's speech, the crowd of citizens declare Brutus and Cassius traitors and run them out of the city. Octavius (Caesar's adopted son), Antony, and Lepidus and their armies defeat the armies of the two traitors, who kill themselves on the battlefield. As they are dying, they declare Caesar has been avenged, and Octavius, Antony, and Lepidus return to Rome to celebrate their victory.

The Chocolate War by Robert Cormier

The Chocolate War, written by Robert Cormier in 1974, has been a long-standing young adult classic. It follows the experience of Jerry Renault, a freshman attempting to navigate the treacherous halls of Trinity High School. The opening scene, like that of Julius Caesar, showcases the division of classes and use of language to shape how the students are perceived. At Trinity, a "secret" student organization known as the Vigils controls both students and teachers, ruling the school from behind the scenes. Through manipulation and social pressure, the Vigils, led by Archie Costello, wreak havoc at the school but also operate with the approval of the brothers who lead the school. Archie doles out "assignments" to students that are designed to test their loyalty to the school and the Vigils. Archie makes a deal with Brother Leon that the students will double the amount of chocolate that they sold last year; this creates an interesting power dynamic for both Archie and Brother Leon. Jerry refuses to participate, pushing back initially against Brother Leon's mandate but then also against Archie. The Vigils attempt to harass and attack Jerry into submission but Jerry stands strong. The final showdown is a spectacle orchestrated by Archie where Jerry fights Janza in front of the entire school. Jerry realizes that he, too, has become a pawn in Archie's scheme too late to change either his actions or the fight. The scheme is not limited to the students, however; Archie tips off Brother Leon, who watches the whole fight from a nearby hill, and later protects Archie from facing consequences for orchestrating the fight.

BEFORE READING

Noticing Rhetorical Devices

Writers employ language to create and develop emotion, characters, plot, mood, tone, and tension. Rich and powerful language choices help readers connect with characters and engage with the story. "Rhetoric" is often used to refer to modes of persuasion and the language or language patterns used to present and support writers' and speakers' opinions, and "rhetorical devices" is a term used more broadly to incorporate more language tools. Writers use language devices in order to persuade, to inform, to entertain, and to engage the reader in the texts. As students read both texts, have them look specifically at the rhetorical questions, patterns of repetition, and comparisons used to manipulate and persuade.

As a pre-reading activity, ask students to write three to five sentences to try to persuade their peers that their favorite food, song, or video game is the best food, song, or video game in the world. Introduce the idea of rhetorical questions by defining what a rhetorical question is and providing several examples (speeches by Martin Luther King, Jr. and other activists offer strong examples of the use of rhetorical questions). Rhetorical questions, those questions we ask that we do not intend to be answered, are tools of language used to draw attention to specific concepts, behaviors, or actions. Rhetorical questions, when left unanswered, become powerful in shaping how the audience responds. When reviewing the examples with students, ask them to identify how the question or questions shaped how they thought about the rest of what was in the speech. Then ask students to revise their sentences to include rhetorical questions. Ask them to share their drafts and talk about how their writing changed when they had to include rhetorical questions. Then, introduce the idea of repetition by defining repetition and showing examples. Ask students to return to their original sentences and add repetition as a tool to persuade others. Pair or team students and ask them to compare and contrast the ways in which rhetorical questions and repetition have changed their writing. Introduce simile and metaphor as rhetorical devices that create comparisons. Ask students to revise their original sentences using similes and metaphors. The students should be able to identify the ways in which their writing changed as they incorporated these rhetorical devices. As they share what they noticed, ask them to explain how incorporating these devices can help a writer influence others.

Shakespeare and Cormier use rhetorical devices to shape how characters act and react. Explain to students that they will be paying attention to the rhetorical tools used as they read. Ask them to develop a list of characteristics that will help them identify these rhetorical tools used in the two texts. The student lists should include pattern, use of words or phrases more than once, questions repeated at least two times, and so on. Students may find it useful to collect their noticing of these tools in a three-column chart with headings such as "Rhetorical Device," "Example," and "How It Is Used in Text."

Defining and Exploring Power

The concept of the use and misuse of power plays an important role in both *Julius Caesar* and *The Chocolate War*. In these texts, readers see how power differentials between generals and citizens, men and women, upperclassmen and freshmen, teachers and students are built and reinforced through both action and language. Move students beyond defining the term "power" and thinking of the multiple ways we use the word in our everyday lives, focusing on how the term is used in our own lives provides a way for us to connect to the multiple ways power shapes the actions of the characters in these texts. Begin by asking students to write as many sentences as they can using the word "power"; the goal is for each sentence to use power in a different way (political power, social power, electrical power, etc.). Ask them to try to write at least five sentences using the word differently. Then, in small teams, have the students sort the sentences and create definitions based on how the word is used in those sentences. Bring students back together and have them pull out definitions of power that focus on political and social power. Ask students to write one or two paragraphs about how those kinds of power play out in their home, school, and social lives. They should consider what the power structures are that are embedded in their lives (home, school, outside of school) and consider how those power structures shape their behavior. For example, a student in the theatre club may talk about firmly established rules about who can go into prop rooms or manipulate light and sound devices. That student may talk about the hierarchy that has been established about who has permission and who does not. This student will likely also incorporate specialized language that means something specific in the context. High school students, in general, might talk about sections of the schools that are segregated by who uses them, when, and how. Asking students to develop their own connections to social and political power allows them to differentiate among the different ways power plays out in the characters' lives and the power structures these characters operate within. Finally, ask them then to think about and describe ways in which characters from books and movies choose to conform or rebel against power structures.

Julius Caesar and Jerry are part of the power structures of Rome and Trinity; Caesar is a war hero and Jerry is a new student. As students think about those roles—war hero and new student—ask them to list what their expectations are for these characters within the world in which they live. Contemporary popular culture has created the idea that a small group of committed fighters or a single hero can rebel against the power of the state, a monarchy, a government, or a universe. While it is an appealing notion that a singular hero who believes strongly can overcome issues within a power structure, is it a realistic one? Readers have come to expect that the hero will be defeated early on in the action but will return stronger to win in the end. Ask students to consider what they know about books, movies, and history in order to answer whether they think that the idea of a heroic rebellion is a realistic one. Neither Julius Caesar nor Jerry win in the end. While neither one wins, they do highlight many of the issues of power in societal structures whether a large empire or a private school.

Battlefields Big and Small

A ninth grade student in a large high school stated that he "had to map the safe way to get through the trenches of the hallways and various student groups" so that he could get to class on time. The battles waged in a school may be as political and dangerous as Rome in *Julius Caesar* and the all-boys private school in *The Chocolate War*. Both texts have settings that contrast with the seeming safety of city and school. Caesar is returning from a battlefield as the play opens, and the last scenes include battles between those who betrayed Caesar and those who are trying to avenge him. To help develop an understanding of setting and how characters act and interact in different settings, ask students to create a map of a school as a battleground. They should consider the following questions: *Who are the multiple groups engaged in the battle? Who is in charge? Who hides and is invisible? Who has authority and power? Where are the safe/unsafe places?*

After the students have created their maps and considered the space of school as a battlefield, ask them to connect back to their definitions of political and social power and about how power—whether political or social—moves through the spaces of the school. Ask them to consider the participants in battles and maneuvering, tools used, and how "winners" are determined. Students could create an annotated map key to help explain the places, tools, and winners on the map. Or, students could create a pamphlet designed for new students to help them negotiate the political landmines and battle sites in the school. The focus for this activity is to create both a shared understanding of how political and social power moves in different spaces and to build connections to the texts by providing a lens with which to analyze the events.

DURING READING

The themes of *Julius Caesar* and *The Chocolate War* center on the roles of power, betrayal, and belonging. Thematically, these ideas emerge in multiple ways in the two texts—in how power is coveted, displayed, and used, how masculinity is defined and judged, and how characters are betrayed by groups and individuals. Both Rome and Trinity are locations in which the battle over social and political power rages—who has power and authority over the actions of the populace of Rome and the student body of Trinity? Power and authority are part of the definitions and portrayals of masculinity in the texts. The question becomes whether or not Caesar and Jerry are the right kind of masculine. Brotherhood and the betrayal of that brotherhood become key in both texts as characters use relationships to justify their actions. Caesar is betrayed by those who are supposed to be closest to him, those that have fought beside him, and those that profess great love for him. Jerry is betrayed by the Vigils, a brotherhood of students who work to maintain control of the student body. Both Caesar and Jerry demonstrate moments of belonging and courage. They have peers who hide behind rhetoric or rules to avoid standing up for them, thus proving themselves to be cowards. The use of language becomes a tool to maintain power, to promote betrayal, and to develop belonging through courageous action.

Battlefields Big and Small Revisited

In a pre-reading strategy, we mapped out the settings in a school that define it as a battlefield for students. The settings in *Julius Caesar* and *The Chocolate War* reinforce the concepts of battle and war. Rome and Trinity, the main settings of the texts, should be safe places for the main characters. Caesar returns to Rome a hero honored for his service to the Republic of Rome. Early in the novel, Jerry is a hero in the halls of Trinity. Much of the political maneuvering that happens in both texts happens in the streets, halls, rooms, and houses—places that are assumed to be safe for the characters. After all, Caesar and Jerry are heroes, how could they be in danger in their own city or school. As students read the texts, ask them to create a map of Rome or Trinity as if it were a dangerous battlefield. Using the same questions in the pre-reading activity, ask students to think about how the characters move and interact in their own battlefields. Add the question, *Who is manipulating other characters by action or language?* After students have created their maps and considered the setting of the text as a battlefield, ask them to connect back to earlier definitions of political and social power and to their maps of the school. Ask them to write a short essay explaining how political power moves through the spaces of the text. They could compare and contrast the battlefields in their school with the battlefields of Rome or Trinity.

Beyond an essay, students could create a series of metaphors and similes that describe the participants, battles, tools and winners. Or, students could create a set of rules that govern the movement of students through the political and social spaces of the text. This activity connects back to the pre-reading activity and helps students visualize the settings as dangerous places for the characters. Both *Julius Caesar* and *The Chocolate War* provide examples of the language of war in their texts that will help support students as they engage with this activity.

Introducing and Developing Masculinity

Appleman (2000) argued for bringing in literary theory when reading literature in school, stating, "Theory helps us recognize the essential quality of other visions: how they shape and inform the way we read texts, how we respond to others, how we live our lives. Theory makes the invisible visible, the unsaid said" (p. 75). Considering the role of gender, and masculinity in particular, as a central tool used in character development in both texts requires readers to look at how roles such as soldier, leader, and athlete are portrayed. Both texts establish expectations for how masculine characters behave in the roles they play, but the expectation for how these roles are defined is often invisible to readers—a soldier just acts like a soldier. Jerry learns in Chapter 1 that the coach likes players with "guts," and Jerry interprets that to mean that he must keep his pain quiet, that he must keep getting up, and he must keep going. Readers need to consider what this means for those people who don't have "guts" or who are not chosen for the team. This expectation begins to set up contrasts because of the assumptions that the characters make and the ones that the readers make. Football players are tough because they have guts could be extended to mean that the people who aren't football players are weak.

Readers need to consider how roles are described and contrasted. *How are masculine characters contrasted or compared to feminine characters? What are the characteristics of masculinity developed in the novel? How do those characteristics or their absence serve as motivation or characterization?* For example, Cassius raises questions about Caesar's masculinity when he says, "Ye gods, it doth amaze me/ A man of such feeble temper should/ So get the start of the majestic world/ And bear the palm alone" (Shakespeare, trans. 1992, 1.2.128–131). In that same speech, Cassius points out that Caesar has epilepsy, that Cassius had to save Caesar's life when he almost drowned, and that Caesar cried out for water when he was ill "as a sick girl" (Shakespeare, trans. 1992, 1.2.128). His goal is to make Caesar appear weak. Janza questions Jerry's masculinity in *The Chocolate War* several times saying that Jerry "lives in the closet" (Cormier, 1974, p. 200). When Jerry asks what that means, Janza caresses his face and says that Jerry is hiding a secret, that he is "a fairy. A queer. Living in the closet, hiding away" (p. 201). Jerry recognizes that in the world of Trinity, "The worst thing in the world—[is] to be called queer" (p. 202). The characters in these texts use the ways that masculinity is defined, along with rampant homophobia at Trinity, in order to manipulate other characters into doing what they want them to do. Students can track the definitions of masculinity throughout the text by collecting quotations and examples. They can then use these quotations to create the definition of masculinity that exists in these texts. Additionally, they can use these quotations and definitions to examine and question the role of masculinity in commercials, television shows, sports, or movies.

Both texts uses images of brutality, violence, and battles to develop ideas about what it means to be part of their respective societies. There are soldiers returning from war, fights in the streets, murder in the Senate, battles, and suicides in *Julius Caesar*. These images further the idea of what it means to be a man in Rome. In *The Chocolate War*, there are images of battle and warfare on the field and in the classrooms. Students are tortured and abused physically and mentally by their peers and their teachers. The novel begins and ends with Jerry in physical pain; first in a football tackle and later in a brutal fight. Jerry is beaten so badly in the "boxing match" that he has to be taken away by ambulance, suffering a broken jaw and possible internal injuries. Even before that culminating moment, Jerry is attacked so viciously that "he was afraid that his body would come loose, all his bones spilling out like a building collapsing, like a picket fence clattering apart" (p. 204). These images show the expectations of what a boy should be at Trinity. Brother Leon also dismisses the extreme violence of the boxing match by saying that "boys will be boys." After Jerry is beaten and taken to the hospital with a broken jaw and other injuries, Brother Leon says, "Renault will get the best of care, I assure you . . . Boys will be boys, Jacques. They have high spirits. Oh, once in a while they get carried away but it's good to see all that energy and zeal and enthusiasm" (p. 250). This normalization of violence as ordinary behavior for boys is indicative of the view of masculinity at Trinity.

Mapping Masculinity

As students read, have them identity moments where the characteristics of masculinity are defined either implicitly or explicitly. Ask the students to use a free online mind-mapping tool (see www.educatorstechnology.com for suggestions) in order to collect and organize the characteristics of masculinity that they find in the texts—including quotes and page numbers. Students should begin noticing patterns in the examples they are collecting and can sort the mind map based on the patterns. As they read the texts, they will revise and resort their examples. After each chapter or act, have students write short summaries of the characteristics they have discovered. Students should return to their maps and summaries at the end of the reading and use the notes to develop an argument about the role of masculinity in the texts. They can then write an essay that explains their argument.

Language and Rhetoric

Language and the use of rhetoric are powerful tools in *Julius Caesar* and *The Chocolate War*. The beginnings of both texts, Act 1 in *Julius Caesar*, and Chapters 1–5 in *The Chocolate War*, incorporate multiple uses of rhetorical devices and language play. *Julius Caesar* opens with a street scene in which large numbers of citizens are gathered in the streets to celebrate the triumphant return of Caesar from battle. This scene sets up the power struggle between the people of Rome and the senators of Rome with Caesar in the center. Cassius, Brutus, and many other leaders in Rome fear that the people of Rome will make Caesar a dictator, thus ending the Roman Republic, and, by extension, their own power. The opening scene shows Jerry getting pummeled on the field and being told that the coach likes guts. Ask students to collect the insults and negative comments used by characters in the opening scenes of the two texts. *What do these particular lines show about the characters in the texts?* Students should notice that the insults used clearly establish a hierarchy in both settings. For example, Murellus has no problem describing the cobbler and other workers as, "blocks . . . stones . . . worse than senseless things" (Shakespeare, trans. 1992, 1.1.34). This shows the reader that he believes he is superior to them. It also highlights the class differences among the people of Rome.

Rhetorical Devices Used to Create/Develop Comparisons

Familiar rhetorical devices such as allusion, metaphor, simile, and personification are used by writers to create comparisons and connections. These may be more familiar to students as literary devices than as tools of rhetoric. Because we are focused on how language is used for specific purposes in the texts, we are calling them rhetorical devices. For this activity, ask students to create a chart to track the rhetorical devices that they see being used in the texts. Charts are useful tools for students to use to collect their examples and ideas as they read. However, if students prefer a different mode of organizing, they can use sticky notes that contain the same information.

Allusion is a reference to a relatively well-known person, place, event, or idea. It is frequently used to build a connection between that person, place, event, or idea in a text and something else. For example, if a student refers to writing a research paper as a Herculean task, we are supposed to realize that this alludes to Hercules and the nearly impossible labors he completed. The student is comparing the work done to write the paper as one of the nearly impossible labors. Writers use this tool to show how what is happening in the text is connected to other important events, people, or ideas. This adds weight to the connection. Allusions in both of these texts serve this purpose and they also foreshadow some of the arguments that will be used to support or betray the characters (see figure 2.1).

Additional allusions in *The Chocolate War* include multiple allusions to Catholicism and Catholic rites (confession, chewing the wafer, etc.), allusions to popular culture of the time (hippies, flower children, grass, James Cagney, etc.), and allusions to literature (T.S. Eliot, disturb the universe). Additional allusions in *Julius Caesar* focus on gods, heroes, and villains from Rome's past such as the Colossus at Rhodes (statue of the Greek god Helios), Tarquin (final king of Rome), and Erebus (personification of darkness and shadows in mythology).

Metaphor and Simile

Metaphors and similes, like allusions, are familiar language tools for students. Identifying how metaphors and similes are used in these two texts can provide a deeper understanding of both the story and the characters. Cassius

Rhetorical Device	Example from text & what it refers to	What I think
Allusion	"...because he was a coward about stuff like that, thinking one thing and saying another, planning one thing and doing another—he had been Peter a thousand times and a thousand cocks had crowed in his lifetime." The Chocolate War, p. 5 This is a reference to the Biblical story of Peter. Peter is told that he will betray Jesus three times before the cock crows, Peter denies that he will do it. But, he does.	I think this allusion in the first chapter is used to show how Jerry will betray what he believes in. It also makes me think that the betrayal will be a big one because of the comparison to Peter.
Allusion	I, as Aeneas our great ancestor Did from the flames of Troy upon his shoulder The old Anchises bear, so from the waves of Tiber/ Did I the tired Caesar. (Julius Caesar, Act 1, Sc. 2) This is a reference to the story of Aeneas and how he carried Anchises from the burning city of Troy. Cassius is comparing himself to a hero that is celebrated for the heroic deeds that he did.	I think this allusion to a hero from the Trojan war is an attempt by Cassius to make himself into a big hero. I think it is important to the story that he compares Caesar to an hold man that needed help. Cassius is using this allusion to make Caesar seem weak and not very tough. Is this something that connects to Caesar's masculinity?

Figure 2.1 Sample allusions in both texts. *Author created.*

believes that Caesar should not be as powerful as he is. He questions, "Upon what meat doth this our Caesar feed/That he is grown so great?" (Act 1, Scene ii). This implies that Caesar is powerful because he has consumed the people around him. Cassius uses this to show that he believes Caesar is feeding on Rome to gain power. Cassius believes that Caesar is gaining power he has not earned and that he has done so by feeding on the people of Rome. This metaphor shows both Cassius's jealousy and his fear. Like Cassius, Brutus also uses a metaphor to describe Caesar's power. Brutus says,

But 'tis a common proof
That lowliness is young ambition's ladder,
Whereto the climber-upward turns his face;
But when he once attains the upmost round,
He then unto the ladder turns his back
Looks into the clouds, scorning the base degrees
By which he did ascend. So Caesar may; (Act II, Scene ii)

In this, Brutus is using a metaphor of a ladder to describe what he thinks Caesar's future ambitions may be—that he may want to ascend even higher on a ladder of power. Cassius plays on Brutus's concerns about the republic and convinces him through discussions and fake letters that Caesar is dangerous and that it is the will of the people that Caesar dies. Analyzing the metaphor used here can help demonstrate how Brutus is beginning to think about what Cassius has been arguing. Ask students to create a metaphor for Cassius or Brutus. Then ask them to share the metaphor and explain what it shows about Cassius or Brutus. Here, teachers can allow students choice in the medium through which they choose to create and share their metaphor. Some students may choose to create memes, while others may use poster boards or create power points.

In *The Chocolate War*, Jerry uses metaphors to describe how he is feeling or to describe another character's actions. For example, after a grueling football practice, Jerry describes his pain, explaining, "a pain appeared, distant, small—a radar signal of distress. Bleep. I'm here. Pain" (p. 7). Metaphors are useful rhetorical tools because, like allusions, they bring additional narrative weight to the comparisons being made. Jerry compares the silence in Brother Leon's class after the teacher has accused Bailey of cheating to that of the silence after a hydrogen bomb. This metaphor adds the emotions of fear and shock to the question the teacher asked. Ask students to create a metaphor to describe a powerful moment in their lives. After they have created it, ask them to write a short explanation of the metaphor. Students can share their metaphors in small teams, or present to the entire class. As described above, teachers could offer students the opportunity to choose how they craft and present their metaphors.

Similes, like metaphors and allusions, are used in both texts to create visual and emotional connections in the reader. The senators surround Caesar and stab him to death. The senators then coat their hands and swords with Caesar's blood. Antony described Caesar's wounds as "like dumb mouths" who are calling on him to speak for Caesar, for his wounds (Act III, Scene i). Brutus described "hollow men, like horses hot at hand" as men who pretend to be strong and brave but, in the end are "like the deceitful jades" who ultimately fail (Act IV, Scene ii). Antony compares the conspirators to apes, dogs, and slaves (Act V, Scene i); these comparisons develop understanding for the readers—the conspirators are not just bad, they are like animals. This adds depth to the descriptions.

Jerry explained that the "[s]weat moved like small moist bugs on this forehead" (p. 7). It is not enough for the reader to know that Jerry is hot after practice, the reader needs the visceral connection to Jerry with the idea that the sweat is crawling down his face like a bug. Brother Leon used his pointer as a tool during lessons—"like a conductor's baton or a musketeer's sword" (p. 38). This comparison shows that Brother Leon likes to control his students.

This section has focused primarily on those that are used to compare one thing to another. Ask students to choose one of the examples from the chart they have created and write a short essay explaining how that example is used in the text and what the effect of that device is on the reader.

Repetition

Repetition is a rhetorical device in which words, phrases, or sentences are used multiple times in a text to create an effect on the reader. Anaphora, a rhetorical device, is the repetition of the first word or couple of words in a set of sentences. There are multiple examples of anaphora in *Julius Caesar*; characters use this type of repetition to make key ideas and actions visible and important. Brutus says,

What you have said
I will consider; what you have to say
I will with patience hear, and find a time
Both meet to hear ad answer such high things.
    (Shakespeare, trans. 1992, 1.1 167–170)

The repetition of "what you have said/what you have to say" and "I will" creates a pattern that both emphasizes the active nature of the betrayal that Cassius is trying to foment and the active nature of Brutus's participation. "I will" is active and indicates that Brutus will be listening and thinking about what Cassius has to say. Brutus acknowledges this that Cassius has said things and will say more. Cassius uses anaphora as well as he talks to Casca, stating,

But if you would consider the true cause
Why all these fires, why all these guiding ghosts,
Why birds and beasts from quality and kind,
Why old men fool and children calculate
Why all these things change from their ordinance.
    (Shakespeare, trans. 1992, 1.3.62–66)

The repetition of the word "why" creates a pattern that almost seems as though Cassius is asking questions, but he is not. He is trying to give the reason why all of the people and animals listed have deviated from their usual behavior. The repetition of "why" becomes almost mesmerizing for his audience. Portia uses the repetition of "I grant I am a woman, but withal" in a scene with her husband Brutus as she tries to prove that she can be a confidant and advisor if he would give her a chance (Shakespeare, trans. 1992, 2.1.291–295). This patterned repetition highlights what she sees as her strengths not just her gender.

The word "beautiful" appears over fifty times throughout *The Chocolate War*. Jerry and Tubs both describe their crushes as beautiful, focusing on the girls as physically attractive objects of their attention. Describing them this way without talking about more than their looks shows the centrality of the male gaze in the novel. Archie uses "beautiful" or "beautiful, beautiful" in the novel when he wants to show his approval of or draw attention to specific events or actions in the novel. The word "beautiful" perversely appears at some of the most disturbing parts of the text, highlighting the stark contrast between the way Archie views the world and the way other characters (and presumably the readers) see it. For example, Archie says "beautiful" to Janza after he pretends to take a picture of him (p. 99). What might make this particularly disturbing to some is that Archie has just found Janza masturbating in a stall in the bathroom. Rather than close the door to the stall, Archie draws attention to what Janza is doing. Janza is so startled that he doesn't even have time to react. Archie later says it to Jerry after Jerry has an argument with Brother Leon about selling chocolates (p. 119) and again when Obie is reporting how other students are perceiving Jerry's rebellion (p. 139). What might make both of these instances troubling for some is that Archie was doing something wrong in both cases (looking for a place to smoke and smoking) and felt it important to name challenges to authority figures at school as "beautiful." Archie notes that the raffle tickets and the description of the punches students want Janza and Jerry to use on each other is "beautiful" (p. 230). He describes the brutality being directed by students as beautiful. He does not consider the harm that it might do to either participant in the fight. After the fight is over and Jerry is taken away in an ambulance, Archie realizes that Brother Leon is on his side and will support him in the brutality and says, "beautiful" (p. 250). This repetition of the word "beautiful" as it is associated with such brutal behaviors highlights the perverse nature of Archie's behavior and how it is rewarded at Trinity.

Students should use a rhetorical devices graphic organizer or Post-its to collect their examples and information about repetition. This organizer can be a resource for them as they write about these texts. Ask students to choose an example of repetition in either text and explain how the repetitions shape either how an action or a character is portrayed. *How does our opinion of Archie change as we consider how and when he uses "beautiful"? How does our opinion of Brutus change when Antony repeats "and Brutus is an honorable man" three times in the funeral speech?*

Analyzing the Speeches

The rhetoric in both *Julius Caesar* and *The Chocolate War* is used to persuade, manipulate, or justify actions. Cassius manipulates Brutus into believing that he is saving the Roman Republic if he participates in the assassination of Caesar. Brutus does not see himself as someone who is betraying Caesar; rather, he sees himself as someone who is protecting the ideas of Rome and keeping it from reverting to a monarchy. Without Cassius's lies and suggestions, Brutus would have continued to see Caesar as a soldier and hero of the Roman Republic. Like Cassius, Archie works to manipulate the people around him to participate in schemes, tricks, and bullying. Archie, through his whisper campaigns and behind-the-scenes actions, successfully manipulates multiple people to act in the manner he wants. Archie recognizes this as he stands looking out at the students who are gathered for the fight. "Now, surveying his handiwork, the crowded bleachers, the frantic comings and goings as the raffle tickets were bought and sold . . . He had successfully conned Renault and Leon and The Vigils and the whole damn school" (p. 223). Jerry was initially controlled by Archie and the Vigils as he refused to sell the chocolate. After ten days, Jerry was supposed to give in and participate in the chocolate sales. Jerry defied that edict and Archie began to manipulate the student body into rebelling against Jerry.

Ask your students to consider what tools Cassius used to persuade Brutus and how those tools shaped how other characters' behavior and actions. In Act 1, Scene 2, Cassius makes several comments to Brutus that show he is manipulating Brutus. Brutus says, "for the eye sees not itself/but by reflection, by some other things" (Shakespeare, trans. 1992, 1.2.52–53). Cassius build on this by complimenting Brutus, stating that he wished Brutus could see his "hidden worthiness" and suggests that Brutus is powerful in Rome just as Caesar is (Shakespeare, trans. 1992, 1.2.55–62). Brutus recognizes this attempt at flattery, asking "Into what dangers would you lead me, Cassius" (Shakespeare, trans. 1992, 1.2.63–65) in order to show that he knows Cassius is trying to manipulate him. Have students analyze Cassius's monologue (Shakespeare, trans. 1992, 1.2.90–132) for three things: (a) appeals to Brutus's emotions, (b) comparisons between Brutus and Caesar, and (c) comparisons to history or fate.

Once students have identified these components, ask them to explain how these appeals and comparisons persuade Brutus to think that Caesar might be dangerous to the Republic. Students might explain that Cassius appeals to Brutus's pride by saying that the names of Brutus and Caesar are equal in Rome and then appeals to his fear by implying that Rome sees Caesar as a possible king.

Archie, like Cassius, used his words as weapons to manipulate other characters in *The Chocolate War*. For example, Archie asks, " 'You mean the finances are bad?' Archie taunted, launching his own offensive. To Leon, it might have sounded like a shot in the dark, but it wasn't" (p. 154). Notice how Cormier uses battle rhetoric ("offensive" and "shot") to describe how

Archie is manipulating Brother Leon, reinforcing the connection between
words and weapons. Archie also makes Janza believe that he has a compromising picture of him, effectively blackmailing Janza into doing his
bidding. He bends the (other) big bully to his will with only a few words
(pp. 98–99).

While many of the monologues show the power of words and language
to shape how the public sees an event, other passages show how a character can use language to defend the choices he is making. Brutus shows his
divided thinking about Caesar in his monologue (Shakespeare, trans. 1992,
2.1.10–34). For this speech analysis, have students identify the sections of the
speech that show the different sides of Brutus's argument with himself. Once
students have done this, ask them to imagine that Brutus's two sides are in
an actual argument and act out the lines. After several teams of students have
acted this section out, ask them to identify the lines that show evidence of
Cassius's manipulations. Then ask them to explain how Brutus builds a case
for himself that "It must be by his death" (Shakespeare, trans. 1992, 2.1.10).

Archie uses his skill with language and persuasion to manipulate the
students in Trinity. He describes how he orchestrated the boxing match by
leveraging what he sees as people's innate greed and cruelty:

> You see, Carter, people are two things: greedy and cruel. So we have a perfect
> set-up here. The greed part—a kid pays a buck for the chance to win a hundred.
> Plus fifty boxes of chocolates. The cruel part—watching two guys hitting each
> other, maybe hurting each other, while they're safe in the bleachers. That's why
> it works, Carter, because we're all bastards. (p. 231)

In addition to using his words to manipulate his fellow students and the
Brothers, Archie also knows when, strategically, *not* to speak: "Archie didn't
say anything . . . When in doubt, play the waiting game. Watch for an opening" (p. 173).

We learn, as readers, that Brother Leon is also a masterful manipulator. He
blackmails a student by giving him an "F" and intimating that he'll change
the grade if the student helps him: " 'Tell you what, Caroni. At the end of
the term, when the marks close, I'll review that particular test. Perhaps I'll be
fresher then. Perhaps I'll see the merit that wasn't apparent before' " (p. 109).
Caroni also notices that he calls him by his first name, David, even though
Leon "seldom called a student by his first name. He always kept a distance
between himself and his pupils" (p. 193). Brother Leon signals by his word
choice that he is treating David differently now, but reverts back to "Caroni"
by the end of the conversation when he wants to show that David is no longer in his confidence. At the end of the novel, we understand the depths of
Leon's depravity, as we learn that Archie tipped him off to the fight and he

did nothing to stop it. He watched the whole thing, and he protects Archie from punishment for orchestrating the whole affair.

Funeral Speeches

The funeral speeches in Julius Caesar contain five major structural components—introduction, development, evidence, response to objections, and summary. These parts provide opportunities for both Brutus and Antony to display their rhetorical skills for the people of Rome. Brutus attempts to justify Caesar's murder, and Antony attempts to show that Caesar's death was not justified. Both introductions begin by calling the people to attention. Brutus says, "Romans, countrymen, and lovers, hear me for my cause, and be silent that you may hear" (3.2.13–14). Antony picks up on the pattern established by Brutus, and says, "Friends, Romans, countrymen, lend me your ears" (2.3.65). This line uses metonymy, one item is used to represent another, and instead of the commanding to listen, he suggests that they do. The openings of each speech then establish the different tones and expectations the speakers have for their funeral speeches. For this activity, ask students to identify the five sections of each speech and then compare and contrast them. Ask them to look for literary elements and repetition in the sections of the speeches and to explain how Brutus and Antony used their language choices to manipulate the Roman people. Students could do a more traditional rhetorical analysis of the monologues and speeches given by Cassius, Brutus, and Antony by examining how they employ logos, pathos, and ethos. These appeals, attributed to Aristotle, are commonly defined as appeals to logic, emotion, and morals, respectively. They are used to persuade other characters to believe or act the way that the characters wish them to do. This can be added as an additional layer of analysis. Additionally, students could write the version of the speech that Cassius or Calpurnia would give using the same five-part structure that Brutus and Cassius used. Students should incorporate fragments of lines that those characters have used earlier in the play as part of the speeches.

Rhetorical Questions

Questions have enormous power as a rhetorical device in both *Julius Caesar* and *The Chocolate War*. Questions have the power to shape how someone responds to the speaker or to characters in a situation. Characters in both texts use questions to draw attention to actions in order to persuade other characters to behave in particular ways. In Act 1 Scene 1 of *Julius Caesar*, Murellus uses rhetorical questions in his speech to the Cobbler, asking, "Wherefore rejoice? What conquest brings he home?" (Shakespeare, trans. 1992, 1.1.31). His purpose is to challenge the Cobbler's idea that Caesar's arrival is to be celebrated. The questions he asks are designed to draw attention away from Caesar and toward the power of Rome.

Cassius asks, "For who is so firm that cannot be seduced?" (Shakespeare, trans. 1992, 1.1.301); with this question, Cassius assumes that his audience will agree that there is no person who cannot be seduced with offers of power. In *The Chocolate War*, Brother Leon asks Bailey, "Are you perfect, Bailey?" (p. 43). He does not mean for Bailey to answer, what he intends is for Bailey and the other students to realize that he (Brother Leon) can do or say what he wishes. Brother Leon is in the middle of what Jerry describes as one of his performances. The questions he asks are rhetorical and the students are largely props.

Archie presents Jerry with the idea that a boxing match is a way to get even with everyone who has harmed him. Jerry asks, "With you too, Archie?" (p. 222). He recognizes that Archie's actions have led him to this point. Archie returns Jerry's question with a series of questions of his own—"Me?" and "Hell, why me?" (p. 222). Archie uses these questions to deflect responsibility for his actions. Brutus and Antony play with questions in their speeches to the populace after Caesar's death.

Ask students to choose a scene that includes rhetorical questions. They should identify the question and the speaker's intent behind using those questions. Additionally, ask students to explain how the questions are used to manipulate other characters. Because rhetorical questions are a useful tool for speakers, it is often challenging to imagine how a scene would change if they were not used. In order to make this more visible to the students, ask them to rewrite the scene so that the questions become statements. They should then discuss how the scene changes.

AFTER READING

Although these paired texts paint a picture of humanity that is overwhelmingly negative, they do contain hope. In both texts, there are characters who demonstrate care and support, even if they falter at times. Take Goober, for example, who is unwaveringly supportive of Jerry. Ask students to seek out instances in either of these texts where a contrast to the negative portrayal of humans—as violent and manipulative, or "cruel and greedy," as Archie believes (p. 231)—is presented. *Are there characters who do the wrong thing for the right reasons or characters who do the right thing for the wrong one?* Students can analyze the ways in which characters behave or don't behave in self-serving ways. Have students create a character analysis or bio poem for a character they find who behave in selfless ways.

The Role of Women in the Texts

Both *Julius Caesar* and *The Chocolate War* are male-dominated texts with very few female characters. Appleman (2000) explained, "Feminist theory invites us to consider a wide variety of issues of gender, of 'the living situations' of men and women, as we read. Feminist theory asks us to attend to the cultural imprint of patriarchy as we read" (p. 76). However, "living situations" should not be limited to men and women as if they are binary categories. While the focus of this unit has been on the portrayals of masculinity in these texts, it cannot be implied that only men can be masculine and women feminine, but rather that gender exists along a spectrum and is not neatly categorizable. For more information on approaching the texts through the lens of gender studies and queer theory, we encourage you to look at Purdue Owl's Gender Studies and Queer Theory webpage.

This activity draws on a feminist theory lens to focus on characters identified as girls or women in the world of the texts. For both *Julius Caesar* and *The Chocolate War*, women, girls, and expressions of femininity are largely absent. The women that are there are defined not by what they do but by the men in their lives. These women are objects of beauty, mothers, wives, or daughters with little autonomy of their own. Ask students to locate scenes in which the women are identified or speaking and determine how they are presented. One heuristic that has become well known for gauging depiction of women in fiction is the Bechdel test. Bechdel (1985) outlined her criteria: the film (or, by extension, work of fiction) must have at least two women in it, and these women must talk to each other about something other than a man. After reading the texts, ask your students to determine whether *Julius Caesar* and *The Chocolate War* would pass the Bechdel test. Ask them to present their Bechdel test results, and an explanation of how they arrived at their conclusion using evidence—or lack of it—from the text to the class.

Calpurnia and Portia are the wives of Caesar and Brutus, respectively. *How are the women in Julius Caesar bound by the expectations of women in Roman culture? How are Calpurnia and Portia situated in their roles as wives? Are they allowed to be confidants, to be heroes?* Both Calpurnia and Portia are defined by who they are married to and/or who their fathers were. While the women attempt to have some sway with their husbands, many of their warnings or concerns are overlooked. Neither Caesar nor Brutus choose to listen to their wives' cautions or use them as confidants. Jerry's mother, Mrs. Hunter, and Ellen Barrett are the women in Jerry's life. The women largely are defined by who they are to the boys and men in the text—wives, mothers, caretakers, and sex objects. *How do these roles shape the way that masculinity and femininity are used in the texts? How does the presence or absence of women shape the lives of the men in the text?* Masculinity, in both texts, is defined in militaristic ways while femininity is limited to discussions of beauty and wifely behaviors. Jerry sees a change in his father after his mother's death; he focuses on the multiple times that his father seems to sleep or respond that things are "fine" when they may not be. He does not want to be like his father who seems to have given up on life and goals. He sees the absence of his mother as the thing that has changed his father. Ask students to find references to women in both texts. Once identified, have students make an argument for how women are portrayed in these texts. Then have them present their argument using Prezi or another preferred technology application. In this presentation, students should use the "results" of their Bechdel test as a starting point.

Beyond identification of references to women in each text, students could choose a scene from *Julius Caesar* or *The Chocolate War* and rewrite the genders of the characters in the scene. *Would the dialogue or action change if the genders were changed in some way? If so, how? Why?* Considering how gender changes may shift the behavior of characters provides an opportunity for students to think about the ways in which gender may inform what characters are allowed to do and say. That these texts are male dominated does not mean that they are not valuable and rich texts to read in schools, but it does mean that we should be critical of gender roles that marginalize some characters and completely omit others.

EXTENSION ACTIVITIES

Both of these texts are period pieces, and readers may wonder how they relate to contemporary society. These extension activities offer ways to help students make those connections. You may opt to use one of the following activity ideas:

- The rhetoric of COVID-19: Watch White House Press Briefing footage to notice rhetoric of speeches about the origins of, spread of, and responses to COVID-19. What words related to battles can you find? Create a video montage of clips of these instances of language. Consider what words get repeated and how the language is used by different stakeholders to create different narratives.
- Campaigns as battlegrounds: Choose a local political race and compare/ contrast the commercials for each candidate. Determine how language is used to create differing views of the candidates.
- Protest sign rhetoric: Search the internet for images of protest signs. What imagery and words do they use to persuade? Design your own, using what

you have learned about persuasive tactics. Share with your classmates and explain why you made the visual and linguistic choices you made.

• Julius Caesar beyond Rome: Watch the filmed production of *Julius Caesar* reimagined by director Gregory Doran to take place in postindependence Africa. How does the meaning of the play change or remain the same when presented this way? Ask students to think of a contemporary conflict that could be represented like this. Who might Caesar, Brutus, and the other characters represent if they changed the setting of the play again?

CONCLUSION

Julius Caesar and *The Chocolate War* are powerful texts that elaborate on the ways in which relationships are made and broken in the quest for power. Both feature power-hungry men with few scruples, and the destruction they leave in their wake. These texts may also serve as a springboard for developing critique; we encourage students to think not only about these powerful themes, but also about the representations and perspectives that are missing or marginalized. The extensions help us recognize the limitations of these texts and encourage students to be critical readers of texts that are frequently read in high school classrooms.

REFERENCES

Appleman, D. (2000). *Critical encounters in high school English*. New York: Teachers College Press.

Bechdel, A. (1985). The rule. *Dykes to Watch Out For*. Retrieved from https://dykestowatchoutfor.com/the-rule/.

Cormier, R. (1974). *The chocolate war*. New York, NY: Alfred A. Knopf.

Shakespeare, W. (1992). *Julius Caesar*. T. Seward (Ed.). New York: Cambridge University Press.

Chapter 3

Revenge, Mental Health, and Suicide

Pairing Shakespeare's Hamlet *and Matthew Quick's* Forgive Me, Leonard Peacock

Joseph P. Haughey

Since its composition over 400 years ago, *Hamlet* has delighted readers and playgoers; its rich language and universal characters connect us, to those who across cultures and centuries studied it before us, as well as within the classroom and theatrical communities in which we continue to ponder its penetrating philosophical inquiries. *Hamlet* makes us reflect deeply within ourselves, rousing us to explore our own innate drives and ambitions: how do we answer when trauma is inflicted; why stomach life's hardships; why "be" when it seems far easier "not to be," disquieting questions for adults and adolescents alike. As a result, the play remains as relevant as ever in the lives of our secondary students, providing a reflective lens as they navigate difficult contemporary young adult issues.

This chapter provides a rationale and strategies for a themed unit pairing *Hamlet* alongside Matthew Quick's young adult novel *Forgive Me, Leonard Peacock*. The two texts side by side open spaces for rich conversations about revenge, suicide, mental health, and gun violence. These issues are not new; rather, they are manifestations of the demons that humankind wrestled with in Shakespeare's time and continue to face. For Leonard Peacock, the title character in *Forgive Me, Leonard Peacock*, this is clear. Leonard immediately recognizes *Hamlet*'s relevance in his own life; the melancholic prince's struggles mirror his own, and by weaving Hamlet's story into Leonard's, the novel illuminates the similarities between *Hamlet* and the anxieties that teens still tackle today. In fact, Quick seems almost to have written *Forgive Me, Leonard Peacock*, explicitly for pairing with Shakespeare's *Hamlet*. Leonard has memorized large swathes from *Hamlet* (as well as a soliloquy from *Macbeth*) and quotes from them freely through the novel. At one point, midway through the novel, it becomes clear that Leonard knows *Hamlet* better than even his own English teacher. In this, Quick provides adolescents an entry point into thinking about Shakespeare's original, a compelling illustration of the Shakespeare text through a character their own age.

Leonard, in many ways, is Hamlet. Theirs are both stories of revenge; both have suffered trauma to such a degree that their sole focus has become trying to kill the one who has wronged them. Theirs are also both stories of isolation, of being alone in a world that has gotten too big for them. Both protagonists have lost their respective fathers. Both lean on and rebel against a mother who has betrayed them. Both are unable to overcome the pain they face, but yet also unable to execute their revenge. Both, though, are also intelligent, witty, and philosophical; their spirits in many ways old and wise, but yet at the same time fiery and impetuous, each of their stories offering insight into the other's. By pairing the two texts, teachers can bring Shakespeare's original to life and highlight just how contemporary *Hamlet* remains still today.

Hamlet by William Shakespeare

Hamlet is a play of revenge and remembrance. The ghost of Hamlet's father returns from Purgatory in the first act to call on his son to both revenge and remember him. The ghost reveals that he had been murdered by his own brother, Claudius, who is also Hamlet's uncle, robbed of life, crown, and queen. Prior to the play, Hamlet, devastated by his father's death and mother's hasty marriage to his uncle, had slipped into a melancholic stupor, but spurred on by his father's ghost, Hamlet had reason finally for action. In the second and third acts, the king and his advisor, Polonius arrange to spy on Hamlet. First, they enlist two of Hamlet's old friends, Rosencrantz and Guildenstern, and then later Ophelia, Hamlet's girlfriend, to try to get Hamlet to reveal what troubles him while they hide nearby and listen. Hamlet sees through the thin plots, though, and brutally berates them.

Hamlet cannot take immediate action against his uncle, at least partially because he is uncertain whether the ghost is really his father or a demon from hell come to trick him, so in the third act he has a group of traveling players act out a scene closely resembling his father's murder and then watches his uncle's reaction. It is enough to prove his uncle's guilt, and in Act 4, Hamlet finds his uncle alone at prayer, but cannot bring himself yet to enact revenge; killing him while at prayer would mean absolved of his sins that his uncle would go to heaven. Hamlet wants to send him to hell, so he waits.

Hamlet chides his mother, Gertrude, in her chambers for having married her husband's brother. Polonius is spying from behind a curtain, though, and when Hamlet hears a sound, assumes it is his uncle, and runs his dagger through the curtain, killing him. Her father's death overwhelms Ophelia emotionally, and she slips into madness and eventual suicide.

In the play's final scene, the king has arranged for Hamlet to be killed in a concocted fencing match. Polonius's son, Laertes—who was also brother to Ophelia—has returned, himself seeking revenge for his own murdered father, and under Claudius's advice, he has poisoned the tip of his rapier and intends to murder Hamlet during the match. Hamlet's uncle further poisons a chalice, which he intends to give to Hamlet to drink from during the match. The poisoned rapier indeed kills Hamlet, along with Laertes when the two combatants change weapons. In his final moments, though, Hamlet is also able to stab his uncle and for good measure force him to drink from his own poisoned cup—Gertrude a few moments before had inadvertently drunk from it and as she died revealed its treachery—and in proper tragic fashion, the dead bodies of the major characters litter the stage as the play concludes. The plot itself is simple enough, but its universal characterization, rich language-poetry, and complex philosophical underpinnings have made it one of the quintessential foundational works of English literature.

Forgive Me, Leonard Peacock by Matthew Quick

Quick's compact storytelling covers just a little more than twenty-four hours of Leonard's life: his eighteenth birthday. Leonard's father, a minor rock-and-roll star from a previous generation, fled to South America years ago to avoid the Internal Revenue Service (IRS) and piles of back taxes. His mother, barely present, is a fashion designer who spends most of her time away from home in Manhattan with her French boyfriend, Jean-Luc. At the beginning of the novel, at breakfast, Leonard makes clear to readers his intentions later that day to take revenge and murder his former best friend, Asher Beal, and then turn the gun on himself. He already has the weapon, a Nazi P-38 that once belonged to his World War II veteran grandfather, and he already has the motive, a series of sexual assaults over a period of two years that Asher inflicted upon Leonard; readers learn later in the novel that these began when Leonard was just thirteen, shortly after a camping trip in which Asher himself was sexually molested, and that he endured them for two years before finally summoning the strength to resist. Before Leonard can carry out his violent intentions, though, he has four gifts to deliver: an old thrift store hat for his elderly neighbor, Walt, with whom he watches Humphry Bogart movies on days he skips school; his grandfather's bronze star for his favorite teacher, Herr Silverman, who teaches a class on the Holocaust; a six-figure check representing Leonard's entire college fund for his Iranian friend, Baback, to support the democratic political movement back in Iran; and a silver cross necklace for Lauren, a girl he met a year before, who passes out Christian pamphlets in the subway station, and for whom he has had a frustrating crush on for more than a year.

Of these four, Herr Silverman proves the book's hero. He is the high school's German teacher, but also teaches a class each year on the Holocaust.

As a closeted gay teacher in a public school, Herr Silverman himself has had to overcome obstacles; he explains late in the novel, "It's sort of don't ask, don't tell for gay high school teachers—especially those of us who teach controversial Holocaust classes" (p. 220). He is not without flaw, as will be addressed in the chapter's conclusion, but he is heroic. He pays attention to his students. He insists on greeting each individually at his classroom door, to the chagrin of some: "Why does he have to shake everyone's hand every day? this kid Dan Lewis says about Herr Silverman as we take our seats. He's so fucking weird, Tina Whitehead answers under her breath" (pp. 106–107). Nevertheless, Herr Silverman sees that Leonard is struggling and takes immediate steps to intervene, giving Leonard his cell number and making him promise to call him before doing anything rash. He knows Leonard is contemplating suicide. Earlier in the novel, he had suggested Leonard imagine loved ones from the future and write a series of letters from them backward in time to himself, and Leonard did; these beautiful letters are inserted at various moments in the novel, providing insight into Leonard's creativity and character, and giving Leonard something to look forward to in the future. At least in part due to Silverman's compassion, the line between intent and action blurs as Leonard's story progresses, and what appears fortitude in early chapters dissolves *Hamlet*-like into inaction. When given the opportunity late in the novel, Leonard can bring himself neither to enact revenge or take his own life, and by the book's conclusion Herr Silverman convinces him instead to throw his grandfather's World War II gun into the river: "As far as [Herr Silverman is] concerned, *all* guns belong at the bottom of rivers" (p. 226).

Forgive Me, Leonard Peacock offers hope; it is the tale of a young man who finds himself incapable of murder and survives a suicide attempt. By the end of the book, while much remains unresolved, Leonard sees a future for himself; he wishes to himself that he "could delete the past twenty-four hours" (p. 240).

BEFORE READING

Setting the Tone

Before reading, students need to be alerted to the dark topics addressed in both *Hamlet* and *Forgive Me, Leonard Peacock*, which can be triggering for some. In preparing students, teachers may want to consider inviting a school counselor or other mental health professional from their district or community into the classroom to share resources. Such professionals can also help set a proper tone for the class on the seriousness of the issues addressed in each of the texts. Teachers might also post on their walls or classroom door the telephone number for the Suicide Prevention Lifeline (1-800-273-8255), which provides free and confidential support for people in distress; their website provides printable resources and pamphlets. In addition, teachers should research and recommend any local resources; many cities and hospitals provide additional services and regular meeting places for struggling teens in their communities. Teachers may find video resources useful as well, such as Mark Henick's Ted Talk, available on YouTube, which explains "Why We Need to Talk about Suicide," or any of a variety of other Ted Talks in which teachers, counselors, and survivors address suicide and mental health.

Conversations on Revenge

Before reading, teachers should lead students in a conversation about revenge. Reflect together on the toxicity of revenge, how unmitigated revenge can cycle endlessly downward, and how only by learning strategies for breaking the cycle can students escape its destructive whirlpool. Explain that in reading *Hamlet*, students will see just how destructive revenge can be; Hamlet's search for revenge on his uncle will lead to the ultimate destruction of almost everybody in the play. Explain that *Hamlet* is an example of "revenge tragedy"; have them share what they already know about "tragedy" and connect this to the outcomes of revenge. Then, explain how in *Forgive Me*, students will encounter a character who finds a way to break the cycle of revenge. The following questions may prove useful as short writing prompts or conversation starters:

- Reflect on a time when you were angry with somebody else and said or did something that you later regretted. What could you have done differently in the situation that might have led to a better outcome?
- Reflect on a time when somebody did something wrong to you and you forgave them. How did forgiving them make you feel? How did it make them feel?
- Recall a character from a story or book you've read (or alternately a movie you've seen) who struggled to control his or her anger, somebody who let his or her emotions control them instead of letting reason control them; what happened to that character?

DURING READING

When pairing the texts, teachers must decide whether students read *Hamlet* or *Forgive Me* first. In a chronological approach, in which students read *Hamlet* first, *Forgive Me* ultimately becomes a richer read, one that speaks backward in time to Shakespeare's original, but does little to enhance students' reading of *Hamlet*. Another approach is to have students first read *Forgive Me* and then *Hamlet*, in which *Forgive Me* serves as a gateway and roadmap into the characters and themes of *Hamlet*, and then enriches the reading of Shakespeare instead of the other way around. A third, and perhaps the better approach, is having students begin with an overview of *Hamlet* through one of the excellent abridged graphic novel adaptations that have been published in recent years followed by the reading of *Forgive Me* with a rudimentary understanding of its *Hamlet* references, and afterward return back to Shakespeare's original for a fuller, more careful second reading.

"I'll Put Another Question to Thee": Herr Silverman's Ethical Question Day

In *Forgive Me, Leonard Peacock*, teacher Herr Silverman conducts an ongoing discussion activity in his Holocaust class in which students debate difficult questions: "We do this thing where someone asks a hard question related to the Holocaust—one with no clear right or wrong solution, like a moral dilemma—and then the class debates the answer" (p. 108). Leonard asks his classmates hypothetically what should happen to a Nazi World War II gun passed down from grandfather to grandson, even as he has his grandfather's World War II gun stashed in his backpack. His classmates' answers range from donating it to a museum to destroying it (pp. 108–113). Students need structured spaces in which they can safely explore difficult ethical questions and Herr Silverman's student-generated discussion activity lets his class delve into complex topics as well as giving him insight into his students' struggles. After class, he talks to Leonard alone and asks him if he indeed has his grandfather's gun and offers to help Leonard.

In adapting this activity for classroom use, set aside discussion time in at least two class periods, and ask students to compose their own ethical questions based on their readings of *Hamlet* and *Forgive Me*. To provide structure, ask students to submit these in writing for your review prior to class. You can also scaffold the discussions by providing guiding topics. Start with revenge: *What moral dilemmas do students see in the revenges that Hamlet and Leonard seek: is the ghost of Hamlet's father wrong to demand his son take revenge; does Leonard have a right to punish Asher for what he did to him? Where do these intersect with their own feelings about revenge: how should students at your school react when they see injustice?* Afterward, allow students to move on in subsequent classes to other topics related to the readings that matter to them. Use Herr Silverman's structure (or adapt it to fit your class) and let students present their own questions, have their classmates answer and provide counterpoints while they listen, and close by having the student who initially asked the question provide concluding thoughts, summarizing the discussion and various student points of view.

Compiling Textual References for Later Use

As students are reading *Forgive Me*, have them compile textual references that they can then use later in their classroom discussions and written work. They can do this in a notebook or digital document. Alternatively, teachers may have students mark the appropriate passages in their texts using color-coded post-it notes. Below are three possible topics—though teachers can use many of the questions in the section after this as well for compiling textual evidence—that students can track as they read. These then align to the after-reading and extension activities provided in the next sections, and will give students material for crafting a thesis and supporting it with textual evidence. These can also serve as points that teachers can return to for discussion at various points during reading.

1. Leonard has memorized most of Hamlet's lines and can quote freely from Shakespeare, as he does throughout the novel. Make a list of all the *Hamlet* references in *Forgive Me*. (Also note, there is one point too when Leonard quotes *Macbeth*.) Write or type out the quotations and corresponding act, scene, and line numbers.
2. In addition to quoting him, Leonard parallels Hamlet in his characteristics as well. As you read, create a list of characters from *Forgive Me* that remind you of characters from *Hamlet*. For example, which character in the play most reminds you of Gertrude, Hamlet's father, Claudius, and so on? Write down what they say or do that reminds you of the characters from *Hamlet*. Keep track of page numbers.
3. In addition to characters, there are a number of scenes in *Forgive Me* that loosely parallel scenes from *Hamlet*. Quick has not made these identical to those from the original, but there are moments in his writing that echo Shakespeare's original. As you encounter scenes that remind you of *Hamlet*, create a list of them, along with brief descriptions of what happens, and their corresponding act, scene, and line numbers.

Exploring Revenge

As students read *Forgive Me*, the following questions can be used chronologically as in-class discussion prompts or as informal writing assignments to lead students' thinking through the novel. These align to the activities in the next sections and will help students brainstorm similarities with *Hamlet* as they work through the play.

Chapters 1–6:

1. Both Hamlet and Leonard have troubled relationships with their mothers. Hamlet is devastated by his mother's marriage to his uncle, while Leonard finds his mother too emotionally and physically distant after she "rented an apartment in Manhattan and left [him] all alone" (p. 9). Later in the book, he will repeatedly say how he hates her. Compare Hamlet's and Leonard's respective relationships with their mothers; in what ways do their complex relationships with their mothers affect their struggles?

2. Hamlet and Leonard are also similar in that both have recently lost their father: Hamlet's father has been murdered and Leonard's father has abandoned him and "fled the country" to avoid prosecution for tax evasion (p. 11). How does losing their respective fathers affect Hamlet and Leonard? What father figures, healthy or unhealthy (e.g. Claudius, Herr Silverman, Walt), does each still each have in their fathers' absences? What do the two stories suggest then about the significance of fatherhood in a young man's life?

Chapters 7–15:

1. As their stories progress, both Hamlet and Leonard have a series of unsuccessful interactions with a host of characters. Hamlet, for example, ridicules and derides Polonius (2.2), Rosencrantz and Guildenstern (still 2.2), and Ophelia (3.1). Leonard likewise reaches out to a handful of adults who fail him: Vice Principal Torres (Chapter 7), the 1970s sunglasses lady (Chapters 9–11), his English teacher, Mrs. Giavotella (Chapter 12), and Baback (Chapter 14). Analyze and compare these various characters; which ones mean to help, which to hurt? Which treated Hamlet/Leonard unfairly; which does he treat unfairly?

2. We do not get to see it, but we know that Leonard wrote an essay for English class in which he argues, as Mrs. Giavotella explains, that "Shakespeare is trying to justify suicide—that the entire play is an argument for self-slaughter" (p. 64). Do you think Leonard is right or wrong? Why does Shakespeare write about suicide? Why does Matthew Quick write about suicide?

3. Leonard is clearly hurt when Baback accuses him of having "first-world problems," and concedes that he is "relatively privileged from a socio-economical viewpoint," but also "so was Hamlet" (p. 94). What does he mean by this; in what ways do privilege and first-world problems differ from the types of struggles that people from Iran face, like Baback? Do you agree with Leonard in his assertion that privileged individuals suffer too, sometimes as much or more than those without privilege?

Chapters 16–23:

1. Analyze and compare the relationships between Hamlet and Ophelia, and Leonard and Lauren. Does Hamlet mistreat Ophelia during the mousetrap scene and at other points in the play; explain why you see (or do not see) his behavior toward her as mistreatment? In what ways does Leonard mistreat Lauren (e.g., the forced kiss)? Why does he mistreat her?
2. Compare Lauren to Ophelia; in what ways are the two characters similar? Is Lauren a strong or weak character (or both)? Do you like Lauren? Do you respect Lauren? There are many possible readings of Ophelia that an actress can employ (strong/weak, chaste/disreputable, etc.); what kind of Ophelia does Matthew Quick create in Lauren?

Chapters 24–30:

1. Compare Laertes from *Hamlet* and Asher from *Forgive Me.* Both young men are secondary characters, but also ones who mirror and contrast their respective protagonists. Laertes, for example, like Hamlet, is compelled to revenge his father's murder, but unlike Hamlet does not pause or soliloquize, but rather moves quickly to action. Asher, on the other hand, like Leonard has suffered sexual abuse (at the hands of his Uncle Dan, his own personal Claudius), but whereas Leonard contemplates his own trauma for several years before taking action, Asher immediately initiates sexual violence upon others. In what other ways are Laertes and Asher similar; in what ways are they different?
2. Compare the scene in *Hamlet* in which Hamlet stands poised to murder the praying Claudius but cannot (4.3) to the parallel scene in *Forgive Me* when Leonard stands outside of Asher's window with the gun but likewise cannot bring himself to pull the trigger (pp. 184–201)? In what ways are the two scenes similar; in what ways are they different? In what ways is Leonard Hamlet-like in this scene; in what ways does he differ here from Hamlet?

Chapters 31–38:

1. When Leonard attempts to pull the P-38 trigger, it "resists and [he] wonder[s] if it might be rusted" and he tries "to straighten [his] trigger finger" but finds that he can't (p. 208). Do you think that Leonard already knew that it would not shoot, or suspected at least that it was unlikely to shoot? Is it possible perhaps that the gun could have shot, but Leonard could not bring himself to pull the trigger, that deep down Leonard never intended to murder Asher or shoot himself? In what other ways are both

Leonard and Hamlet unwilling or unable to take action; is their hesitation to enact violence a weakness or strength?

2. Terms like "protagonist" and "antagonist" are relevant. Hamlet and Leonard are the protagonists in their respective stories, yet both threaten throughout to carry out violence. Had their stories been told, though, through the lens of another—perhaps Laertes or Asher—then Hamlet and Leonard could be the antagonists instead. With that in mind, evaluate how the two stories would have changed had they been told from different perspectives? In what ways might we see Hamlet and Leonard as culpable? How might our perspectives of characters like Claudius or Herr Silverman potentially change?

3. In some ways, both *Hamlet* and *Forgive Me* can be read as stories of redemption. Even though Hamlet's is indeed a tragedy and he dies at the end, he also forgives and is forgiven by Laertes in his last lines. Leonard similarly survives his eighteenth birthday without hurting himself or Asher, and his story ends with a sense that he will get help and survive. What hope do you see in the two works? What good might come afterward?

AFTER READING

"I Hope All Will Be Well": Ophelia's Letters from the Future

Before the events of the novel, in *Forgive Me*, Herr Silverman suggested that Leonard write letters to himself from the future (p. 118). At the end of the book, Herr Silverman explains, "maybe you won't find those exact people, but friends will arrive at some point." He adds that he "used to write letters to [him]self from the future" and "it helped [him] a great deal" (p. 217). Interspersed throughout the novel are four letters that Leonard has composed in response: one from his future father-in-law (pp. 27–34); one from his future wife, who he first bonded with over recitations of *Hamlet* in a hospital ward; she doesn't like it when he calls her Ophelia (pp. 69–77); and two from his future daughter (pp. 101–104, 267–273). His responses to Herr Silverman's assignment are beautiful and well-crafted; in just a few pages, Leonard creates an apocalyptic world reminiscent of favorite young adult dystopian book series like *Hunger Games* and *Scythe*. In his imagined world, Leonard tends a lighthouse in a flooded Philadelphia in the not-too-distant future with his family and pet dolphin, Horatio. Sea levels have risen and swallowed the city, but Leonard and his little family nonetheless have found happiness. It is these letters later in the novel that Herr Silverman draws on as he pulls Leonard back from suicide, and it is an activity that teachers can borrow for their own students. Have students write letters to themselves from future loved ones: a future in-law, a future spouse, a future child, or any of a host of imagined family and friends.

There are also a number of variations teachers can draw on, such as one. For example, have students write "affirming letters to peers" (Rumohr-Voskuil, 2019, p. 43). Another possibility with a Shakespeare twist, ask students to write from the perspective of Ophelia and from her future family and friends, an activity that has students imagine an alternate ending for *Hamlet*. In this, students could create a different future for Ophelia and then write two to four letters from twenty years into her future, writing backward in time with encouragement from those who want her to survive into her future. Have students imagine what Ophelia might have written had she had her own Herr Silverman advising her. Alternatively, students can write from the perspective of Hamlet, Laertes, Gertrude, or even Claudius, imagining letters from loved ones from a different future in which each lived on. *If they had survived, what future might each have found? What might their Denmark have become had they taken different steps in acts four and five? What might they have said to their younger selves, what advice to avoid the tragedy that unfolded at the end of the play?*

"I Thank You for Your Good Counsel": Inserting Herr Silverman into *Hamlet*

In *Hamlet*, a character gets advice that steers them from tragedy. Have students add a scene to *Hamlet* in which Herr Silverman is transported into the play. Students can either keep him as Herr Silverman, or imagine a new character inspired from him. This scene should be inserted into a key moment in *Hamlet*, with the ability to alter the events of the tragedy. Have students determine exactly where in the play they would insert their Herr Silverman. For example, in the case of Laertes, imagine if Herr Silverman had been there after 4.7 to intercept Laertes just after his conversation with Claudius. Claudius had just convinced Laertes to join his plot to murder Hamlet, but if Herr Silverman had been there, as he had been there for Leonard, he perhaps could have changed the outcome of the play and saved both Laertes and Hamlet. Have students write out the dialogue and appropriate stage directions in which Herr Silverman intercepts Laertes and averts the tragedy.

Alternatively, students could write their scene with an emphasis on Hamlet or Ophelia, inserting Herr Silverman into a scene after Hamlet finds himself unable to kill Claudius (3.3), but before Hamlet has killed Polonius (3.4); or rather into a scene after Ophelia's flower scene (4.5), but before her suicide. After reviewing the appropriate scenes, have students create a dialogue in which Herr Silverman talks down Laertes, Hamlet, or Ophelia, getting them over their immediate distress and pointing them toward help. If students think of others in Shakespeare's original who have faced trauma, encourage them to get creative with other Herr Silverman visits.

Closing Conversation with a Counselor

If before the unit you invited a school counselor or other professional to present to your class, invite that individual as a guest for a second visit. This time, though, instead of requesting a presentation, ask the counselor to be part of a class conversation. Have students reflect on how their own feelings about revenge, suicide, and mental health have evolved through their reading of *Hamlet* and *Forgive Me. In what ways do the readings reveal the destructiveness of cycles of revenge? In what ways do the readings reveal the need for compassion for those facing mental health concerns or contemplating suicide?*

We do not read plays like *Hamlet* and novels like *Forgive Me* just to make students better readers, score better on standardized tests, or to get into a good college—as Leonard protests, "If my classmates put as much effort into making our community better as they give to the college-application process, this place would be a utopia" (p. 62), but because they make us more empathetic to those around us. Literature makes us human. It can help make us aware that there are those around us who need help. It can reaffirm that there are those around us, particularly in our schools, who are suffering and that their struggles are genuine and real and warrant our attention. To this end, provide a few minutes at the end of the conversation for the school counselor or other guest to reiterate what district and community resources are available to students. In addition to providing the counselor opportunities to better know the school's students, part of the goal of the conversation is to reiterate to students that there are resources available to them where they and their classmates can turn when they need help.

EXTENSION ACTIVITIES

"I Swear I Use No Art at All": Comparing Characters through Art

Have students match characters from *Hamlet* to *Forgive Me*, and then create art posters with each character on opposing sides with images and quotations that highlight their similarities: for example, Leonard and Hamlet, Lauren and Ophelia, and Linda (Leonard's mother) and Gertrude (Hamlet's mother). Have students draw a diagonal line from the bottom left corner of the poster to the upper right corner of the poster: the left side will be for the *Hamlet*

Figure 3.1   Sample art. *Created by Levi Bradley (permission granted).*

character, the right side for the *Forgive Me* character. On the left side, they should write the *Hamlet* character's name in big, block letters that will make it easily readable from a distance; then draw a picture of their Shakespeare character. Lastly, have students write out three to five quotations from Shakespeare, either quotations that the character said or quotations about that character. On the right, they should write out the name of the *Forgive Me* character they have selected, draw his or her picture, and add three to five quotations from *Forgive Me* (see figure 3.1). Get creative in how you assign this and let students get creative in their work too. It is fine to stick to these guidelines, but allow your and your students' creative muse to alter it to fit your own classroom. After the activity, hang students' art on the wall or create bulletin board(s) that feature student work. Incorporating art in the English language arts curriculum can be therapeutic for many students and it provides opportunities to showcase artistic skills that only rarely get attention in the classroom. Your doodlers will appreciate the opportunity to demonstrate their learning through art.

"It Will Discourse Most Eloquent Music": Compiling an Uplifting Playlist

Music plays a role in both *Hamlet* and *Forgive Me*. In the third act, Hamlet plays on a recorder and then chastises Rosencrantz and Guildenstern because they do not know how to play too, and for their failed attempt to "play" him: "there is much music, excellent voice in this little organ, yet cannot you make it speak. 'Sblood, do you think I am easier to be play'd than this pipe?" (3.2.337, 348–349). Hamlet can make music; Rosencrantz and Guildenstern cannot. Hamlet can "play" others; Rosencrantz and Guildenstern, though, cannot "play" him. And music is just as central to most adolescents today as it is to Hamlet's metaphor. Leonard is a good example. Since tenth grade, he has spent his lunch hours listening alone in the auditorium to Baback practicing his violin; he tells him, "you have no idea how much your violin music has saved me over the past few years . . . your music gives me something to look forward to each day—and it's like a friend to me" (p. 91). Music also was the force at one time over which Leonard and Asher bonded: seven years before, "back before all the really bad stuff started to happen," Leonard's father had been able to procure first-row Green Day concert tickets for him and Asher, which Leonard gave to him for his birthday. It was the "best concert [that Leonard] ever attended," not because he was a big Green Day fan himself, but because "it was so much fun to see Asher experience *his* favorite band live," and being able to be "the hero that night" (p. 126). He expounds, if somebody would have asked him "if Asher and I would be best friends for life, I would have said yes on that night without hesitation" (p. 128).

For this activity, lead students in discussion as to why music is so powerful. Start by playing a video of a musician playing the recorder. Excellent examples can be readily found on YouTube. After listening, ask students how seeing the recorder played professionally influences their understanding of Hamlet's metaphor; *how does the artist "govern these ventages with [his or her] fingers and thumbs, give [the recorder] breath with [his or her] mouth"* (3.2.337–338)? Next, play "American Idiot" by Green Day; *what do Asher's music choices reveal about who he was "before all the really bad stuff happened"?* Next, play a violin concerto from Niccolò Paganini, the Italian violinist whose work Baback practices while Leonard listens; these too can be found on YouTube. Baback's tastes reveal him as a counterpoint to Asher, his serene and contemplative personality contrasted against Asher's abrasive and abusive nature. That Leonard so deeply appreciates Baback's music suggests likewise his own intellectual thoughtfulness as he struggles to find his own inner peace. *What else do Baback's and Asher's musical choices reveal about their characters?*

Last, have students create a playlist of five songs that build them up when they are feeling down, along with a one-paragraph explanation of why they chose the songs they did. Have students share the playlist and rationale with a classmate, preferably not a close friend, but rather somebody they do not know very well yet and preferably somebody with different musical tastes than their own. Have them listen to the five songs and write an uplifting response to their classmate. Emphasize the need to be open-minded about music they may not normally listen to. The objective of the activity is to build one another up, so keep critique positive. *What mood does the music create? What do the lyrics say? What do the selections reveal about the classmate who put them together?*

A NOTE TO TEACHERS

In closing, it must be noted that teachers need to be careful in comparing themselves to the teachers and school professionals that Leonard interacts with over the course of the novel. Leonard is not a reliable narrator when he portrays Mrs. Giavotella, his English teacher (Chapter 12) or Mrs. Shanahan, his counselor (Chapter 16) in a negative light. In fact, his comments about both women reek of misogyny: he describes Mrs. Giavotella as looking like a "cannonball," "short and round," wearing "overstuffed pants that are about to explode," and expresses gratitude that her "knees [are] clamped together" when she sits on the desk in front of him, so he doesn't "get a direct view of her overly taxed zipper" (pp. 62–63). She nonetheless makes it clear she wants to help Leonard—"when you're willing to talk straight with me, I'm willing to listen" (p. 67). Her inability to connect with Leonard has as much to do with his own biases as it does with any of her faults. On the other hand, Leonard finds Mrs. Shanahan attractive. He does not think her intelligent or a particularly insightful counselor, but he likes her because "she keeps a jar of lollipops on her desk" (p. 97). He imagines that she flirts with him, explaining that a lot of female teachers "flirt with male students" and ponders whether it is "the only way they know how to interact with men," to "use their sexuality to get what they want" (pp. 97–98). Despite Leonard's perceptions, though, both women genuinely reach out to Leonard, using their training and the structures in place at the school, and Leonard rejects their helping hands.

Leonard can connect with Herr Silverman, in part because he is a young, tall, White male, and because Leonard can see himself in Herr Silverman in a way he never could with Mrs. Shanahan or Mrs. Giavotella. Students often connect more easily to those who reflect their gender, race, and other demographic characteristics. Herr Silverman serves as a mentor to Leonard, and the one character every reader can agree that they like, but he too is flawed, even though Leonard adores him. Herr Silverman takes actions and makes decisions that put himself and his career at risk, and that in other circumstances could have put Leonard and other adolescents at risk too. In Chapter 18, for example, Leonard praises Herr Silverman for closing his door when they talk, "which makes me trust him. He doesn't play by their rules; he plays by the right rules" (p. 115). As a general rule to which many teachers adhere, teachers should not be alone with a student behind a closed door, and even though this is an exceptional circumstance—Herr Silverman can tell that

Leonard is contemplating suicide—he is taking on Leonard's problems alone, instead of leaning on the systems in his district meant to help at-risk youth in the way that Mrs. Giavotella and Mrs. Shanahan do. By the end of the novel, sitting together under the bridge with him, even Leonard acknowledges, "how much Herr Silverman is risking coming out . . . to deal with [his] crazy ass" (p. 226).

Herr Silverman saves Leonard's life, but there is nothing in the text to suggest that he ever reached out to his administration, his colleagues, or any other of the various apparatus set in place meant to help young adults like Leonard. He took it on alone. And that makes him less heroic; that makes him flawed too, just like every other character in the novel. That Herr Silverman took Leonard to his private residence to spend the night is particularly troubling. As readers, we can forgive Herr Silverman this because it is clear that Leonard should not be home alone, and Herr Silverman explicitly makes sure he is not. We admire him for taking action to protect Leonard. But as professionals, we also see the inherent liability in Herr Silverman's actions, in bringing a student home to spend the night (as does Herr Silverman's partner). It screams against all the rules regarding how teachers and students interact. And there are good reasons why these boundaries exist.

Just like teachers today, Herr Silverman works in a school that has systems in place to help at-risk students and while the stories of the children and adolescents who fall through its cracks are often shouted in the headlines, we only rarely hear the far more numerous stories of those the system saves. It can give the impression that the system is broken when in fact it helps countless adolescents every day. Our counselors, administrators, and teachers, and the system they have built and maintained, is sound. It is overburdened and underfunded, stretched too thin, but nonetheless it is a good system, and educators must work with one another, rather than alone. Be brave. Be courageous for your students. Make decisions about curriculum that create spaces for difficult, but necessary, conversations. Reach out and make sure all of your students know that you see them, that you care not just about their academic success, but also about them as human beings too.

CONCLUSION

Hamlet and *Forgive Me*, paired together, can be powerful texts for pushing students to reflect deeply on difficult issues. They are texts that push us as adults and educators to ponder what it means to be a good teacher. Taught together, these open up spaces in the ELA classroom for teachers to reach out and to teach their students that these are necessary conversations. Revenge, suicide, mental health, our anxieties: these are not issues to be swept under the rug, but rather issues that schools must bravely face together, conversations that we must learn to embrace even when they make us uncomfortable. Together, we can continue to make a difference for the better in the lives of the adolescents we work with every day.

REFERENCES

Quick, M. (2014). *Forgive me, Leonard Peacock.* New York, NY: Little, Brown.
Rumohr-Voskuil, G. (2019). Looking for hope—and helpers—in *Forgive me, Leonard Peacock.* In S. Shafer, G. Rumohr-Voskuil, and S. Bickmore (Eds.), *Contending with gun violence in the English language classroom* (pp. 41–47). Abingdon: Routledge.
Shakespeare, W. (1994). *Hamlet.* Boston, MA: Bedford.

Chapter 4

Reading *Hamlet* and *Monster* to Study Identity

Amy Connelly Banks and Chris Crowe

In Shakespeare's play *Hamlet,* a grieving and confused Prince Hamlet kills Polonius and escapes to England before returning home to exact revenge for his father's murder. Throughout the play, Hamlet wonders not only about what he should do, but who he is. In *Monster,* Steve Harmon is on trial for being a lookout in a robbery that led to a murder, events that have deeply disturbed his sense of identity.

Monster, a multi-genre, high-interest, contemporary story that can serve as an effective pre-reading bridge to the more complex and canonical *Hamlet* by engaging students in thinking critically about issues of identity. Both texts feature a protagonist who is driven by, maybe even tortured by, his struggle to answer the question, "Who am I?" In *Hamlet* and *Monster,* the technique of writing for catharsis guides the characters in their search for the answer to this question: the play within a play that Hamlet writes and Steve's reflective personal journal and his film script about his involvement in the crime. In their respective stories, both characters write to make sense of complex and tragic circumstances they cannot untangle and project their real-life dramas on stage. By doing this, these scripts make the audience voyeurs in both narratives. This chapter explores how William Shakespeare's play *The Tragedy of Hamlet, Prince of Denmark* and Walter Dean Myers's young adult novel *Monster* can be paired to examine the complexities of personal identity.

The Tragedy of Hamlet, Prince of Denmark by **William Shakespeare**

Hamlet, prince of Denmark, follows his friend, Horatio, to find the ghost of Hamlet's recently deceased father, the king. The ghost tells Hamlet he was murdered by Claudius, his brother, who just married Hamlet's mother, Gertrude, and will become the new king. Hamlet soliloquizes about life and death while contemplating his next move. Meanwhile, Ophelia, Hamlet's former love, seeks advice on Hamlet's apparent madness from her brother, Laertes, and her father, Polonius, famous for his proverbs: "To thine own self be true" (Shakespeare, n.d., 1.3.84) and "Neither a borrower nor a lender be" (Shakespeare, n.d., 1.3.81). Hamlet instructs an acting company to put on a play reenacting the murder of his father, in order to assess Claudius's guilt, and it proves true. Hamlet goes to kill him, but Claudius is praying. Hamlet decides to wait because he doesn't want Claudius to be saved. Hamlet visits his mother to condemn her for her hasty marriage, while Polonius is hiding in her room. Hamlet kills Polonius (assuming him to be Claudius), and the king's ghost reappears to instruct Hamlet to support Gertrude and avenge his death.

Because of the murder, Hamlet is sent away to England to evade trial, but the plot to execute him is thwarted when pirates attack the ship. Hamlet discovers the plot and rewrites the orders to execute his friends Rosencrantz and Guildenstern. Hamlet then returns to Denmark and meets Horatio by the gravediggers burying Ophelia, who was found drowned after her father's death and her own speech on death and madness. Laertes, convinced by Claudius, challenges Hamlet to a duel. Claudius poisons the drink to toast a victor, as well as the tip of Laertes sword, in a double plan to kill Hamlet. Toasting to Hamlet during the duel, Gertrude drinks from the cup and dies. Laertes and Hamlet are both wounded by the poisoned blade, and Laertes dies. As Hamlet is dying, he kills Claudius. Horatio is the only one left to explain the events to the new king, Fortinbras.

Monster by Walter Dean Myers

A National Book Award finalist and winner of the inaugural Michael L. Printz Award in 2000, *Monster* is the story of sixteen-year-old Steve Harmon, who faces felony murder charges in a trial related to his involvement in the robbery of a neighborhood convenience store in Harlem. The novel uses multiple genres, primarily screenplay and personal journal writing complemented by a few marginal notes and occasional photographs, to tell Steve's story of the trial and what got him there.

The novel opens with a journal entry in which Steve describes the harsh environment of jail and his decision to write a film script as a way to make sense of his experience. He will title the script "Monster" because that's what the prosecutor called him. The narrative then moves between screenplay scenes of the trial interspersed with journal entries that provide insight into Steve's reflections on and reactions to what had happened and what is happening. The extent of Steve's involvement in the crime is ambiguous, and the prosecutor works hard to play on the jury's racial biases to paint Steve as yet another young Black thug terrorizing New York neighborhoods. Her characterization disturbs Steve and casts doubt on the likelihood that he'll avoid being convicted with the gang members who committed the crime. After the trial and Steve's acquittal, he decides to examine his identity through the production of a film about the entire experience.

BEFORE READING

Before reading either text, students could practice identifying and analyzing what composes an individual's identity. Through pre-reading activities like viewing and writing on short films, as well as writing identity poetry, students will be better equipped to analyze the more complex characters of Hamlet and Steve, as well as creating their own definition of identity.

Hair Love and DeAndre Arnold's Story

Given the genres of a play for *Hamlet* and a screenplay for *Monster*, film and media texts could be included in this unit to teach students about the differences between their roles as readers and as viewers. To begin, students could connect ideas of identity through the viewing of the Oscar-winning animated short film, *Hair Love*. This short film, which is being adapted into an animated series for HBO Max, is available on YouTube and explores the theme of personal identity through a seven-year-old Black girl, Zuri, trying to style her hair. With her father's assistance, and her mother's online tutorials (as she battles cancer in a hospital), she is able to embrace her hair and its role in her identity. This video primes students for conversations about the roles race and family play in defining identity, preparing them to consider how family affects Hamlet's identity and how race and family intersect as important aspects of Steve's experiences and identity in *Monster*.

A discussion of *Hair Love* can be richly enhanced when viewing the film along with reading the story of DeAndre Arnold, the young man who was recognized in conjunction with the film at the Oscars. The newspaper account about Arnold could be read, or students could watch on YouTube, his interview with Ellen DeGeneres to get some insight into the kinds of racial experiences endured by some students. In January of his senior year of high school, administrators told DeAndre, after years with no such warning and no academic or behavioral concerns, that he had to cut off his dreadlocks in order to participate in graduation. DeAndre has explained in interviews the connection his hairstyle has with his identity, from his family, as "he grew out his dreadlocks to honor his father's Trinidadian heritage" (D'Zurilla, 2020). He was invited by the *Hair Love*'s director Matthew A. Cherry and producers

Gabrielle Union and Dwayne Wade to attend the Academy Awards with them because of his experience. DeAndre's story is a particularly poignant example of how race and family define identity. It also prepares students in considering some of these issues as presented within *Hamlet* and *Monster*, as both deal with the much darker repercussions of murder as it relates to identity.

After discussing both *Hair Love* and DeAndre's story, students could write about themselves or about a favorite character, identifying a physical characteristic like hair or an item of clothing that represents that person's identity. This writing assignment could include a visual component, with students drawing or bringing to class an object to demonstrate how an object or identifying physical characteristic can be representative of a person's identity. Have students share these representations with their classmates. In doing so, it provides students a chance to get to know their peers on a more personal level.

Identity Poetry Reading and Writing

Poetry provides another accessible genre for exploring identity. Students could read several poems that deal with identity. Through poetry, conversations on gender and race, in conjunction with identity, can be explored. Readily accessible online, Emily Dickinson's "I'm Nobody! Who are you?" (Dickinson, 1951) and Maya Angelou's "Phenomenal Woman" (Angelou, 1978) are both excellent poems about defining a person's self. Dickinson's poem invites the reader to consider what it means to be nobody or somebody, akin to Hamlet's famous "To be or not to be—that is the question" (Shakespeare, n.d., 3.1.6). Dickinson concludes that anonymity is better than being known as somebody. Students could debate and discuss this theme and contrast it with Angelou's well-defined, declarative "Phenomenal Woman," where she outlines the features and characteristics that make her phenomenal. Students could mimic the stylistic structure of either poem by writing a version about themselves, with Dickinson's two stanza, eight-line poem a good mentor text for emerging writers, and the much longer and more complex "Phenomenal Woman" better for more advanced writers. Students could even just write a simpler identity poem, like an acrostic poem or another formulaic name poem, that defines and examines their own identity.

Considering Justice in the Legal System

An examination of justice in the legal system could be included in classroom conversations, specifically discussing appropriate sentences for crimes. Students could study the work of Laura Bates, a professor at Indiana State

University, who taught Shakespeare's plays to inmates in minimum to maximum security prisons. Students could listen to interviews with Bates and reflect on the transformative nature of literature in helping readers mindfully process their experiences (Bogaev, 2018; Martin, 2013). A particular prisoner, Larry Newton, has a real-life story that parallels what might have been for Steve in *Monster* if he had received a prison sentence. In talking about Newton, Bates explained,

> at the age of 17 he and three other peers were arrested for a murder. Larry pled guilty 'cause he was at that time facing a death penalty. And evidence suggests that it may not have been him who was the actual person who pulled the trigger, it's uncertain, but he is doing a life without parole sentence. And he did also at the age of 17 waive his right to ever appeal the sentence. So he's going to be there forever. (Martin, 2013, para. 25)

After hearing Newton's story, students could discuss the consequences of severe sentences, such as the solitary confinement units, life in prison, and the death penalty. This would allow for more nuanced analysis of the punishments considered for any crime, but particularly in the murder cases of Hamlet, King Claudius, and Steve that students will encounter while reading.

DURING READING

The two texts have disparate lengths, requiring dedicated amounts of time for considering and developing a character analysis of Steve and Hamlet. They each offer a unique opportunity for students to compare a play within a play and a film script as both genres expose characters' intentions and personal beliefs.

Relationships and Justice in Forming Identity

As they read and consider how justice is fairly or unfairly meted out in *Hamlet* and in *Monster*, students may want to explore the theme of justice in both texts, both in legal terms and in general considerations of justice between characters. Hamlet obviously murders Polonius, but students may want to examine a more complex relationship, between Ophelia and Hamlet. How is Hamlet unfair to her? As Ophelia reminds him, right after his "To Be" monologue, "My lord, I have remembrances of yours / That I have longèd long to redeliver. / I pray you now receive them," and Hamlet denies it, "No, not I. I never gave you aught" (Shakespeare, n.d., 3.1.102–105). What does he owe to her, especially as he pretends not to remember their previous romantic relationship? What do characters owe to each other? Students could write journal entries, choosing either Hamlet or Steve, in which the character must examine his personal guilt and what justice they either experienced or still owe. They could begin considering Steve's words: "I wonder if [the prosecutor] knows what I'm really like" (Myers, 1999, p. 89), and try to capture his voice in their writing. Students could also write a letter calling for a trial to determine culpability for Hamlet in Ophelia's death. Hamlet holds a type of mock trial for Claudius in his play within a play, as he succeeds in exposing his uncle's guilt publicly. Students, then, could examine Hamlet's guilt in his relationships with others, particularly with the injustices suffered by Ophelia. With Steve, however, students will read a trial, and so they could further examine the justice between Steve and his family, integrating textual evidence of Steve's relationships with his parents, like with his mother: "I could still feel Mama's pain. And I knew she felt that I didn't do anything wrong. It was me who wasn't sure. It was me who lay on the cot wondering if I was fooling myself" (Myers, 1999, p. 148). And with further complexity, with his father: "Miss O'Brien said things were going bad for us because she was afraid that the jury wouldn't see a difference between me and all the bad guys taking the stand. I think my dad thinks the same thing" (Myers, 1999, p. 116), and "My father is no longer sure of who I am. He doesn't understand me even knowing people like King or Bob or Osvaldo. He wonders what else he doesn't know" (Myers, 1999, p. 281). After considering how Steve starts thinking about his former and current relationships with his parents, students could write about how Steve could reconcile these relationships and what his home life might look like after the trial.

Body Biographies as Venn Diagrams

In order to better understand the identities of Hamlet and Steve, students could engage in character analysis throughout the reading. Body Biographies, a visual representation of a body of a character with textual evidence written on the image, could be an excellent project for students to chart character development, create visual symbolic representations, write as a class or in reading groups, and have a gallery walk at the end of the reading. These body biographies can be created in a variety of ways, depending on the needs and constraints of the classroom. Mandy Perrett (2018) suggests the options to "use butcher paper and outline a fellow student; use a premade outline provided by you, the teacher; or use digital tools to develop the image" (para. 3). There are also several options for organizing students in the project: independent creation, reading groups, or whole class body biographies with individual students assigned to contribute to either body poster. However the class is arranged, a modified body biography that splits the bodies in two, one-half for

Hamlet and one-half for Steve, offers the greatest opportunities for comparison and contrast analysis. The body becomes a Venn Diagram, to explore the distinct differences between the characters and the places where they overlap. A space could be placed, running through the middle of the body, for students to write out the similarities of the two protagonist teenagers.

If the class is arranged by reading groups or working as a whole class, the body biographies can be displayed in the classroom visual representations of a split Hamlet and Steve in the classroom for students to view and continually update throughout the reading. Students could know the specific expectations for the body biographies, such as the parts of the body to label, requirements on color choices, symbols/images, and quotes from the texts.

ELA instructors could begin with a model for students, such as a quote for the heart of each character. For Steve, his part of the heart could contain the lines:

> Miss O'Brien looked at me—I didn't see her looking at me but I knew she was. Who was Steve Harmon? I wanted to open my shirt and tell her to look into my heart to see who I really was, who the real Steve Harmon was. "That was what I was thinking, about what was in my heart and what that made me. I'm just not a bad person. I know that in my heart I am not a bad person." (Myers, 1999, pp. 92–93)

Hamlet's heart could be modeled with more complexity, broken in two with Claudius's mocking "A heart unfortified, a mind impatient" on one side, and Hamlet's "But break, my heart, for I must hold my tongue" on the other (1.2.100; 1.2.164). Lines can be drawn that connect each of these textual quotes to the other significant parts of the body, with a line to the mind, and another to the mouth. This will model for students how to connect a body biography together for all of the different significant parts of a person.

At the conclusion of their creation, the body biographies could also be displayed for a classroom gallery walk, requiring each student artist to write a museum label for their creations. Students would then walk around the room, taking notes and writing questions about the body biographies to ask their fellow artists. Students would then meet in groups to discuss the different interpretations of Steve and Hamlet together.

AFTER READING

Perhaps the most productive examinations of identity will take place when students have completed their reading of *Hamlet* and *Monster*. At this point, teachers might simply ask students to identify thematic parallels between these stories—stories that were written centuries apart—and then to consider what those parallels say about literature, human nature, and society in general.

Identity

As a continuation of their examination of identity, students could be directed to some of Erik Erikson's basic ideas about identity formation. Erikson suggested a series of stages to describe the developmental progress of people as they mature, beginning with Stage One, "Trust vs. Mistrust," which occurs during infancy, and ending with Stage Eight, "Ego Integrity vs. Despair," which begins around age sixty-five. Generally, Erikson was interested in the effects of social interaction and relationships on development and growth, and his description of Stage Five, the period from about age twelve to age eighteen, the stage he called "identity vs. role confusion," is most relevant to this discussion of identity in *Hamlet* and *Monster*. In Stage Five, young people are considering the roles they will assume when they are adults, and part of that consideration requires them to evaluate critically their identities to determine who they are (Cherry, 2019). At various times in their respective stories, both Hamlet and Steve Harmon seem to be working to determine their own true identities. Throughout the play, Hamlet is clearly not himself. In Act 2, Scene 2, he tells Rosencrantz and Guildenstern, "I have of late, but wherefore I know not, lost all my mirth, forgone all custom of exercise" (Shakespeare, n.d., 2.2.318–320). Early in *Monster*, Steve shows a similar awareness when he writes, "When I look into the small [mirror], I see a face looking back at me but I don't recognize it. It doesn't look like me. I couldn't have changed that much in a few months. I wonder if I will look like myself when the trial is over" (Myers, 1999, pp. 1–2). In their respective stories, both young men are working to understand and define/redefine themselves and their roles.

Students could be asked to examine each character's attempts to address their identity-versus-role confusion and to point out what contributed to, or hindered, their attempts to understand their true nature and their place in the world. Part of this examination of the characters' identities could include the consideration of their internal (monologues for Hamlet and journal entries for Steve) and external (dialogue and interactions with other characters) conversations about themselves and their actions.

After reading both stories, students could also use the traditional methods of characterization as a way to analyze the identities of Hamlet and Steve: *What do other characters say about the two young men that teach readers about the nature of Hamlet and Steve? How can readers use what the two characters say about themselves as a way of determining the authentic identity of each main character? How and why might these sources of information be unreliable? Finally, what do the actions of Hamlet and Steve say about their identities and values?* In this activity, have students utilize a graphic organizer to keep track of scenes that answer each question. Students could do this in pairs or teams, with a whole class sharing when complete.

Monologues, a Play within a Play, and a Film Script

Both Hamlet and Steve's monologues reveal their innermost thoughts, with Hamlet's "To Be" and his monologue at the end of Act 2, Scene 2, where he is determined to stage a play. Steve's entire story is a running monologue, as he reflects at the beginning of the novel: "When I look into the small [mirror], I see a face looking back at me but I don't recognize it. It doesn't look like me. I couldn't have changed that much in a few months. I wonder if I will look like myself when the trial is over" (Myers, 1999, pp. 1–2). These monologues function as cathartic writing for the respective characters, an opportunity for them to process and to explore their feelings, particularly during challenging circumstances. After considering some aspects of these monologues, students could write a monologue for themselves, one that considers who they are by talking to an imagined audience. Students could either perform these for their peers or video record them in an application like Flipgrid. If students video record these monologues through Flipgrid, teachers could pair or team students and have them view each other's videos and provide a video response to their peer as a way for students, and the teacher, to get to know each other on a deeper level.

More than just monologues, Shakespeare's play is also layered "playing," with a protagonist intent on using a play to expose evil deeds, layering the dramatic irony and doubling the audiences' role in viewing the scenes. As Hamlet famously believes, "The play's the thing / Wherein I'll catch the conscience of the King" (Shakespeare, n.d., 2.2.633–634). But in using a play, Hamlet not only reveals Claudius's intent, but Hamlet also reveals a lot about his own character, believing that "murder, though it have no tongue, will speak / With most miraculous organ" (Shakespeare, n.d., 2.2.622–623). Hamlet prefers to watch rather than directly address his uncle: "I'll observe his looks; / I'll tent him to the quick. / If he do blench, / I know my course" (Shakespeare, n.d., 2.2.625–627). Hamlet could try to interrogate Claudius, but because he believes that murder will not reveal itself through tongue or speech. He prefers to set the scene and watch what happens. Hamlet believes a play will be more accurate in determining the guilt of the King, just as Steve believes a film script will better tell the story of his innocence.

Steve explains, "Maybe I could make my own movie. I could write it out and play it in my head. . . . The film will be the story of my life. No, not my life, but of this experience" (Myers, 1999, p. 4). He even further explains the necessity of film for his life: "That is why I take the films of myself. I want to know who I am. I want to know the road to panic that I took. I want to look at myself a thousand times to look for one true image" (Myers, 1999, p. 281). Students could take this cathartic modeling of processing through playwriting, or screenwriting, and write a short scene of their own. It could be either a play or a film script genre, to reveal their inner motivations. Students could use the texts as models, to see what the formulas of the genres expect: italics for stage directions, all caps for characters' names, correct line spacing, and so on. But these pages can also model the types of themes students want to explore for themselves: family, identity, race, gender, revenge, justice, and more.

EXTENSION ACTIVITIES

Identity in Other Forms of Text

To extend their encounters with stories centered on identity and role confusion, students could be directed to find other narratives that deal with similar issues. They could start with poems and short stories in their classroom literature textbook and then broaden their search to look for YA novels (*Make Lemonade, Mexican Whiteboy*, and *Long Way Down* to name a few), movies (*Finding Forrester, Lion King*, and *Spider-Man: Into the Spider-Verse*), and even popular music ("Who Are You" by the Who, "What's Your Name?" by Lynyrd Skynyrd, "You Belong with Me" by Taylor Swift) to investigate how the search for identity is represented in other texts and media. Students could present their found narratives, along with their analysis of how the narrative explores identity, in a formal presentation to the whole class.

Exploring Villains

As demonstrated in the activity above, there are plenty of texts in which characters struggle with their sense of identity and how they're perceived by others. And some of the most interesting may be characters who might be considered villains. Mary Shelley's *Frankenstein* and Robert Louis Stevenson's *Strange Case of Dr. Jekyll and Mr. Hyde* are some early examples, but the trope carries on into our own century and even popular media examples abound (consider King Kong, Darth Vader, Hannibal Lecter, Thanos, and the Joker). Students could conduct their own search for villains (or characters who are considered by others to be villains) in literature or media and examine how those beings transformed from good to evil or evil to good. *Are they misunderstood, are they victims of circumstance, or are they responsible for their own descent into evil? Do they consider themselves villains or heroes?* Students could also consider how the justice system of the society in which that person/villain exists treats the person/villain: *Is it sympathetic? Judgmental? Vengeful? Biased? Forgiving? What do the representations of villains and their actions and the reactions of their societies say about justice and about how society views them?*

Cathartic Writing

After becoming familiar with the ways Hamlet and Steve used writing in their respective stories, students could consider the cathartic effects of writing. In Aristotle's definition of tragedy, the narrative involves "incidents arousing pity and fear, wherewith to accomplish the catharsis of such emotions" (Abrams, 1999, p. 322). The events of *Hamlet* and *Monster* provoke those emotions in their audiences, but at various times, the stories also provide the protagonists a release—a purge or catharsis—of those emotions. More recent uses of the term apply catharsis to personal writing (often just journal writing) with therapeutic and reflective potential for the writer. Choosing a text of their own, like *The Outsiders*, for example, students could read closely to see how a character uses writing as a tool of healing. In *The Outsiders*, Ponyboy writes about his experiences as a make-up assignment for his high school English teacher. Reviewing the events of his tumultuous school year help him to process the experience and to start on the path to healing. Using that story or one of their own choosing as a mentor text, they could then select a key passage and use it as a prompt for some cathartic writing of their own—or, if that's too personal, cathartic writing for a character from a favorite novel or movie. They might also take a key line/advice from *Hamlet*, "To thine own self be true" (Shakespeare, n.d., 1.3.84), or from *Monster* "Think about all the tomorrows of your life" (Myers, 1999, p. 205), and use it as a prompt to write a letter of advice for a younger friend or relative.

CONCLUSION

Though they were written centuries apart, *Hamlet* and *Monster* have multiple points of contact that enable them to be used in tandem to help students examine identity and identity formation. Both protagonists face challenges that require them to reconsider themselves and their actions, and by reading, analyzing, and writing about how these characters engage and are shaped by conflict, students can come to a better understanding of themselves and their place in society. The activities outlined in this chapter will also help students to appreciate people whose lives and life experiences are nothing like their own, making them better prepared to live, learn, and work in a modern, diverse world.

REFERENCES

Abrams, M. H. (1999). *A glossary of literary terms*, 7th ed. Boston, MA: Heinle & Heinle.

Angelou, M. (1978). *Phenomenal woman*. Retrieved May 8, 2020, from https://www .poetryfoundation.org/poems/48985/phenomenal-woman.

Bogaev, B. (Host) (2018, April 2). *Shakespeare in solitary* (No. 58) [Audio podcast episode]. In Shakespeare Unlimited. Folger Shakespeare Library. http://www.folg er.edu/shakespeare-unlimited/solitary-prison.

Carras, C. (2020, July 7). *A "Hair Love" series from Oscar winner Matthew A. Cherry is coming to HBO Max*. Los Angeles Times. https://www.latimes.com/entertainme nt-arts/tv/story/2020-07-07/hair-love-series-matthew-a-cherry-hbo-max.

Cherry, K. (2019, December 7). *Identity vs. role confusion in psychosocial stage 5*. Retrieved from https://www.verywellmind.com/identity-versus-confusion-27957 35.

Cherry, M. A. (Director). (2019). *Hair love* [Film]. Sony Pictures Animation.

Dickinson, E. (1951). I'm Nobody! Who are you? (260). Retrieved May 8, 2020, from https://poets.org/poem/im-nobody-who-are-you-260.

D'Zurilla, C. (2020, February 9). *"Hair Love" team brings teen who wouldn't cut his dreadlocks to the Oscars*. Retrieved May 8, 2020, from https://www.latimes.com/ entertainment-arts/movies/story/2020-02-09/oscars-2020-hair-love-deandre-arnold -dreadlocks.

Martin, M. (Host). (2013, April 22). *Teaching Shakespeare in a maximum security prison* [Audio podcast episode]. In Tell Me More. NPR News. www.npr.org/2013 /04/22/178411754/teaching-shakespeare-in-a-maximum-security-prison.

Myers, W. D. (1999). *Monster*. New York, NY: Scholastic.

Perrett, M. (2018, September 25). *Body biographies: Deepen character analysis in English and History class*. Duke TIP. blogs.tip.duke.edu/teachersworkshop/body -biographies-deepen-character-analysis-in-english-and-history-class/.

Shakespeare, W. (n.d.). *Hamlet* (B. Mowat, P. Werstine, M. Poston, and R. Niles, eds.). The Folger Shakespeare. https://shakespeare.folger.edu/shakespeares-works /hamlet/.

Chapter 5

What Is the Price of Ambition? Teaching *Macbeth* with *On the Come Up*

Jen McConnel

"I might have to kill somebody tonight. It could be somebody I know. It could be a stranger. It could be somebody who's never battled before. It could be somebody who's a pro at it. It doesn't matter how many punchlines they spit or how nice their flow is. I'll have to kill them" (Thomas, 2019, p. 3). In this opening line of *On the Come Up*, Brianna Jackson sounds like she could saunter into the pages of *Macbeth* and compare notes with him about personal ambition and their shared ability to be ruthless. Either one of them could have said, "And damned be him that first cries, 'Hold, enough!' " (Shakespeare, Act 5, Scene 8, Line 39): Bri and Macbeth are ready to take down all who oppose them, even though Bri faces them in rap battles that promise stardom, while Macbeth wields a sword to claim a kingdom.

Shakespeare's *Macbeth* and Angie Thomas's *On the Come Up* draw on the theme of ambition, claiming power without waiting for an external authority to recognize the characters' potential, and a willingness to fight for personal beliefs even in the face of opposition and hostility. These texts diverge, however, on themes of madness and isolation. While Macbeth becomes increasingly alone and tormented through his bloody decisions, Bri faces isolation but pulls herself back from the edge of tragedy. Unlike Macbeth, Bri returns to the council of her friends and family, and she trusts them enough to support her even when they know the truth of her near-deadly choices. Bri pauses on the precipice of ambition and steps back before teetering into the amoral darkness that consumes Macbeth. Because of these parallels, these two titles offer rich possibilities for paired teaching.

The unit presented in this chapter offers students multiple opportunities to engage in inquiry, reflection, and sharing. Students can form meaningful connections to the content of both *Macbeth* and *On the Come Up*, bringing

Shakespeare out of the past and into their lives in diverse ways as they work
to answer the driving questions at the heart of this unit: *What is the price of
ambition?* And, *How do you decide if that price is too high?*

Macbeth by William Shakespeare

Macbeth is noticeably shorter than most other Shakespearean tragedies, but
a multitude of betrayal and action is packed into the pages of this play. The
story centers on Macbeth, a Scottish lord who starts the play as a fierce war-
rior, loyal to King Duncan. Before the end of Act I, however, Macbeth has
been snared by ambition, spurred on by the promises of three witches that
he will one day be king. As the act ends, Macbeth and his wife have made
plans to murder Duncan in pursuit of the throne. From that point on, both
Macbeth and Lady Macbeth descend into madness. Macbeth adds violent act
to violent act to secure his claim to the throne, killing not only the king and
his servants, but hiring assassins to kill Banquo, Macbeth's best friend, in Act
III. In Act IV, he doubles down on his cruelty by sending men to slaughter the
wife and children of Macduff, another Scottish lord whom Macbeth sees as a
threat to his throne. In the final moments of the play, Lady Macbeth commits
suicide, plagued by her role in the regicide that elevated herself and her husband to their new status, and although Macbeth mourns her, he proceeds to
defend his ill-gotten throne on the field of battle. However, the bloody price
of Macbeth's ambition is all wasted, for Macduff fulfills the prophecy of the
witches and defeats Macbeth, killing him and passing the crown of Scotland
onto Duncan's heir, Malcom.

On the Come Up by Angie Thomas

Angie Thomas's YA novel *On the Come Up* focuses on sixteen-year-old
wannabe rapper Brianna Jackson. The daughter of a hip-hop artist murdered
by a local gang when she was only five, Bri is the baby of her family. She
is her mother's miracle baby following multiple miscarriages, her brother
Trey's reason for staying off the streets, and her paternal grandparents'
mostly joyful reminder of the son they lost. Bri is also the beloved only niece
of her mother's younger sister, her Aunt Pooh, who joined a rival gang after
her brother-in-law's murder in hopes of pursuing her own brand of justice.

  Because Bri's dad, Lawless, is something of a legend in the neighborhood,
and because none of the adults in Bri's life want to get into tough conversations about his death with their "Lil' Bit," Bri jumps head first into a series of
decisions that lead her dangerously close to becoming the next victim of the
gang that killed her father. Like the hip-hop artists she adores, Bri doesn't shy
away from strong language and tough topics, and she doesn't try to sugarcoat
the hardships she and her neighbors face on a daily basis. Her career takes

off after she records a song about playing into ghetto stereotypes, but most people are not reading between the lines like she wanted. However, her ambition to make it big at any cost overrides her values for a while. Ultimately, she steps back from the brink and leans heavily into her growth over the course of the novel in a heartfelt freestyle, ending with the lines "I'm not for sale." And, as often happens in fiction, even though Bri decides she is not willing to sacrifice everything for her ambition, her choice to seemingly throw it all away gets her the kind of industry attention she's been seeking for her music, and the novel ends with a sense that there's a chance Bri might be able to get her come up, after all.

BEFORE READING

Defining Ambition

Since this unit revolves around the theme of ambition, a great activity to engage students throughout the course of their reading is the creation of a class annotation wall centered on ambition. The annotation wall can include both an evolving definition of ambition and a compilation of quotes pertaining to this theme from both texts. To start this activity, consider if you want to develop a virtual or physical annotation wall: for a physical wall, consider using butcher paper to cover a wall of the classroom for the duration of the unit or build a class wiki for a virtual wall, as in the example here created using Padlet (see figure 5.1).

To start your word wall, have students brainstorm synonyms for "ambition." You might encourage them to do this in a word map structure, with "ambition" in the center and the synonyms radiating out, or you might suggest a T-chart, with synonyms on one side and antonyms on the other. Brainstorm directly on the wall, if space allows: it is good practice for the students to see the ways in which their thinking changes shape over the course of the unit. Once the class has agreed on a working understanding of what constitutes ambition, cue them to add to the wall as their reading progresses.

Personal Ambition

When starting a new unit, especially one that centers around a text that students might, at first glance, find inaccessible (like Shakespeare), students should consider the core themes of the text in relation to themselves before they have even started reading. Teachers might integrate a "vote with your feet" anticipation activity that primes students to consider the driving

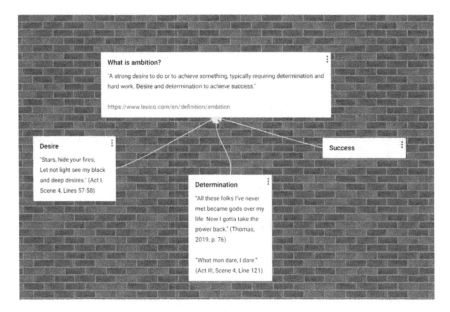

Figure 5.1 Word wall (in-progress) on Padlet. *Author created.*

questions of the unit: *What is the price of ambition? How do you decide if that price is too high?*

For this activity, you will need: signs to label the four corners of the room (and the center, if you want to include a "neutral"/"neither agree nor disagree" response option). One sign each should say "strongly agree," "agree," "disagree," and "strongly disagree." Make sure the font is large enough to be visible to cut down on student confusion, especially if you have never done a four corners exercise like this before with your students.

Begin this anticipation activity by reading out the prompts one at a time and asking students to move to the corner that most represents how they respond to the statement. Once there, students can chat in their groups and even share with the large group, or students can move through the activity with less conversation. It is up to you how much time you want this to take. You might invite students to talk and share their ideas, and it would be best to allot at least a half hour to work through the questions in that way. However, there are multiple reasons to do the activity silently, especially since some of the questions might elicit emotional, private responses from students. Asking students to consider these prompts will create space in the classroom for them to work through their individual perceptions of personal ambition and its cost before engaging with Bri and Macbeth in their quests to achieve their dreams. This activity primes students to make personal connections by asking them to articulate their own beliefs around ambition (see table 5.1).

Table 5.1 Anticipation activity

Anticipation Activity Prompts
I would do anything to achieve my dreams.
If you are not with me, you are against me.
Sometimes the people you trust most let you down.
Revenge is never worth it.
If I knew I was on the right path, I would not let anything get in my way.
It is lonely at the top.
The price of fame is loneliness.
Love is weakness.
It is okay to lie to get what you want.
I would sacrifice anything for my family.

These prompts, while generic enough to elicit responses from students prior to reading either text, can also be brought into conversation about the texts as students read. For example, the statement "If I knew I was on the right path, I would not let anything get in my way" can be reintroduced following Act 1, Scene 3 in *Macbeth* where, after the witches' prophecy, Macbeth and Banquo learn that part of the prophecy has already been fulfilled. Additional ways to circle back to this activity are included later in the chapter.

Gender and Ambition

In both *Macbeth* and *On the Come Up*, gender intersects with personal ambition in interesting ways. In *Macbeth*, for example, Lady Macbeth's ambitions are discussed as being beyond what is expected for a woman, and she also accuses Macbeth of not being manly enough (in this case, ruthless) in pursuit of his ambitions (Act 1, Scene 7). In *On the Come Up*, Bri's ambitions and talent are patronized by some of the men around her, and comparisons between her songs and her late father's work raise the issue explicitly:

> "Look, I'm not trying to come at you," Hype claims. "I love the song. I can't lie though, knowing that a sixteen-year-old girl is talking about being strapped and stuff like that, it caught me off guard." Not that a sixteen-year-old rapped about it. But that a sixteen-year-old *girl* rapped about it. "Did it catch you off guard when my dad rapped about it at sixteen?" "No." "Why not?" "Aw, c'mon, you know why," Hype says. "It's different." (p. 352)

In both texts, men are permitted to pursue their ambitions more aggressively than women, and for Bri and Lady Macbeth, their unwillingness to back down in pursuit of their ambitions raises tension among the characters around them connected to the ways in which their fierceness appears to conflict with their femaleness. Examples of gender in power in *Macbeth* can be found in the following: Act 1, Scene 5, Lines 38–41; Act 1, Scene 7, Lines 39–84; Act 2, Scene 2, Lines 1–73; Act 3, Scene 4, Line 98; Act 4, Scene 3, Lines 220–235. Examples of gender in power in *On the Come Up* can be found on the following pages: 9, 23, 352–355, 378–384, 440–441.

The idea of skewed expectations based on binary gender conventions will not be unfamiliar to your students. To guide an initial conversation around this topic, ask students to consider the differences between terms like "bossy" and "assertive," which are often gender-coded. A good text to prompt this discussion might be the short video "Ban Bossy—I'm not Bossy. I'm the boss."

Before reading, invite students to explore music for evidence of the intersection between gender and ambition. Songs you might want students to consider include: "Don't Stop Me Now" (Queen), "Dark Horse" (Katy Perry), or "Girl on Fire" (Alicia Keys). As a way to model the process of connecting the song lyrics to the essential questions, provide them with the examples of Taylor Swift's "The Man" and the song "Make a Man Out of You" from Disney's animated film *Mulan* (see figure 5.2).

After students have completed a graphic organizer, they could present their observations on one of the songs to the class, or have a listening party

Title of Song (Artist)	Summarize the song in 2-3 sentences.	What does the song say about ambition and gender? Is there a price to ambition in the song? Include one or two quotes to explore.
The Man (Taylor Swift)	In this song, Swift imagines the differences between a man and a woman when it comes to success. Singing in the first person, Swift says that she feels all her efforts are ignored because she is a woman, and that if she were a man, she would have more recognition and external support, even if her behavior was morally questionable.	The song hinges on the idea that ambition is gendered; that women will be ridiculed for the same ambitious behavior that men are praised for (mostly revolving around money and power dynamics). "They'd paint me out to be bad, so it's okay that I'm mad". Swift implies that the price of ambition is higher for a woman than a man, particularly in terms of social interactions and other people's opinions.
Make a Man Out of You (Donny Osmond)	In this song, the leader of the new recruits to the Chinese army presents his expectations of manhood (and worthy soldiers). The song emphasizes speed, strength, and mystery, encouraging the new soldiers to be "tranquil as a forest but on fire within".	This song hinges on the idea that "being a man" is necessary for bravery and strength in a fight. Gender is used to shame the soldiers ("Did they send me daughters when I asked for sons?"). Without attaining the examples of manliness in the song, the perceived honor of the battlefield will be out of reach. For Mulan, then, the price of her ambitions to be a soldier is the surrender of her femininity.

Figure 5.2 **Songs emphasizing gender and ambition.** *Author created.*

based on their submissions. Afterward, students can be invited to add insight to the songs that their peers selected, always pinning back to the driving questions: *What is the price of ambition? How do you decide if that price is too high?*

DURING READING

Macbeth and Bri's Ambitions

When you encounter examples of ambition in either text, point it out and ask students to add the quote, author, and page number (or act, scene, and line for the play) to the word wall. Here are some suggestions to get you started: "I have almost forgot the taste of fears" (Act V, Scene 5, Line 11); "What man dare, I dare" (Act III, Scene 4, Line 121); "I approach, you watch close, I'm a threat" (Thomas, 2019, p. 111); "My crown cannot be taken" (Thomas, 2019, p. 441).

In further exploring ambition in both texts, teachers can pause during reading and pose discussion questions spotlighting this theme at the following places within Macbeth:

- Macbeth meets three witches who tell him he will be Thane of Glamis (which he already is), Cawdor, and King. He and Banquo discuss the prophecy, but are interrupted by the announcement that Macbeth is now Thane of Cawdor, and Macbeth begins thinking out loud about what this might mean for his future (Act 1, Scene 3, Lines 40–175). Pose the following questions: *Thinking back to the anticipation activity, reconsider your answer to the following statement: If I knew I was on the right path, I would not let anything get in my way. How should Macbeth behave?*
- Banquo begins to doubt the story Macbeth shared about Duncan's murder, and Macbeth makes plans to have Banquo and Fleance killed, remembering that the three witches promised him kingship, but promised Banquo that his descendants would be king (Act 3, Scene 1): Pose the following questions: *How do you think Macbeth would respond to the statement: If you are not with me, you are against me? What price has Macbeth already paid for his ambition? What will be the price if he goes through with his plan to kill Banquo and Fleance?*
- Prior to the battle against Macbeth, some of the men who have shifted allegiance to Malcom, Duncan's son and heir, discuss Macbeth's current situation. They reveal that "those he commands move only in command, nothing in love. Now does he feel his title hang loose upon him, like a giant's robe upon a dwarfish thief" (Act 5, Scene 2, Lines 22–25). Macbeth is king, but friendless and without true support as he prepares to fight to keep his

crown. Pose the following questions: Do you think Macbeth regrets his actions? Is the loneliness he is now experiencing worth the cost? Do you think being lonely/without close confidants is something inescapable for kings and other leaders?

In *On the Come Up*, teachers could pause at the following places and pose discussion questions:

- There are multiple points in the story where Bri chooses to lie to her family and friends as she pursues her come up. For example, she ignores her aunt's advice and lies about uploading the song (Chapter 13), and she chooses not to tell her mom about the song, only telling her after her mother has found out from a news report about the student protest at Bri's school (Chapter 17). Like Macbeth, she runs the risk of alienating everyone around her as she pursues her ambitions to become a famous hip-hop artist. Pose the following questions: *Who is Bri willing to lie to in order to pursue her ambitions? Is it okay for her to lie to these individuals? What might be the eventual cost of Bri's lies? What wouldn't Bri do to get her come up?*
- One of the tensions Bri grapples with is her loyalty to her aunt and her desire to make it big in the music industry. She wants fame for herself, but when Supreme begins courting her and working to be her manager, the increasingly dire financial situation of her family is one of the deciding factors that pushes her to drop Aunt Pooh as her manager and make a deal with Supreme. Before agreeing to work with him, she extracts a promise that he'll "make sure you and your family are good [. . .] you got my word" (Chapter 18, p. 256). Pose the following questions: *Do you believe that Supreme can take care of Bri's family? What is Bri sacrificing to work with Supreme? What is driving her motivation in this chapter? What is Macbeth's driving motivation? How do they align or differ?*
- Bri's bargain with Supreme forces her to decide if she wants to play the role of the "ratchet hood rat" that Supreme seems to think will make her famous. That description doesn't sit right with Bri, but when Supreme takes her to a studio to record a song that someone else wrote for her, with lyrics that make her feel ill, Bri has a moment where she is ready to set her ambition aside. She is not entirely ready to try doing things her own way yet, though, and she "follows him back into the studio like the desperate idiot that I am" (Chapter 30, p. 383). However, she ultimately walks away from Supreme and the persona he wants her to assume, but at this point in the book, Bri shows that there is nothing she would not do in pursuit of her goals. Pose the following questions: *Do you agree with Bri's choice to record the song? Why or why not? What kinds of ethical issues are raised in this chapter? Is Bri still a character you can root for? Was she ever? Do you think it will be*

worth it for Bri to record this song? What might be the cost of her actions? In what way is Bri like Macbeth right now?

This activity facilitates cross-textual connections and conversations, while also creating an ongoing collaborative annotation practice as students add to the word wall. For example, you include questions about the lyrics from Bri's song on the word wall when you write down the lyrics: prompts like "I wonder . . ." and "this reminds me of" are a good place to start encouraging students to engage with the text through the word wall. You might also pose the driving questions throughout the process, asking students to think through ways a particular quote on the word wall addresses the unit's guiding questions.

What Makes a Character Ambitious?

Students will have the opportunity to develop character profiles for some of the characters in these texts. These character profiles might also serve as prewriting for the final team project, explained later in this chapter. You can add more characters from each text to this activity, but the core characters to consider are Macbeth, Lady Macbeth, and Macduff from the play, and Bri, Supreme, and Aunt Pooh from the novel.

These character profiles can take a variety of forms: students can answer questions about each character during reading, returning to the profile and adding to it as they understand more about that character and their motivations. Students might also make an image to accompany their profile. A fun way to approach this exercise is to have students follow the structure of a profile page on Facebook or another social media site.

While students create these profiles, prompt them to consider the ambitions of these specific characters during reading. For example, students could assess the price of ambition after reading the banquet scene where Macbeth encounters Banquo's ghost, considering the loss of trust his nobles have when they see his breakdown (Act III, Scene 4), or after reading the chapter in which Bri signs on with Supreme and gives up on working with her aunt (Chapter 18). Some character-specific prompts are included in figure 5.3.

AFTER READING

Deciding if the Price Was Worth It

For this team activity, students should work together to pick any character from either text, and then form an argument based on the driving questions

Character Prompts	When to Offer
What might it cost Macbeth and Lady Macbeth to carry out their plan?	Before Act II, Scene 2
What is the price of Macbeth's ambition in the banquet scene? (What does he lose/gain?)	After Act III, Scene 4
What price do the characters who oppose Macbeth pay (such as Macduff, or Malcom)?	During Act V
What do you predict might happen now that Bri has recorded her song?	After Chapter Eight
What might it cost Bri to work with Supreme?	After Chapter Eighteen
Was it worth it for Bri to vent on Instagram? Why or why not?	After Chapter Twenty
What might Bri's actions cost Supreme?	After the End of the Book

Figure 5.3   Character profile prompts. *Author created.*

in terms of that specific character. For example, if a group wanted to focus on Bri, they would work to craft a compelling argument that takes a stance on whether or not the price Bri paid in pursuit of her ambition was worth it. Teams might decide to explore secondary characters, too: they could argue, for example, that Banquo paid the ultimate price for remaining loyal to Macbeth, despite his own doubts: he ends up murdered, and with no one to seek justice on his behalf. Or they might decide that the price Banquo paid was worth it, since his descendants would eventually sit on the throne of Scotland. Help students avoid taking the easy way out by choosing to argue that Macbeth's ambition was not worth the cost because he ends up dead, or that Bri's was because she gets what she wants in the end. They can still argue that Macbeth's actions were not worth it, but they need to present more evidence and nuance than the above example.

For the presentation, teams should include a clear thesis statement arguing if the price the character paid for their ambition was worth it. They should also present at least two pieces of evidence to support their thesis, as well as at least one counterclaim and a rebuttal. Presentations should be no longer than —five to seven minutes each. The goal of this assignment is not to write an essay or match a word count: the point is for students to develop a cohesive argument collaboratively that they then present in simple, defendable terms to their peers. This assignment helps students strengthen their rhetorical skills and collaboration.

This team activity also lends itself to full-class collaboration. Students can vote on the validity of the arguments: the class could do a show of hands before a team starts on how many agree with the central argument the team is making (it was or was not worth it for Character X) before they hear the reasons, and then vote again after the presentation to see if anyone changed their mind. It would be interesting to keep track of the "winning" arguments, and this voting process could also be used to spark conversation and encourage students to search for their own rebuttals to their peers' arguments.

Freestyling Ambition

The final assignment for this unit centers on a verbal performance. Students will answer the driving questions of the unit, *What is the price of ambition? How do you decide if that price is too high?* in a composition that they will perform, in a final project gala. To prepare for this final public product, spend some time at the end of the unit focusing on spoken word and slam poetry by exploring the flow in both texts, or in widely available videos of poetry slams and rap battles. You might bring in the video *Epic Rap Battles of History: Guy Fawkes vs Che Guevara* to give students a sense of Bri's battle in the ring while also providing an historical context for an inquiry into the Gunpowder Plot, sometimes attributed as an influence on *Macbeth* (due to the timing of the plot and the first staging of the play).

For this final public product, build in time for discussion, peer review, and workshopping in whatever ways work best in your classroom. Students might be encouraged to write a song, compose a piece of spoken word or slam poetry, or deliver their answer to the questions in the form of a Shakespearean soliloquy. In fact, Bri's final freestyle (pp. 440–441) could serve as a template for students to consider when crafting their own compositions, since she effectively answers the question about the price of ambition throughout the piece—"I refuse to be their laugh, I refuse to be their pet, I refuse to be the reason some kid now claims a set" (p. 440). Or, students can look to the example of Macbeth's final lines, where he decides that surrender is a price he will not pay and that even death is not too steep a price for his ambitions, declaring, "I will not yield to kiss the ground before young Malcolm's feet [. . .] Lay on Macduff, and damned be him that first cries 'Hold! Enough!' " (Act V, Scene 8, Lines 32–39). In both of these scenes, Bri and Macbeth each offer multiple examples of the things they will (or will not) do in pursuit off their ambitions.

For whichever genre students choose to compose in, they should include a clear answer to the driving questions, with textual support from both the novel and the play. Consider including an option for students to prepare and rehearse their presentation before the big day, and depending on the technology access in your classroom, students might even be invited to record a video of themselves ahead of time, to help with the jitters of a live performance.

EXTENSION ACTIVITIES

Ambition Onscreen

This unit lends itself to a number of extensions that you might consider. A comparative element can easily be brought into the unit by asking students to compare the texts through a film comparison. You could use either selected scenes from the multiple adaptations of *Macbeth* that exist (including the contemporary retellings, such as *Scotland, PA*), or asking students to select two adaptations to watch independently and compare to the text of the play, either in note-form or as a formal comparative essay. The films can be used to compare against each other or the source material, or even cross-genre, with a film adaptation of *Macbeth* being paired with the text of *On the Come Up*. And when it comes to bringing in film adaptations, *On the Come Up* has recently been slated for film production, so incorporating that film into this extension is an additional choice. Guide students in their explorations by prompting discussion about elements of each movie, from cinematography to costuming and casting choices, and ask them to reflect on the ways the films do or do not line up with their mental image of the texts.

Collective Ambition

Throughout the unit, the questions of the price of ambition have been mostly addressed with a lens on personal ambition. An interesting possibility for extension lies in continuing the conversation with students, but instead of focusing on individual ambitions that have widespread consequences, ask students to consider the price of collective ambition, and the potential personal costs of such ambition. One way to approach this conversation would be through Dar Williams's song "Southern California Wants to Be Western New York." As the title indicates, the entire song focuses on the ambition of one place to be more like another. Using this song as a prompt, invite students into a Socratic seminar centering on these modified questions: *What is the price of group ambition? Who decides if that price is too high?* Ask students to explore the song lyrics with these questions in mind. For example, at one point, Williams says, "Sometimes the stakes are bogus, sometimes the fast lane hits a fork, sometimes southern California wants to be western New York." Some questions to offer students for these lyrics might include: what stakes is Williams talking about? What does the image of the fast lane hitting a fork make you think of? Separate the metaphors: what is the idea of the fast lane? What does it mean to come to a fork in the road? These open-ended questions can be used to prompt discussion, and you can guide students toward an understanding that this song is contrasting the idea of the "fast lane" with a lifestyle that is more focused on family and community rather than high stakes and success. It would also be interesting to ask students to consider ways in which individual ambition might collide with collective ambition: do they think there are people living in western New York who long for the pace of California? Are there people in California who are perfectly content with the pace of their lives? Encourage students to probe these complexities in the course of the seminar discussion.

CONCLUSION

The possibilities presented by pairing *Macbeth* and *On the Come Up* are diverse. Both texts invite a deeper examination of the ways in which gender expectations and individual ambition are connected, and both texts offer protagonists who are single-minded in pursuit of their goals. By exploring the driving questions in a variety of ways for both texts, students will develop a deeper understanding of the themes of gender, ambition, and the price of ambition as they engage with Shakespeare and Angie Thomas's works through this unit. As part of the process of working through these texts, this chapter suggests that students consider the driving questions from multiple angles throughout the unit, including answering them from the point-of-view of the characters in both texts, and from their own perspective. *What is the price of ambition? How do you decide if that price is too high?* Exploring these questions in relationship to the two texts at the heart of this chapter will offer students multiple, nuanced ways to make meaning and develop their own answers that connect the texts beyond the classroom and into their everyday experiences.

REFERENCES

Cook, B. (Director). (1998). *Mulan* [Film]. Buena Vista Pictures.

ERB. (2019, May 4). Guy Fawkes vs Che Guevara. Epic rap battles of history [video]. YouTube. https://www.youtube.com/watch?v=Yow_BJeb8TI&list=L LHhlOkTgMv6fP7jvCpQBdag&index=2339.

ILA/NCTE. (2020). *Read write think*. Readwritethink. http://www.readwritethink .org/.

Lean In. (2014, March 9). *Ban bossy—I'm not bossy. I'm the boss* [video]. YouTube. https://www.youtube.com/watch?v=6dynbzMlCcw&feature=emb_title.

Lopez, E. (2020). *Teaching slam poetry*. Scholastic. https://www.scholastic.com/tea chers/unit-plans/teaching-content/teaching-slam-poetry/.

Poetry Out Loud. (n.d.). *Poetry out loud*. https://www.poetryoutloud.org/.

Shakespeare, W. (2013). *Macbeth.* Eds. Barbara A. Mowat and Paul Werstine. New York, NY: Folger Shakespeare Library, Simon and Schuster.

Swift, T. [Taylor Swift]. (2020, February 27). *The man (official video)* [Video]. YouTube. https://www.youtube.com/watch?v=AqAJLh9wuZ0.

Thomas, A. (2019). *On the come up.* New York, NY: Balzer + Bray.

Williams, D. (1996). Southern California wants to be western New York. On *Mortal City* [CD]. Razor & Tie.

Chapter 6

Using *All American Boys* to Contextualize *Othello*

An Exploration in Alterity

Jennifer S. Dail and Michelle B. Goodsite

Jennifer's first teaching position placed her as a supply teacher in an urban school with a predominantly African American student population who could not have diverged more from her own student teaching and personal schooling experiences. Jennifer received instructions to teach *Macbeth* by having students read along as she played audio cassette tapes, pausing for summary discussion and key points. The students received no opportunities to make any meaning with the text for themselves, nor did they receive opportunities to make connections between the text and their own lives. They not only hated the reading experience, but they also left the class hating Shakespeare. Now, as teacher educators, we strive to actively engage students in constructing meaning from texts by making authentic textual connections.

While thinking about teaching Shakespeare's *Othello* in conjunction with the young adult novel *All American Boys* (2015), one of the students in Jennifer's class observed that it was practically impossible to overlook the issues of prejudice and stereotype in the novel, thus highlighting the need of an opportunity for both teachers and students to make connections between texts and to current social issues. Such connections allow students to engage with their own identities, cultures, and social constructs. Our students cannot afford for us to turn away from the ways the world in which they live impacts how and why they read literature and the ways in which they see the world around them through the literature we put before them. The issues of prejudice and stereotypes to which Jennifer's student referred hinge around the concept of alterity, or otherness of characters—a concept prevalent in Shakespeare's *Othello* as well. Making the lens of alterity accessible in *Othello* lies at the core of our rationale for pairing it with *All American Boys*.

Alterity as a lens aligns with the marginalization of groups of people frequently focused on in social justice curricula. Reading *All American Boys* in conjunction with *Othello* engages students in examining the issues of social class disparities and police brutality, all relevant in their current world. Our overarching goal in this thematic text pairing is to align students as critical readers empowered to take action in their schools, their communities, and the larger world.

Othello by William Shakespeare

In *Othello*, Desdemona, a fair-skinned Venetian, falls in love with and marries Othello, an African general in the Venetian army. Over the course of the play, Othello is tricked into suspecting his wife of adultery by a jealous Iago. Iago is determined to destroy Othello's happiness as revenge for being passed over for promotion by Othello. Iago begins his destruction by informing Desdemona's father of her marriage to the Black Moor. Desdemona's father becomes enraged at the marriage and pushes for the punishment of Othello by the Duke of Venice, but eventually realizes his daughter's true love for Othello. This further pushes Iago to continue his attempts to ruin Othello. Through continued deceit Iago pushes the story of revenge against another made to seem inferior at all costs with little attention to human consequence. Iago does this by positioning Othello as an outsider both in racial identity and social status. While *Othello* is a play of sexual jealousy, it explores issues of racial prejudice and of conditional plausibility since a contest of stories allude to the possibility that Othello somehow charmed Desdemona to marry him which exacerbates the racial tensions.

All American Boys by Jason Reynolds and Brendan Kiely

In *All American Boys*, Rashad, an African American teenager, receives a brutal beating when he is arrested by the police as a suspect in a convenience store theft. Assumptions are made about this JROTC and wildly talented art student because he is Black. Quinn, a White teenager, witnesses his friend's brother—the police officer—beating Rashad. While Quinn does not completely understand what he witnesses, it quickly becomes clear that he cannot be a bystander because the larger issues of marginalization are at play when issues around racism and prejudice become part of the public outcry surrounding police brutality. The boys alternating viewpoints tell the story offering a hint of conditional plausibility where stories align and misalign given the differing backgrounds and experiences in and out of their school and community settings. In the end, Rashad and Quinn come face to face and recognize the importance of being seen and being counted in the larger conversation of racism and equality even at their young age.

BEFORE READING

Defining "Alterity" through Concept Mapping

Simply put, "alterity" is a term that means *otherness*. It is used in postcolonial literary theory to point to ways characters are developed as radically alien or different in cultural orientation from the dominant group. It is a term with which students can relate when given some support and a lens that facilitates incorporating some literary theory, even subtly, into literary study with secondary students. Applying a postcolonial perspective, "Western values and traditions of thought and literature, including versions of postmodernism, are guilty of a repressive ethnocentrism" (Selden & Widdowson, 1993, p. 188). Students should understand that *alterity* means otherness, but they also should understand the greater implications embedded within that. They should understand the systemic oppression and repression of cultures other than the dominant, typically Western, culture by the dominant culture. In *Othello,* the main character, a Moor with dark skin, is actively plotted against to destroy his marriage to the fair Desdemona, a Venetian of the dominant culture in the play. In *All American Boys*, Rashad, a Black teenager, experiences the effects of systemic racism and his White classmate Quinn struggles with the realities of the situation and recognizes his own role in an unjust system. In both texts, characters are othered by being marginalized and even harmed by those representing the dominant culture. Looking at these texts through a lens of *alterity* offers readers a critical means of examining the cultural systems at play in these texts and extending that examination into the world in which they live to consider the ways in which systems they assume support everyone actually marginalize or "other" some groups of people.

The idea of becoming or even feeling different offers an entry point with which students can relate. They likely already recognize that the world does not treat everyone fairly, even if they cannot clearly articulate why and how that is. Defining *alterity* or *otherness* is a good point for bringing students into this conversation. We want students to understand that *alterity* means "other" or some manner of being different from the mainstream culture. Even when students may not themselves feel culturally different, they likely feel different in some manner since that lies at the crux of adolescence. Begin by discussing this definition with them and ways they might feel different from dominant or mainstream culture and societal expectations. Use a journal entry to get students thinking about and making these connections to their lives because it offers them a space to unpack their thinking without judgment from peers. You can support students by discussing ways that people might differ from cultural norms and expectations or even ways they might feel they do. Some questions that support this journaling include: *What expectations do you feel that society has of you? Who creates these expectations? Do you ever feel like an outsider and that you don't fit into these norms? In what ways? Do you notice different social norms for different groups of people (maybe based on gender, race, socioeconomic class)? Why do you think that is? Where do you notice that groups of people are underrepresented or not represented at all? Do you think that makes them feel included?*

After students have had time to think through writing, invite them to share their responses in small groups prior to the whole group discussion, offering them an additional layer of safety from sharing with an entire class. Use the resulting discussion to guide them in making connections and to help them better understand the concept of *alterity*, which ultimately relates to the relationship between self-perception and the larger world and the ways in which people feel like an "other" or that they don't fully belong.

Next, move this into visually supporting students in building this concept beyond personal experiences or observations. Point them back to the question of who creates societal expectations and norms. You might also ask them to think about why this group is the one to decide this. Visually building the concept offers students an entry point to comprehension by engaging them in building a concept map aimed at concept attainment. To do this, students name the concept, in this case, *alterity*. They then record a definition of the concept which should have been unpacked more concretely through the writing and discussion. On their map, students should offer examples where alterity occurs in the world around them. They may notice similar demographics in the community around them as well. Perhaps the local library offers an underrepresentation of books for adolescents, leaving them out of the mainstream audience served by that cultural institution. Students should then record words that connect to the concept of *alterity* on their map. Such words might include "other," "outsider," "different, marginalized," or "excluded." Finally, students should include resources for more information related to the topic on their concept map. This is an area where they can connect to specific instances they may have noted or want to investigate further.

Alterity through Contemporary News Stories and Micro-Readings

Connecting the definition of *alterity* and discussion of the concept to contemporary news stories supports students' meaning making by highlighting examples of where instances of alterity are enacted around them. To do this, identify news articles that are current. At the time of this chapter, a current example is the killing of George Floyd, a Black man in police custody who had a White officer kneel on his neck cutting off his breathing for over eight minutes, contributing to his death. The incident led to an amplification of the Black Lives Matter movement and offers some good material for textual analysis around the lens of *alterity*. It also offers direct connections to events portrayed in *All American Boys.* The *New York Times* article "How George Floyd Was Killed in Police Custody" (2020, May 31) reconstructs a timeline of the May 25 death of Floyd, which will give students some solid background information on the incident. As students read and discuss the article, engage them with the following discussion points: *Why did this incident occur? Who was involved? Why does race matter in what happened here? How do you think this could have been prevented?*

Next, move students into other readings about George Floyd. As students engage in these readings, discuss with them how the media portrays the victim in these readings. One reading is the *New York Times* article "George Floyd, from 'I want to Touch the World' to 'I Can't Breathe'" (2020, June 18), where a former classmate of Floyd's recalls his aspirations to "touch the world." The article then begins by painting a picture of Floyd that most people in mainstream culture can relate to—college on a basketball scholarship as a means out of a neighborhood with a reputation for poverty, gangs, drugs, and violence. The cultural norms have positioned us to appreciate this sort of drive and hard work to overcome circumstances in people; however, the article then takes a turn. It starts discussing a string of arrests for Floyd and prison time, things that put him outside the mainstream cultural narrative of improving oneself. These things position George Floyd and "other," and the manner in which some of the media construct narratives around those who experience violent encounters with police. One way students can explore this is through an activity that has them examine media bias. Have students watch a clip from CNN, one from FOX and one from BBC all on this same event. Students could explore these clips and discuss how media is not monolithic. They should pay close attention to how narratives are driven: *How do media outlets—typically labeled as left, right, and so on—portray Blacks who have violent interactions with police?*

DURING READING

Repeated, Socially Constructed Readings from *Othello* and *All American Boys*

Although a class might read the play *Othello* in its entirety, we suggest focusing on select scenes that illuminate a topic and engage students in grappling with Shakespeare's language more deeply than when they are confronted with an entire play. Some scenes to emphasize because they are easily viewed through the lens of alterity are suggested in figure 6.1.

Scene in *Othello*	References dealing with alterity	Diving Deeper
Act I, scene i	refers to Othello as a black man/Moor	We learn that Othello is a Moor when Iago refers to him as "his Moorship" (I.i.35). Moor is used as a derogatory term by Iago, who views Othello as an outsider and resents his rise in the Venetian army. We learn that Iago also dislikes Othello because of his recent promotion of Cassio over him to a higher post in the army. This positions Iago as a character serving his own self-interest. When Brabantio, a Venetian senator believes he has been robbed, Iago speaks against Othello by telling him that his daughter, Desdemona, and Othello are "making the beast with two backs" (I.i.118). This phrasing refers to a sexual relationship between Othello and Desdemona, setting Othello to be marginalized for stepping outside of his social class and, in doing so, crossing racial lines.
Act I, scene ii	society rocked by interracial marriage	Iago tells Cassio that Othello has married. We know from scene i he married Desdemona. Here Brabantio comments that Othello must have enchanted Desdemona, otherwise she would not have gone "too the sooty bosom of such as thing as though" (1.2.70-71). This results in orders to seize Othello. Barbantio's language here is undergirded by racial prejudice and the horror of an interracial relationship. Language such as this, coupled with the order to seize Othello, serves to further marginalize him by positioning him as an outsider.
Act I, scene iii	refers to Othello as "more fair than black"	In trying to cheer up Brabantio, the Duke comments that Othello is "more fair than black" (I.iii.317). Brabantio, hurt because Desdemona is choosing to go with Othello instead of staying home, warns Othello that Desdemona is likely to deceive him, just as she deceived her father. Statements such as this subtly work to marginalize Othello by planting the seeds of doubt that eventually lead to the destruction of his relationship with Desdemona.
Act 3, scene iii	Othello blames his complexion for Desdemona's fading love	Growing suspicious of Desdemona and his relationship with her, Othello's mental state continues to decline when Iago plants the idea of an affair between Cassio and Desdemona. At the conclusion of the scene, Othello expresses concern that it is unrealistic to expect Desdemona to love him when he is black, older, and of a lower social status than she is: "Haply, for I am black And have not those soft parts of conversation That chamberers have, or for I am declined Into the vale of years--yet that's not much" (III.iii.304-307).

Figure 6.1   Selected scenes from *Othello*. *Author created.*

To participate in these readings, divide students into four teams prior to engaging in whole class discussion. Students will likely need some background summary so that they understand where their assigned scene is positioned within the broader context of the play. Each team member should receive a copy of their scene that they can write on. Ask students to individually conduct three repeated readings where they mark points that cause confusion, ask questions of the text, indicate words they do not understand, and make connections across texts and experiences. As example, in Act I, Scene i, you might anticipate that students mark the phrase "making the beast with two backs" (p. 118). They likely will not know what this means, so they might put a question mark beside it to indicate that. Others in the group may have heard the phrase before, which will help them when they come back together to socially construct meaning. What is marked for each student will be highly individual, as they all bring different skills as readers to interpreting this text.

For each of the three individual readings, have students use a different color pencil or pen so that the shifts in understanding across readings is visible to both the reader and the teacher. After each reading, students should rate their understanding on a scale of 1–10. On this scale, a rating of 1 indicated, "Huh? What the heck is going on here?" A rating of 5 indicates, "I think I get what is going on," and a rating of 10 indicates, "I am a rock star and could publish a scholarly article!" We recommend telling students that it is normal for ratings to decline across readings as deep, sustained readings often lead to greater confusion. After students complete their final rating, ask them to write a three-to-five-sentence summary of the scene.

Students should then work in their assigned teams to talk through their understanding of the text. They can start by sharing their summaries and using the discussion to make revisions. For example, a student may be misunderstanding which characters have positions of power and how deceit is being used to manipulate others and leverage power against Othello. Other students may pick up on this. Their summary conversations will reveal this and help them make revisions. As the teacher, you should also be listening in and asking questions to help lead them to these conclusions. As students work in their groups, the overall goal is that each one is able to point to the text to support their decision. Questions you might ask students to support them in this process include: *Who is in a position of power? How is he/she using that power against Othello, especially in regard to his marriage to Desdemona? Who has the listening ear of those in power? How is he/she using that power against Othello, especially in regard to his marriage to Desdemona? Where do you see language that positions Othello as an outsider to the Venetian army leadership?*

This process of repeated readings accompanied by social construction of meaning can also be used with *All American Boys* if your students need that support. Engaging students in this process with *All American Boys* for one or two select passages offers a good opportunity to transition students from reading drama to prose and to examine those different textual demands (see figure 6.2). Questions you might ask students to guide them in reading and summarizing scenes from *All American Boys* include: *How are Rashad and Quinn treated differently in their school and community? How does this relate to their difference in racial identity? How do Rashad and Quinn perceive the events at the convenience store differently? What factors account for these differences? In what ways do Rashad and Quinn change in their perception of the events at the convenience store and social constructs informing those events and their reactions?*

Scene in *All American Boys*	References dealing with alterity	Diving Deeper
Pages 21-23	assumptions by a police officer before ever hearing Rashad's side of the story	Rashad is shocked by the accusation of the store clerk of something he never would have done. The police officer grabs Rashad by the arm before he can explain what really happened in the store. "I said shut up!" he roared, now pushing me, grabbing me by the arm. "Did you not hear me? You deaf or something?"
		The police officer shoves Rashad to the ground face first cutting his face and breaking his nose. Rashad tries to move to avoid the pain but not run. The cuffs are tightened and Rashad receives another blow and a knee in the back with an arm to his neck. "Oh, you wanna resist? You wanna resist?" The police officer keeps pounding on Rashad. "My brain exploded into a million thoughts and only one at the same time-- please don't kill me."
Page 132	The use of the word thug by Quinn's mother places otherness and fear on those different.	Rashad has not been to school in days and everyone is talking about the video from the Sunday morning news. Quinn refuses to watch the video to not remember what he had witnessed at Jerry's. He doesn't think the beating Rashad took was justified. Quinn remembers back to when he was a freshman and is passed by a large black senior in the hallway. "Fear. Like the way Ma told me to cross the street to the other side of the sidewalk if I was walking home along and I saw a group of guys walking toward me. Guys. That wasn't the word she used. Thugs. Fear of thugs. Just like what some people were saying on the news. Rashad looked like a thug."

Figure 6.2   Selected scenes from *All American Boys*. *Author created.*

Making Students' Thinking Visible

During reading, students can complete sketch notes, a visual doodling of comprehension, questions, and tensions through the use of illustrations, symbols, and words on paper. These can be constructed through shapes, colors/ shades, and idea connectors among other graphic possibilities. Text can be used as little or as much as needed. Sketch notes are constructed during the reading of both *Othello* and *All American Boys* not only allow students to retain new and difficult information while reading, but also allow a place for students to make visual connections across both texts. More importantly, the sketch notes become a visual representation of their growing understanding of alterity and developing empathy during reading.

Start by having students select various symbols to represent different character identities and events. For example, when considering *Othello*, students may select a handkerchief to represent Desdemona's perceived deceit. They might select a sword to represent Othello and his service in the army. When considering *All American Boys*, students may select the ROTC symbol or pencils to represent Rashad, a JROTC member and budding artist. They might select a basketball to represent Quinn, a senior athlete. Both boys have troubled paternal relationships that inform how they personally move through issues of racism. Students might then use connectors, such as arrows, to show how the boys are similar in the troubled relationships with their fathers. Through the use of illustrations and connecting emotions, students can express deeper understanding of characters than they may be able to verbally.

Ultimately, these sketch notes become a synthesis moving students to be successful in after-reading and extension activities. It is worth noting that students do not have to be artists to create sketch notes, as the focus is on content and representation of thinking, not artistic ability. If artistic ability intimidates students, you might connect them with some online platforms for this process; however, most are fee-based in some form or another.

AFTER READING

Revisiting Definitions

This is a good time to have students revisit the concept maps they did pre-reading and build it out more with textual evidence from the two readings. From the work they did analyzing the texts to construct meaning and engaging with the guiding questions you used to support them, ask them to return to their concept maps and include specific instances from all of the texts pointing to alterity with characters. Remind them that this relates to how they are othered or are a victim of "oppressive ethnocentrism." Any of the specific passages above are ones you are looking for students to include and discuss.

Exploring Systemic Issues of Discrimination

We like infographics as a means of engaging students with data about topics while also honing in on students' inference skills. Start by having students brainstorm to identify issues of marginalization and inequity in both *Othello* and *All American Boys*. Guide students in this by asking them what they see as the root causes of those issues in each text. In *Othello*, it is manipulated by people, such as Iago, of the dominant culture trying to maintain power. In *All American Boys*, it results from societal systems, such as the police force, in place. Both inform the other, and that is something you might discuss with students as well. If people did not seek power or use power to appoint others into similar positions, larger systems would be less likely to fail marginalized groups.

Next, have students generate some researchable questions around these issues. You should refer back to the specific passages they worked with from both texts and draw from those. Examples of questions they might ask include the following:

- How do social or cultural groups gain and maintain power in society? Here they could narrow it down even more by looking at historical examples of the rise and fall of power where others were marginalized and oppressed as a result. The Nazi party in Germany offers a good example of this. Apartheid in South Africa does as well.
- How many Black Americans are killed by police as compared to White Americans? With this, you want to have students explore beyond the numbers and examine some cases to look at the circumstances surrounding those.
- How does the media portray Black victims of police brutality? You can connect this back to the micro-readings relating to George Floyd.

Next, engage students in reading some infographics as mentor texts. One we recommend is "Police Shootings: Black Americans Disproportionately Affected" [Infographic] (2020, May 28) because it aligns well with the core texts for this study. Have students examine the infographic and related article. Ask students the following questions: *What does this infographic say about Black shootings? What does this infographic not say (or what might be absent) about Black shootings? What were the sources of this data? Are these reliable sources? Why or why not? What other sources might the author have used?*

We also recommend talking with students about how to read the data. One way to do this is to have them look at the percentages these numbers represent because that paints a different picture than a number alone. There are a multitude of types of infographic out there for students to examine as mentor texts. Visually (2020) is an excellent source to send students to for identifying infographic mentor texts because it offers user-created infographics on race with a variety of variables examined, including racial tolerance around the world, racial representation in youth and professional sports, and the racial wealth gap in America. However, because they are user-created, students will also need to thoroughly examine each infographic in terms of validity and reliability. They will need to look closely at who created the graph and why. The goal here is to have students thinking about what type of infographic might best represent the data generated from the topic they want to research.

The final step is to have students conduct research around their question and create an infographic to share that research. Their questions should have been generated from the examination of alterity through the textual pairings, so students should be required to represent the texts in their infographic. For example, if a student is researching Black shootings by police, they might put their research up against *All American Boys* to show how the text fits (or does not fit) with what they are finding. Another example might be researching views on interracial marriages in a particular culture and comparing that to the treatment of Othello's marriage to Desdemona in *Othello*.

EXTENSION ACTIVITIES

Race, Bias, and Identity—Viewing Mini-Documentary Films

It is important that teachers help students not only connect issues of alterity in the texts, but to extend those issues to themselves and the world around them. One way to accomplish this is to have students view several short mini-documentaries; "A Conversation with White People on Race," a five-minute film focusing on the difficulties White people may have when discussing race and racial biases, and the seven-minute film, "A Conversation with Police on Race," which presents police officers' viewpoints on dealing with race within larger community constructs and systems. Watch these films with students and then springboard into a discussion about racial issues. Ask students to move into discussion by having them identify a golden moment—a moment that stood out to them or one that connected to the reading of either *Othello* or *All American Boys*. Students should work to connect the information in the selected films with the reading of the texts. To guide students, the teacher could ask the following questions: *What issues of marginalization or othering of people do you recognize in these two films? How do those issues connect to Othello and All American Boys? What role do you feel you play in these issues in your world?*

Students' responses should be supported with instances in the original texts that illustrate issues or complicate these issues. For example, from "A Conversation with Police on Race," students may consider the discussion of how officers might target African American adolescents in particular, and how that directly relates to the very beginning of *All American Boys* where the brutal beating of Rashad is overwhelming and excessive. The goal here is to guide students in making both text-to-world connections and text-to-text connections.

You also might ask students to identify any information or perspectives that proved surprising for them and maybe even points of tension that make them uncomfortable. This ties to the guiding question of identifying their role with these issues. If students have points of tension or disbelief, ask them to articulate the reasons behind that if they can. We suggest doing this not only with these short films, but also during the reading of the texts. While you should invite whole class discussion, respect that students may not be comfortable sharing because of the sensitive nature of the content. Finally, invite students to submit their writing and mark something specific they would like us to read or respond to.

Remixing the Texts

In asking students to extend their understanding of alterity through the texts read, teachers could move them beyond the role of consumer and into the role of producer in creating new texts. Remix is when we take something that is well known and already exists and rework or revise it into a different, yet still recognizable, format. Remixes extend beyond polishing something a little bit or adding one or more elements; they involve reseeing and rethinking texts—transforming them so that the meaning of the original text is altered. It also involves multiple modes of composition—text, image, sound, motion—which may all come together in a variety of possible formats including, but not limited to, video. Ask students to create multimodal remixes of the texts and using those remixes to highlight the issues of alterity explored in the readings. In creating their remixes, students can have the choice of working individually or collaboratively. We suggest offering students benchmark deadlines in order to allow them opportunity to receive feedback on their ideas before submitting the final project. Those benchmark moments appear with asterisks in the following description.

Before delving into the steps of the assignment, articulate the following goals for students' remixes. They must:

- remain recognizable as having *Othello* and/or *All American Boys* as the source material,
- alter/add to/advance the story substantially—transform the text and its treatment of alterity,
- take risks and push boundaries to present a creative product,
- integrate multiple modes of composition, and
- communicate the message clearly.

Present the assignment as steps for students to better support them in long-term work for the project. Step 1 is for students to create a statement of intent*. Here they draft an author's agenda articulating their intent as authors. In their author's agenda, they should address the following questions:

- Who is your audience?
- What do you want your audience to learn about alterity or marginalization of others from your remix?
- What do you want your audience to feel from your remix?

- What is your overall message?
- What message, tone, information do you want to avoid in your remix?
- Into what genre(s) does your remix fit?
- How does it fit into that genre(s)?
- What modes of storytelling will you use to accomplish your intent?

Step 2 is for students to consider and plan the design of their project*. Ask them to create an organized, detailed plan for their remix. Remixes may take shape in any genre (e.g., narrative, poem, song, play, video), so their plan needs to consider the genre, as well. They should include important points, images, characters, words/phrases/dialog, music/sound, and so forth. The best way to do this is to have students create a storyboard aligning elements such as text, image, and sound. We recommend using sticky notes with one color representing each element because sticky notes allow students to easily move elements as they revise their plans. Ask them to consider how these multi-modal elements line up and to directly tie them back to their statement of intent. If students are working in a collaborative group, they should determine individual tasks and group meeting times and spaces at this point.

Step 3 is for students to produce a final remix. The platforms students use will depend upon their final genres. If students are producing some type of video, we recommend either MovieMaker or iMovie, installed on most computers or WeVideo, a free, online movie-making platform. We also advise students to allow extra time to attend to any technical issues for final editing prior to publishing their products. Step 4 is for students to consider the impact of their remixes. Assign them to groups to review each other's remixes and provide feedback. In reviewing remixes, have students address the following:

- How does this remix address alterity and connect to *Othello* and/or *All American Boys*?
- In what ways is the original text we read still recognizable (e.g., characters, events, language)?
- In what ways has the original text been transformed?
- What new perspectives did this remix provide you with about alterity?

Finally, for Step 5, students write a reflection on the process. We include this element because it is entirely plausible that a students' technical production may fall flat, and that is okay! The reflection allows them to demonstrate learning by unpacking their behind-the-scenes thinking. The prompts we use to guide students in reflection on remix are as follows:

- What effects does your remix have on the viewer/reader/listener/user? (This would come from peer feedback in Step 4.)

- What rhetorical choices did you (the author) use to create these effects?
- Where are your original sources from (*Othello* and/or *All American Boys* and any other readings they draw from should be addressed here), and what was their original meaning/purpose? How was the concept of alterity addressed in the original sources?
- How has the meaning/purpose of the original texts and their presentation of alterity been transformed through your act of remixing?

For these remixes, students could imagine any number of possibilities. Perhaps they take a selected scene from *Othello* and rewrite it with language that no longer marginalizes Othello and present a multimodal product around that. Or they could take a scene from *All American Boys* and revision it with a reformed police system where Blacks are not brutalized. They could discuss alterity through a mode such as poetry or song. The possibilities here are as limitless as the students' imaginations.

CONCLUSION

Although work around issues of alterity and race have become more prevalent in the curriculum, especially through the teaching of literature, the work must continue. Canonical Shakespearean texts such as *Othello* do not appear to be moving out of the standard curriculum in the near future, and while they have value, we must continue to reenvision the ways in which we teach them. We must find ways to connect them to students' lives in non-superficial ways so that they see the value in studying them. Through the pairing of this text with a more current, young adult novel like *All American Boys*, students have the opportunity to explore topics and issues that not only resonate across time but are relevant to the current world in which they live.

REFERENCES

Fernandez, M., & Burch, A. D. S. (2020, June 18). George Floyd, from 'I want to touch the world' to 'I can't breathe'. *The New York Times.* https://www.nytimes.com/article/george-floyd-who-is.html.

Gonchar, M. (2017, March 15). *26 mini-films for exploring race, bias and identity with students.* Retrieved from https://www.nytimes.com/2017/03/15/learning/lesson-plans/25-mini-films-for-exploring-race-bias-and-identity-with-students.html.

Hill, E., Tiefenthäler, A., Triebert, C., Jordan, D., Willis, H., & Stein, R. (2020, May 31). How George Floyd was killed in police custody. *The New York Times.* https://www.nytimes.com/2020/05/31/us/george-floyd-investigation.html.

McCarthy, N. (2020, May 28). Police shootings: Black Americans disproportionately affected [infographic]. *Forbes.* https://www.forbes.com/sites/niallmccarthy/2020 /05/28/police-shootings-black-americans-disproportionately-affected-infographic/ #28bbcc859f7c.

Reynolds, J., & Kiely, B. (2015). *All American boys.* New York, NY: Atheneum Books for Young Readers.

Selden, R., & Widdowson, P. (1993). *A reader's guide to contemporary literary theory.* Lexington, KY: The University Press of Kentucky.

Shakespeare, W. (2004). *Othello.* New York, NY: Simon & Schuster.

Shakespeare, W. (2017). *Othello: Updated edition Folger Shakespeare Library.* New York, NY: Simon & Schuster Paperbacks.

Visually. (2020). *Race.* Retrieved from https://visual.ly/tag/race.

Chapter 7

Othello and *My Friend Dahmer*

Examining the Beast Within

Lisa Scherff

Othello is one of nearly a half dozen full-length canonical works (*Lord of the Flies, Native Son, The Crucible, Frankenstein,* and *The Great Gatsby*) traditionally taught under the umbrella of "the beast within" during sophomore year at my high school. This construct helps to unify the curriculum and asks students to make connections between and among the texts they study over the course of the year. The topic of "the beast within" also requires students to consider a range and types of beasts in the world (local to global), which often cross over and connect to each other: figurative, psychological, systemic, and societal. For example, a figurative beast is the dead parachutist in *Lord of the Flies*; a human beast is in *Frankenstein*; psychological beasts are examined in *The Great Gatsby*; and, systemic, societal, and human beasts are exposed in *Native Son* and *The Crucible*. These canonical texts have stood the test of time. However, in looking for another text to connect to the beast within, I wanted something modern and "different." The perfect option to expand our collection is Derf Backderf's graphic novel *My Friend Dahmer*, the story of Jeffrey Dahmer, who was Derf's friend and classmate during middle and high school. Pairing *Othello* with *My Friend Dahmer* provides an opportunity to study the influence of psychological beasts.

In this chapter, I offer different methods to approach these two texts using the broad idea of the beast within. Some of the ideas presented relate to one text more than the other; however, using the idea of the beast or monster within provides a way to make these two very different works work as a good pairing. Before moving to a discussion of instructional methods, summaries of both works are provided below.

Othello by **William Shakespeare**

First performed in 1604, Shakespeare's *Othello* is a tragedy that centers on how deception and jealousy can cause a man's downfall. In it, Othello, a "moor," former slave, and legendary war hero, falls in love and elopes with the much-younger daughter, Desdemona, of a well-to-do Venetian senator, Brabantio. Because of Othello's background—he could be from Spain, Africa, or the Middle East—and history (former slave), the union is frowned upon. In addition, Iago, Othello's ensign is angry because Othello does not promote him to lieutenant, a position he feels he deserves, and bestows the honor on Cassio, a young and inexperienced soldier. Thus, Iago hatches a plan to ruin Othello by convincing him that Desdemona and Cassio are having an affair. The play takes place over the course of a few days and, despite the short time frame, like other tragedies, several deaths occur. One of the major themes in the play is how jealousy can cause a person's downfall.

My Friend Dahmer by **Derf Backderf**

Published in 2012, and 2013 Alex Award winner, Derf Backderf's graphic novel *My Friend Dahmer* recounts the middle and high school years of one of America's most notorious serial killers, Jeffrey Dahmer, who murdered seventeen young men and boys during the late 1980s and early 1990s. Told entirely in black-and-white panels, Backderf, who was Dahmer's classmate and friend, provides insight into Jeff's home life and idiosyncrasies, and—most importantly—how the adults in Dahmer's life (school staff, parents, etc.) failed to provide him with the help he desperately needed. Dahmer displayed warning signs early on, which grew progressively worse in high school (alcohol abuse, for example), but were ignored by those who could have done something to ensure Jeffrey received mental health treatment and counseling.

BEFORE READING

Before students engage with the texts they need to consider what qualifies as a beast, which can be accomplished through a discussion of beasts and making inferences based on small excerpts of dialogue. Another pre-reading activity is to introduce students to reading graphic novels for students who are unfamiliar with the genre; an extended discussion is beyond the scope of this chapter, but there are many excellent resources out there.

The Beast Within

Because the theme of the year is "the beast within," an appropriate before-reading activity for *Othello* and *My Friend Dahmer* is to have students consider what the term "beast" might mean. It is easy for students to identify obvious beasts that they have read, watched, or heard about. For example, some students might bring up the book and/or movie *Frankenstein*, the Disney classic *Beauty and the Beast*, or even *Bigfoot*.

Start by exploring literal, traditional definitions of the word, from the animal (four-footed, under human control, etc.) to the human (despicable) to a tough situation. Then, move on to more current definitions, for example, from Urban Dictionary ("a person that is extremely talented at whatever they do and always displays great determination, dedication, and resilience to always win or want to win").

Building off this, to get students thinking more deeply, encourage more figurative associations. How are some athletes described? NFL player Marshawn Lynch has often been described as a beast. *What qualities make people call him a beast? Is the beast connotation positive or negative?* However, to encourage students to dig deeper, one can bring up the seven deadly sins: pride, greed, envy, gluttony, lust, anger, and sloth. *How could each of these be a beast? Do we have representations of these throughout history and in popular culture?* Here, bring up names like Bernie Madoff, and then see what names students will generate. *What if the beast is not a person or an animal? What about COVID-19? Are there aspects of a beast or being a beast tied to the pandemic?* Showing images of people ravaging stores, protesting wearing masks, or health care workers showing the bruising on their faces from personal protective gear can spur discussion.

There are a number of directions one could take with this brainstorming and discussion: small group posters, mini-research projects with presentations, and so on. The key idea is to expand students' understanding of the word "beast" before reading the texts.

Shakespearean Musical Chairs

The idea for Shakespearean musical chairs comes from Brian Sztabnik (2014), who devised the lesson to help his students "develop a way to reduce their inhibitions, build their close-reading skills, front load information about the play, and make it fun and inviting at the same time." In brief, the teacher pulls key quotes from the first act of the play and cuts them into strips. Then, a quote strip is placed on each student's desk. Students are told that the activity is similar to musical chairs except chairs are not pulled away. The desks are arranged in a circle and as music is played, students circle around the chairs, and when the music stops they sit down at a desk in front of them where they fill out a graphic organizer noting what is revealed in the quote (something about a character, setting, conflict, etc.). After —two to three minutes, the process continues. After roughly twenty minutes, the activity stops and the class discusses what they learned so far.

In regard to the idea of the beast within, modify the lesson for students, pulling quotes that ask them to think about how each one might pertain to some sort of beast in the play—literal or figurative. This activity can be accomplished by making it into a paired gallery walk. For example, stations can be set up around the room, each with a large Post-it containing the quote, character, and scene. Give students a few minutes to work together to paraphrase and speculate about the quote before moving to the next station. Below are examples of quotes and explanations from *Othello*, each of which gets to the idea of comparisons between people and beasts/animals, which is a key component of the play.

- "Even now, now, very now, an old black ram/Is tupping your white ewe" (Iago, Act 1, Scene 1)
  - In this quote from the opening of the play, Iago is speaking to Brabantio, informing him—using crude animal/sexual imagery—that Othello has secretly married his daughter, Desdemona. Because Othello is a Moor, the black-and-white imagery and the comparison to male and female sheep is meant to shock and offend him beyond the mere fact that his daughter married someone without his blessing or permission.
- "You'll have your daughter covered with a Barbary horse; you'll have your nephews neigh to you" (Iago, Act 1, Scene 1)
  - The animal motif is shown again in this quote, where Iago—in the same speech to Brabantio—now moves to compare Othello to not just a horse, but a "Barbary" horse. The term "Barbary" refers to the coastal area of North Africa, so Iago is continuing the racist overtones with the reference to people with darker skin color. He extends this by suggesting Othello and Desdemona will produce animal-like offspring.
- "I am one, Sir, that comes to tell you your daughter and the Moor are now making the beast with two backs" (Iago, Act 1, Scene 1)
  - To continue to rile and create a feeling of disgust in Brabantio, Iago continues using crude, sexual references when speaking of Othello and Desdemona as making the beast with two backs refers to having sex.
- "Ere I would say I would drown myself for the love of a guinea hen, I would change my humanity with a baboon" (Iago, Act 1, Scene 3)
  - Roderigo is infatuated with Desdemona, and because he now cannot have her since she is married to Othello (he never could have married her anyway), Roderigo threatens to drown himself. In response, Iago speaks these lines, which show his contempt for love and women, equating Desdemona with the common barnyard fowl and anyone who loves like the primitive baboon.

For *My Friend Dahmer*, the musical chairs activity could be modified; instead of using quotes, panels from the book could be pulled and students could work to make inferences about them and what is happening in the story related to the concept of beasts or the beast within (a variation of this follows in the During Reading section of this chapter).

Teaching Graphic Novels

If students are not familiar with graphic novels, several elements should be taught upfront in order for students to gain the most from *My Friend Dahmer*. A full discussion of the form and content of graphic novels is beyond this chapter; thus, some main components are discussed below.

Panels and Gutters. Panels are the individual frames on each page, which can be bordered or borderless; a page can contain one panel or several (of differing sizes). Panels can contain words, images, or a combination of both, and they serve a variety of purposes to move the story forward—characterization, setting, plot, and so on. Gutters are the spaces between panels. The amount of space between panels can indicate the amount of time passing or where one is placed as a reader, and this space is used to "take two separate images and transform them into a single idea" (McCloud, 1993, p. 66).

Description and Word Balloons. Description, dialogue, and thoughts can be placed in enclosed balloons (sometimes, for effect, such information might be borderless). Where and how does the narrator provide description, if any? What do we learn from characters' thoughts and speech?

Sound Effects and Motion Lines. Sounds (think onomatopoeia) in graphic novels are often shown in description and/or word balloons. What sounds does the author include, and why?

Art. Just like an author has a writing style (Faulkner versus Hemingway, for example), each graphic novelist has their individual style. Is the story told in black and white? Shades of gray? If in color, what colors and shades are used? What is the effect of the author's artistic choices? Students could look at differently styled graphic novels and compare and contrast how the use of different colors and shades impacts the tone and mood of the information conveyed.

There are many online resources for learning about graphic novels. Even though some are not actively updated, the information is still helpful. Here are a few: Graphic Novel Resources (graphicnovelresources.blogspot.com/), Graphic Novels & High School English, the Center for Cartoon Studies (www.teachingcomics.org), and ComicsResearch.

DURING READING

While reading the play and/or the graphic novel, focusing on characterization and the beast within is critical. The concept of the iceberg works particularly well given how the main characters present only some aspects of themselves to others while hiding most of their true natures and/or motivations. In Shakespeare's play, while Othello is the tragic hero, it is Iago who is more interesting and complex, revealing little to no version of his true self to other characters (while creating outward versions of those around him for other characters); it is only the audience who sees his true nature. And, in *My Friend Dahmer*, we have a young man who presents different aspects of himself to classmates and his family, each one disturbing and alarming, and as readers—although we see his inner demons—we really do not understand the depth of what lies beneath.

Characters as Icebergs

It's often difficult for students to fully understand a character because they often have to read between the lines and try to see what is "beneath the surface." The visual image of an iceberg helps students remember the importance of looking deeper than the surface in order to better understand a character. With *Othello*, this method is also a good reminder of the purpose and importance of asides, soliloquies, and monologues.

Readers must analyze Iago and Othello to understand how the beast within each contributes to their outward actions and eventual downfall. Iago's internal beasts are envy (of Cassio's promotion), revenge and jealousy (for both Cassio and Othello supposedly sleeping with his wife, Emilia), and hatred (for Othello); they manifest themselves through his words and behavior—including how he manipulates other characters to act for him. Othello's internal beast is jealousy, which is created and sustained through Iago's manipulation.

One of the most striking means by which the beast motif is carried out is through the use of animal references. In *Othello*, Shakespeare often expresses a person's ruin by repeated use of animal imagery. In fact, "there are forty-five mentions of creatures or beasts in the play: dog (×5), hound, horse, hobby horse, jennet, toad (×2), ass (×2), monkey (×2), baboon, cats, wildcats, wolves, puppies, ram, ewe, goats, flies (×2), locusts, moth, snipe, (jack)daws, raven, parrot, lion, crocodile, bear, minx (×2), cod, salmon, asp and viper (both snakes), beast (×4), and monster or monstrous" (Creatures and beasts, 2020). Thus, one approach to looking at the beast within is to study how and when beast comparisons are made and what they accomplish.

For example, in Acts 1 and 2, it is Iago who most often utilizes beast references (e.g., goats, asses, Barbary horse, black ram) in an effort to create negative images of Othello and Desdemona in the other characters (that he is manipulating); however, this strategy also shows the reader Iago's own contemptible nature as a beast or monster. After being misled by Iago, Othello—who at the beginning of the play was respectful, well-spoken, and admired—begins to use derogatory animal terms about and toward Desdemona: snakes, minx, bear, and crocodile tears.

In the end, it is these men uttering bestial terms that commit beastly acts: Iago kills his wife, Emilia, and friend, Roderigo; Othello smothers his wife, Desdemona.

Analyzing Panels

With *My Friend Dahmer*, students will need to make inferences about what is happening and why in the panels because unlike traditional texts the novelist does not always know or provide that information. In analyzing the beast within, students need to study the text on two levels: (1) How do we see Dahmer's inner beast portrayed, and (2) in what ways is that manifested outwardly?

For example, the graphic novel Prologue opens with Dahmer walking down a two-lane hilly country road (p. 13). We zoom in closer from above, to see the crunch of his footsteps written in the panels (pp. 14–16). As if seeing things from Dahmer's perspective, a dead cat lies on the ground, which he nudges with his foot and then picks up (pp. 16–17) and carries past a driveway and house through the woods (pp. 18–19). It is here that Dahmer encounters some boys who question his carrying a dead cat. He explains that he is going to dissolve the animal in acid, which the boys doubt, so he takes them to his "hut" (pp. 21–22), where over a half dozen jars of dead animals in acid are displayed (p. 22). Four panels show the process Dahmer uses to dissolve dead animals, with the dead cat as his example for the boys. When questioned by them why he does, Dahmer says he likes "to . . . study . . . the bones" (p. 23).

When the boys doubt what is inside the jars, Dahmer gets upset and throws one to the ground (pp. 24–25), causing the boys to run away retching and calling Dahmer a "freak" (p. 26). The final full-page frame is Dahmer standing alone, head lowered, on a path in the woods (p. 27).

In these opening pages, there are several examples of inward and outward beasts: Dahmer's picking up and carrying the dead cat, his collection of dead animals, and his explanation above that he is interested in what is inside a body. We are introduced to his internal motivation for outward actions and—in addition, we also notice how Dahmer is perceived by others. He is a freak, a monster, to some peers his age. This internal/external analysis can be carried out through the remainder of the novel to understand the beast within.

AFTER READING

After finishing the texts, instruction should build off the during-reading analysis and discussion, connecting to an exploration of the different types of protagonists, antagonists, and heroes in literature and which descriptions Othello, Iago, and Dahmer most closely fit. Provide students with definitions (see below for abbreviated explanations from litcharts.com); then, students work in whatever structure works best (alone, pairs, small groups) to explain what type of hero, protagonist, and/or antagonist each character is and to provide text evidence for their assertions. This activity can also be utilized as prewriting for a literary analysis paper for students who might need scaffolding with this type of academic writing.

- **Hero/Heroine**: A character who overcomes a struggle or conflict to reach some sort of success because of their own determination, courage, or intellect. Heroes frequently have to make sacrifices, always for the greater good and not for personal benefit.
- **Antihero/Antiheroine**: The antihero is markedly unlike the hero; they are often shown to lack honorable or virtuous intentions. Antiheroes often act on behalf of their own self-interest, but they aren't completely unethical or corrupt, like a villain.
- **Tragic Hero**: A type of character in a tragedy, usually the protagonist. They usually have heroic traits that gain the sympathy of the audience; they also have flaws or make errors that lead to their downfall.
- **Villain Protagonist**: The villain is clearly the bad guy, dedicated to wrongdoing. Frequently a story's villain is the antagonist; villains can also be protagonists when they are the main character propelling the story forward and creating sympathy in the audience.
- **Villain Antagonist**: A villain antagonist has malicious or self-centered aims and wants to stop or thwart the protagonist.
- **Hero Antagonist**: A hero antagonist has noble intentions; their main goal is to stop or hinder the protagonist. If a story has a villain protagonist, chances are there will be a hero antagonist. Including a hero antagonist does not always mean the protagonist must be a villain.
- **Internal antagonist**: Some authors use this term to illustrate a situation where an internal flaw or concern of the protagonist stands in his or her way.

Othello

In *Othello*, determining whether Othello or Iago is the protagonist, antagonist, and/or hero, readers must consider their role in the play and the extent to which the action revolves around them and, in the end, how the audience feels about them. Written responses and/or class discussion should focus on determining what type of character each is. Contemplating Othello first, Walthall (2016) raised several points to consider:

Is Othello the protagonist? Is he the main character? He's certainly the *title* character. . . . Does he have the most speeches? Yes, but barely; Othello has 274 speeches, two more than Iago. . . . Do we as an audience focus on him? Do we root for him? I'd argue yes, but even those who would argue against this would have to admit that we root for him more than just about any other character.

However, in that same vein, we must apply the same questions for Iago. Walthall (2016) noted that even though Iago has two fewer speeches than Othello, he has over 200 more lines. Further, he has seven soliloquies of ten lines or more; Othello has only three. Thus, including all of Iago's asides, he is *in* the play more. However, the typical reader does not cheer for or admire him. His overt goal is to ruin those around him. Based on the evidence, and the definitions above, it appears that Iago is a villainous protagonist.

So, what is Othello? He fits the description of a tragic hero. Walthall (2016) argued that using the term "tragic flaw" is incorrect; analysis goes beyond simply noting a "character flaw or personality defect" that causes a hero's downfall. Instead, it is Othello's hamartia, or "error in judgment," that brings about his downfall. He also recognizes "his situation and position in the world" at the end of the play, what Aristotle calls *anagnorisis*. We can sum up Othello in the following way: his fortune is reversed (respected general with a loving wife to a weak, controlled, jealous man); his error in judgment is not only willingly believing what Iago tells him (Desdemona is unfaithful) but quickly deciding that his wife and her lover must be killed; his *anagnorisis* in Act 5 occurs on two levels—one is the overt and abrupt recognition that Iago was behind all of it, the many lies, tricks, and manipulations, and the other relates back to the beginning—he is a beast (a Moor), an outsider in this White world.

My Friend Dahmer

In *My Friend Dahmer*, we have only one main character—Jeffrey Dahmer— who is clearly a villain protagonist. Dahmer is unmistakably the "bad guy." We know the ending before the book begins: Dahmer kills, mutilates, and sometimes eats the males he encounters. Yet, there is sympathy for him. Why? The unanswered questions are what creates sympathy. *What if his parents hadn't been so clueless and absent? What if teachers and school staff said something and intervened? What if Dahmer's classmates and friends had been able to turn to and tell adults what was happening? Could Jeffrey had been stopped? Could he have been saved?* These questions are explored in more detail in the interview with Derf Backderf presented at the end of this chapter.

EXTENSION ACTIVITIES

For an extension activity for *Othello*, students could perform a close analysis of the text to attempt to answer the question that has plagued readers and scholars for hundreds of years: "What the f*ck, Iago?" (Gladstone, 2015), as "no unanswered question in all Shakespeare beats that one." Othello, for all his misfortune and suffering, is at the core a man whose good sense was used and sabotaged by Iago. Iago's techniques are not cryptic for readers. The question is, *why did he employ them in the first place?*

Students should carefully study not only what Iago says and thinks but also what other characters reveal, especially in Act 5. For example, in Scene 1, Iago is encouraging Roderigo to get ready to attack Cassio and as an aside reveals his feelings about the murderous plot and both men and Othello. The audience learns of his disdain for Roderigo and why it is imperative that both men die.

I have rubb'd this young quat almost to the sense,
And he grows angry. Now, whether he kill Cassio,
Or Cassio him, or each do kill the other,
Every way makes my gain. Live Roderigo,
He calls me to a restitution large
Of gold and jewels that I bobb'd from him
As gifts to Desdemona;
It must not be. If Cassio do remain,
He hath a daily beauty in his life
That makes me ugly; and besides, the Moor
May unfold me to him; there stand I in much peril.
No, he must die. Be't so. I hear him coming.

As another example, in Scene 2 when everyone is gathered trying to sort out what happened, Emilia reveals the truth about the handkerchief. Desdemona did not give it to Cassio. She (Emilia) found it by accident and gave it to Iago, who had asked her to steal it many times; it was he who planted it to frame Cassio. This revelation makes Othello start realizing how much he was duped by Iago. Once students share their answers, the whole class can read and discuss Gladstone's post in the Shakespeare on Tor.com series.

The same process of analysis can be completed for *My Friend Dahmer*. To analyze the monsters in the text, students could be reminded that monsters exist "near or outside the farthest outlier of acceptable human behavior" (Stesienko, 2011, p. 92). They could then be directed to explain why (or why not or to what extent) Jeffrey Dahmer is a monster. Students could pull from articles about mental illness and/or psychopathic behavior as part of their explanation (and there is much armchair/pop psychology about Dahmer). Because the reader lacks internal motivations students can refer to the Notes section at the end of the book, which includes some annotations from news sources. After analysis and discussion, teachers could share the interview with Derf Backderf, which took place in April 2020.

Essay Options

Students could also be assigned the type of writing they may face on the AP literature exam or in college by choosing among several prompts and writing to the one that they feel can best showcase their knowledge and writing skills:

- In literary works, cruelty often functions as a major motivation or a main social or political factor. Write a well-developed essay analyzing how cruelty functions in Othello as a whole and what the cruelty reveals about the perpetrator(s) and/or victim(s).
- Acts of betrayal occur in literature and in life. Friends and/or family may betray someone; main characters may likewise be guilty of treachery or even betray their own values. In a well-written essay, analyze the nature of the betrayal in *Othello* or *My Friend Dahmer* and show how it contributes to the meaning of the play as a whole.
- Writers often highlight the values of a culture or a society by using characters who are alienated from that culture or society because of gender, race, class, disability, and so on. Using *My Friend Dahmer*, write an essay showing how Dahmer's alienation reveals the surrounding society's beliefs or moral values.
- In novels and plays, some of the most significant events are mental or psychological (awakenings, discoveries, changes in awareness, etc.) rather than physical. In a well-organized essay, describe how the author in *Othello* or *My Friend Dahmer* gives these internal events the sense of excitement, suspense, and climax usually associated with external action. Do not merely summarize the plot.
- Superior works of literature sometimes produce in the reader a healthy confusion of pleasure and unease (or anxiety). Think about how *My Friend Dahmer* or *Othello* produce this "healthy confusion." Write an essay in which you explain the sources of the pleasure and unease/anxiety experienced by readers.
- Othello or Jeffrey Dahmer, on the basis of their actions alone, might be considered evil or immoral. In a well-organized essay, explain both how and why the full presentation of the character in the work makes us react more sympathetically than we otherwise might.

Interview with Derf Backderf (April 8, 2020)

While Derf Backderf has been interviewed many times, I wanted to get his perspective on some aspects of the novel that related to the idea of beasts within Jeffrey (and, really, anyone) and places where artistic choices might be brought up by students or teachers during their analysis and classroom discussions. Below are excerpts from the interview that teachers could utilize in class for discussion.

Lisa: You talk about the adults' culpability and absence throughout (pages 11, 67, 87, as examples), which, to me, is a key theme. It makes me wonder what you think might have most contributed to the beast within Dahmer.

- **Derf:** I have no answers on why Dahmer became a monster. Nor did he. He was at a loss to explain why he did what he did. The criminal psychologists who worked with him in prison couldn't come up with a diagnosis either. The monster bubbled up from deep in his psyche and took him over completely. Sometimes there IS no explanation. Sometimes monsters just happen. However . . . mistakes WERE made, and the indifference and failures of the adults in Jeff's life allowed him to continue on his path. If just one had noticed and interceded in a substantive way, could he have been diverted? Unclear, but it would have been nice had someone tried. And Jeff's behavior was SO out of control, it's stunning that no adult stepped up. Not one. They either couldn't be bothered, or were too wrapped up in their own issues, or just blew it. That still makes me mad. The cost of that failure was a pile of bodies.

Lisa: I love the juxtaposition of Dahmer alone on the road on page 13 and then standing at the meeting of two paths on page 27. Could you speak to that?

- **Derf:** Isolation is a major theme of the story. Jeff later describes that he killed his lovers so that they would never leave him, like everyone else in his life had. The fear of being alone, with only the insane voices pounding in his skull, consumed him. That first scene opens and ends with twelve-year-old Dahmer alone, but by the last page of that scene, we realize the reason he's alone is because of his own bizarre behavior. That's a powerful scene. Many read a hidden message into the page with Dahmer and the forking paths. Honestly, that wasn't my intent! I was simply trying to compose a striking image. Nothing is implied there. Besides, Dahmer in reality only had ONE path. Now, I don't believe all those people had to die, but Dahmer was always going to wind up a monster. At best, he would have spent his life institutionalized and pumped full of meds. That's a fate he would have gladly chosen over the living hell his life became.

Lisa: Something that really struck me was the description on page 33—"the loneliest kid I ever met." Looking back now, any ideas about that . . . being introverted, afraid (like you write at the end) of talking to his parents, made small because of his home life, his own inner demons? All of it?

- **Derf:** Something within, I imagine. Jeff was never "normal." His wiring was always off. He didn't have many friends when he was young because he couldn't relate to others. As he grew older, he drove everyone away with behavior that was increasingly dark and frequently scary. That's what happened with me and my friends.

Lisa: Like Othello, it is a tragic story. But while Othello is a tragic hero, Dahmer just seems tragic. Othello is demonized and ridiculed because he is a "Moor"; Dahmer (and the group) engages in "disablist" mockery. And, in school, Dahmer is ridiculed because, really, it seems nothing else than he is just Dahmer. Not sure that's much of a question, just something that strikes me as very sad.

- **Derf:** It's incredibly sad. What resonates with readers is that everyone knows a kid like Dahmer, the class freak, the oddball who doesn't fit in. And we all wonder later in life, man, what happened to that guy? As incredibly unique as Dahmer was—we're talking about the most depraved fiend since Jack the Ripper—there's much in this story that is disturbingly familiar to everyone.

Lisa: Why is MFD a book that high school kids should read?

- **Derf:** It's a cautionary tale. Maybe we'll be more aware, more concerned, more vigilant, maybe we'll stop letting disturbed kids fall through the cracks. Is it a lesson we, as a society, are willing to learn? Considering how many of these damaged kids go wrong, how often serial killers and mass shooters pop up, I fear the answer is no. But I have hope.

CONCLUSION

Beasts are all around us. Crooked politicians. Greedy corporations. Systems of inequity. One need only turn on the news or open a social media app to understand that. But, sometimes confronting those beasts and working to create change is overwhelming. This is where literature comes in. Works like *Othello* and *My Friend Dahmer* provide spaces for readers to recognize and understand the beast-like forces that shape actions. Moya (2016) wondered *what is the power of a work of literature to affect a reader's perception of his or her world? How might a nuanced and insightful interpretation of a given text affect our perception of that text—and by extension, of the worlds it represents?* One answer is this: "In and of itself, [literature] cannot change the world. Yet [literature] itself and the way we engage with it can indeed effect change—both within ourselves and eventually within the public worlds we inhabit" (Eshel, 2019, para. 4).

REFERENCES

Backderf, D. (2012). *My friend Dahmer.* New York, NY: Abrams ComicArts.

Beast. (n.d.). Retrieved from https://www.urbandictionary.com/define.php?term=beast.

Creatures and beasts. (2020). *Othello. Crossref-it.info.* Retrieved from https://crossref-it.info/textguide/othello/41/3128.

Eshel, A. (2019). Narratives of narcissistic democracy and rational tyranny. Stanford University Press Blog. Retrieved from https://stanfordpress.typepad.com/blog/2019/11/narratives-of-narcissistic-democracy-and-rational-tyranny.html.

Gladstone, M. (2015). What the f*ck, Iago? *Shakespeare on Tor.com.* Retrieved from https://www.tor.com/2015/05/07/what-the-fck-iago/.

McCloud, S. (1993). *Understanding comics: The invisible art.* New York, NY: HarperCollins.

Moya, P. M. L. (2016). Why study literature? Stanford University Press Blog. Retrieved from https://stanfordpress.typepad.com/blog/2016/01/why-study-literature.html.

Shakespeare, W. (2004). *The tragedy of Othello, the Moor of Venice* (Folger Shakespeare Library). New York, NY: Simon & Schuster.

Stesienko, A. (2011). The monster in the moor. *The Oswald Review: An International Journal of Undergraduate Research and Criticism in the Discipline of English, 13*(1), Article 7. Retrieved from https://scholarcommons.sc.edu/tor/vol13/iss1/7.

Sztabnik, B. (2014). Shakespearean musical chairs. Retrieved from http://www.aplithelp.com/shakespearean-musical-chairs/.

Walthall, B. (2016). *Protagonist antagonist villain tragic hero.* Retrieved from https://thebillshakespeareproject.com/2016/01/othello-herovillainprotagonistantagonist/.

Chapter 8

Monsters Matter

Reimagining Caliban Using Monster Theory

Laura Bolf-Beliveau

La Llorona. Chupacabra. Candyman. Babadook. Krampus. Slender Man. Monsters are found in all cultures and societies. They are feminine, masculine, or gender nondeterminant. They have been photographed, drawn, and painted. They appear in film and television. Our students have been inundated with monsters since they were young, reading children's classics like *Where the Wild Things Are* or Sesame Street's *The Monster at the End of This Book*. As they grew older, monsters may have also helped many deal with more painful realities such as grief, as evidenced in *A Monster Calls* by Patrick Ness. Monsters scare, entertain, and help us envision other worlds, or, perhaps, reenvision our own. Monsters matter.

Monsters matter so much that there's actually *monster theory*. Developed in 1996 by Jeffery Cohen, this work builds a fundamental and theoretical understanding of a monster's purpose. Monsters recur in cultures because they speak to something at the core of humanity: our long-held beliefs. When the world shifts, those beliefs can be questioned, changed, rediscovered. Monsters help that happen. Although Cohen's *monster theory* outlines seven theses describing the functions of monsters, this chapter focuses on four: *crossroads, embodiment, difference, and dependency.*

Monsters are born when cultures are at some kind of *crossroads*, metaphorical or literal (Cohen, 1996). As such, monster's bodies are more than symbolic holders; they *embody* the fears, desires, anxieties, and fantasies of the culture (Cohen, 1996). This embodied monster is "difference made flesh, come to dwell among us" (Cohen, 1996, p. 7). These differences can be cultural, political, racial, economic, and sexual, and they make the monster an outsider (Cohen, 1996). Although monsters are often considered outsiders, they mirror humanity's limitations, reflecting our monstrous behavior. Cohen pushes us to think about our *dependence* on monsters when he asks, "Do

117

monsters really exist? Surely they must, for if they did not, how could we?" (1996, p. 20). We need monsters, and determining why we need them helps us see our (in)humanity.

These focal concepts can help students discover why monsters matter in William Shakespeare's *The Tempest* and Akwaeke Emezi's *Pet*. This pairing argues that Caliban can be reimagined through exploration of the crossroads, embodiments, differences, and dependencies placed upon him. Using textual evidence and building on stage productions of the play, Caliban becomes less of a monster and more of a sympathetic character that provides insight into the other characters. Pet, the monster in Emezi's novel, becomes an excellent supplemental character to help draw comparisons between the two texts.

The Tempest by William Shakespeare

Most likely Shakespeare's last play, *The Tempest*, focuses on Prospero, a scholar-turned-magician whose machinations affect all other characters. He and his daughter Miranda are shipwrecked twelve years before the play opens. The only other inhabitants of the island are the spirit Ariel and a native Caliban. Caliban's mother, Sycorax, imprisons Ariel in a tree, but Prospero's magic releases the spirit, and Ariel is now indebted to him. Caliban is then enslaved and controlled by Prospero. The play's action begins when Prospero, with assistance from Ariel, creates a tempest that causes a shipwreck. The ship is carrying the royal court of Naples: King Alonso, his son Ferdinand, Prospero's brother, other lords, and two comedic characters, the drunken butler Stephano and a court jester Trinculo. They find themselves separated on the island and are manipulated by Ariel as an agent forced to further Prospero's agenda. Three major subplots emerge. First, Miranda and Ferdinand meet and fall in love. The second subplot focuses on the royal court. Believing his son Ferdinand died in the storm, King Alonso ruminates on fatherhood. Unbeknownst to the king, others are plotting his assassination. The interaction between Caliban and Stephano and Trinculo, the third subplot, highlights a significant contrast: Caliban's love of the island and its beauty and the men's desire to take Caliban to Europe and exploit him for financial gain.

Pet by Akwaeke Emezi

Pet is about Jam, a transgender girl, who lives in a utopia named Lucille. Before Jam is born, the adults rid Lucille of monsters (rapists, abusers, etc.). Those adults are now called angels, and they created a revolutionary cry for the people of Lucille based on a Gwendolyn Brooks poem: "*We are each other's harvest. We are each other's business. We are each other's magnitude and bond*" (Emezi, 2019, p. 14). Jam's idyllic childhood changes drastically when an entity from one of her mother's paintings comes to life. This "monster" is Pet, and it challenges everything Jam thought about Lucille and its citizens. The monster Pet forces Jam and her best friend Redemption to look for evil in Lucille. Throughout this magical story, Pet starts acting less as a monster and more as a protector. Jam is confused; she's been told her entire life that monsters are bad and angels are good. But nothing is as it appears, and Pet eventually tells Jam: "You humans and your binaries. . . . It is not a good thing or a bad thing. It is just a thing" (Emezi, 2019, p. 118). This phrase, "just a thing," is at the heart of the novel. It is only when Jam willingly agrees to look at the gray areas that she finds a deeper truth about herself, Lucille, and the way "things" are.

BEFORE READING

Monster theory is challenging, and the texts suggested below help build schema and basic understanding before applying the concepts to *The Tempest* and *Pet*. As mentioned in the introduction, this chapter focuses on four elements of monster theory: embodiment, difference, crossroads, and dependency (definitions appear in bold in introduction). The texts and activities presented as before-reading approaches can function independently of one another; however, they do grow in complexity, so using all three in order offers the best preparation. The goal of each pre-reading strategy is to establish a baseline definition of the concept and then apply it to an accessible text.

Embodiment and Difference through Children's Literature

Quit Calling Me a Monster by Jory John and Bob Shea (2016) is an excellent text to explore a monster's embodiment and differences. There are several YouTube videos of the book being read (author Jory John has his own version). The story follows a monster named Floyd Peterson as he explains how his monstrous body and actions are not necessarily different from the children he sees. It may be helpful to start with the first two images of Floyd on his bike. Ask students to make inferences about the book's message based on the contrast between these two. Then ask them to think about why we fear monsters—*what about their bodies and actions cause that fear?*

Building on the opening discussion, stop after the first ten pages, and ask students to name the most frightening aspects of the monster's body. How does Floyd seem like a typical monster? Atypical one? Then, as students hear the rest of the book, focus on the emerging comparison and contrasts between what the monster does and what the children do. A Venn diagram works well to note these. When they are done reading the book, students should discuss why the authors chose these particular images and words: How do they contribute to the book's message about monsters and children who fear them? How are the children in the book monsters themselves?

Crossroads and Music

Metallica's (1991) "Enter Sandman" and Billie Eilish's (2019) "Bury a Friend" are excellent examples of how monsters are created at crossroads and speak to our fears, especially the fears connected with sleep. To best understand this as a crossroads, begin with a discussion of that not-quite-asleep or not-quite-awake feeling students have when either falling asleep or waking up: *How does it feel? Have unusual things ever happened at that time? Why might storytellers use it as a setting?* The emphasis should be on how the in-between state allows for different feelings and sensibility.

Next, students could annotate the song lyrics looking for examples of crossroads. For example, "Enter Sandman" includes these two lines in its chorus: "Exit light/Enter night/Take my hand/We're off to never-never land" (Hetfield, Ulrich, & Hammett, 1991). The speaker of that song is the monster, but "Bury a Friend" approaches sleep from the perspective of a person speaking to the monster under her bed, asking it:

What do you want from me? Why don't you run from me?
What are you wondering? What do you know?
Why aren't you scared of me? Why do you care for me?
When we all fall asleep, where do we go? (Eilish, 2019)

If time permits, students may find the creator's explanation of the songs interesting. Metallica's "Enter Sandman" is about the Sandman who supposedly puts a bit of sand—dried discharge—in children's eyes to help them sleep. Instead of helping the child, he "kinda freaks. He can't sleep after that and it works the opposite way. Instead of a soothing thing, the tables turned" (Revolver Staff, para 6). In regard to her song, Eilish told *Rolling Stone* "anything could be the monster—it could be someone you love so much that it's taking over your life. I think love and terror and hatred are all the same things" (Weiner, 2019, para. 2).

After discussing the crossroads depicted in the lyrics, show each music video and ask students to look for images that connect with the crossroads noted in the lyrics. Students might take screenshots of particular images that show the crossroads. Bruce (2012) discussed videos in terms of their "grammar," so have students look for establishing shots (how the crossroad is set), reaction shots (responses to the crossroad), and perspective shots (how the viewer is put into the crossroad) (pp. 34–35). If possible, curate the screen-shots into a slide show and ask students to discuss how each produces an effect of displacement and upheaval, two characteristics of Cohen's *monster theory*.

Crossroads, Embodiment, and Dependency through Urban Legends

Monsters are often the focus of urban legends. Chris Clark's infographic includes dozens like Bigfoot, Demogorgon, and Kraken, and all intrigue and scare people, and while all are terrifying, a relatively new one, Slender Man, works well to frontload *monster theory*. Slender Man is an internet sensation, one that began as a meme and then became the focus of numerous YouTube videos (Boyer, 2013, p. 243). This urban legend is summarized in a six-minute video, "Slender Man: The Documentary." As students watch this, they should focus on the following:

• What does Slender Man look like?
• What are his most monstrous actions?
• What happens to those who interact with him?
• What is Slender Man's history?
• Why do you think this monster was created?

Slender Man was born on the internet, a crossroads itself where Slender Man "walked the invisible line between reality and fiction" (Boyer, 2013, p. 241). A discussion about the ways in which the internet functions as a crossroads would prove helpful to begin the discussion of Slender Man. Then discuss what Slender Man looks like: *In what ways does his facelessness mirror the anonymity of the internet? How does that allow for monstrous behavior?*

Slender Man introduces a more complex aspect of *monster theory*: dependency. Monsters matter because we need them. They are children of our imaginations, put on the page or internet, because they help us think about who we are and what we value. However, some monsters are used to justify our own monstrous actions. This was the case when, in 2014, two twelve-year-old girls from Waukesha, Wisconsin, stabbed their friend nineteen times and left her for dead. The victim was able to crawl from the scene and get help. When asked why they stabbed her, they told the police, "Many do not believe Slender Man is real." They wanted to prove those skeptics wrong (Neuman, 2017).

Dewey's 2016 article, "The Complete History of 'Slender Man,' the Meme That Compelled Two Girls to Stab a Friend" is an excellent overview of the case. After students read the article, they could apply TQE Method

(Gonzalez, 2015), a focus on their thoughts, lingering questions, and epiphanies. Writing prompts conducive to this method might include the following:

• What thoughts do you have about monsters and our need for them?
• What questions do you still have about our dependency on monsters?
• What epiphanies or surprise discoveries did you experience about this topic?

DURING READING

Once the key concepts are explored and applied to popular culture examples, students can move to the focal texts. Although this section applies each aspect of *monster theory*—crossroads, embodiment, difference, and dependency— teachers may opt to use those most relatable to their instructional goals for the unit. Figure 8.1 serves as a menu of choices when approaching the play and the novel. Each part of *monster theory* is explored in more depth, often discussing more of the theoretical underpinnings before applying it. Please note the supplemental material for *The Tempest* is found in the Cambridge School's Shakespeare edition of the play.

Crossroads

Why was the monster created? Monsters are engendered at a time of cultural flux, often tied to political, historical, or societal changes (Cohen, 1996, p. 4).

Monster Theory Concept	Focal Section(s) in *The Tempest*	Focal Section(s) in *Pet*
Crossroads	2.2.25-31 5.1.263-265 Supplementary Material, p. 66 & pp. 152-155	Pages 1-4 Pages 48-51
Embodiment	1.2.283-4 2.2.23-25	Page 10 Page 23-25 Page 108
Difference	1.1.353-365 1.2.331-346 Supplemental Material, pp. 30 & 154	Pages 71-75 Pages 125-134 Pages 200-201
Dependency	1.2.311-314 1.2.348-349 2.2.3 5.1.292-294 Supplementary Material, p. 6	Pages 200-203

Figure 8.1 **Monster theory connections in *The Tempest* and *Pet*.** *Author created.*

The monster represents the fears and anxieties of that time. This crossroad, whether literal or metaphoric, provides background or motivation for the monster itself or for the way others treat the monster. Cohen argued: "the monster signifies something other than itself: it is always a displacement, always inhabits the gap between the time of upheaval that created it and the moment into which it is received, to be born again" (1996, p. 4). Perhaps revisiting Slender Man would help to understand Cohen's claim. The creation of this urban legend was dependent on the rise of the internet and technology that allowed that medium to produce and propagate the myth. Given the large number of followers, including the girls who attacked their friend, Slender Man filled a need for those who sought him out.

Crossroads in The Tempest

The Tempest takes places against the backdrop of exploration and was most likely inspired by stories circulating in London about a group of ships sailing to the New World One ship, the *Sea Venture*, became separated from the others during a storm and wrecked on Bermuda. Eventually, the lost colonists arrived in Virginia with stories about their adventure and pamphlets about their experiences no doubt influenced Shakespeare (Brady & James, 2015, pp. 152–153). This background proves important when reading Caliban. He is made a monster because of his bodily differences and behavior, but it is important to see that the colonization of the Americas was, in part, a purposeful demonstration of ethnic superiority: Caliban's name could be an anagram of cannibal, and Prospero's an anagram of oppressor. Europeans believed that a "masterless man" like Caliban was a threat to social order (Brady & James, 2015, p. 154). This crossroads is evident in two places in Shakespeare's text. When Trinculo first sees the fish-like Caliban, he says:

> Were I in England now—as once I was—and had but this fish painted . . . there but would give me a piece of silver. . . . When they will not give a doit to relieve a lame beggar, they will lay out ten to see a dead Indian. (2.2.25–31)

Later, Antonio reiterates this sentiment calling Caliban "marketable" (5.1.265). Historical realities shape the way others see Caliban; he becomes a placeholder for the fears of exploration and of economic greed. Explorers often brought back Indigenous people and used them as sideshow attractions. Students should consider the ramifications of being made a monster in this way. How might Caliban feel as a monstrous freak?

Crossroads in Pet

The opening line of *Pet* is: "There shouldn't be any monsters left in Lucille" (Emezi, 2019, p. 1). However, Pet comes to life when Lucille, supposedly a utopia, is at a time of upheaval. Thinking they had rid their culture of monsters,

Jam's parents, Bitter and Aloe, are astounded when Pet becomes a corporeal body. Aloe asks Pet, "What do you want? Why did you come here?" (Emezi, 2019, p. 48). Pet responds that he must hunt a monster. Aloe does not believe him, but Bitter reminds him that "they always come for a reason, remember?" (Emezi, 2019, p. 48). Aloe tells Pet that there are no more monsters in Lucille, and Pet responds: "You keep lying that lie, liar" (Emezi, 2019, p. 49). At the end of this scene, Jam asks what the monster looks like, but Pet responds:

> I don't know yet, I am rife with unknowns, part of the hunt is to make the not-known known. Not just to me, or us, but to the not-knower, so that they may know, the truth is in the knowing. (Emezi, 2019, p. 51)

Pet signifies the displacement, the unknown, caused by his emergence at this time of upheaval. However, something else is at work in Pet's statement; any truths about who is monstrous depends on if we seek to know why monsters are constructed. What need are they fulfilling?

Crossroads Activity—Creating Metaphors

Literal or metaphoric crossroads engender monsters, and this is an opportunity to think about setting as more than the time and place of a story. What from that moment in time helps to produce monsters? Using "Metaphorical Thinking" (K-20 Learning), students might write metaphors for the crossroads in either or both texts. Begin with an example from one of the two songs from the Before Reading section. The metaphor should focus on crossroads and define them using examples from the song (i.e., "Crossroads are the moment when your back feels 12 syringes stabbing it").

Embodiment

What does the monster embody? Bodies are more than flesh; societal beliefs are embedded or housed in bodies. For example, fat bodies are often considered unhealthy. This generalization produces narratives resulting in fat shaming. As we saw in the children's book *Quit Calling Me a Monster*, Floyd is shamed for his body when, in many ways, the children share some of the same qualities. Caliban and Pet contain markers that make them different, but the word "monster" comes from *monstrum* that means "that which reveals" (Cohen, 1996, p. 4). What do these monsters reveal about our culture? Caliban's appearance, different than the Europeans who discovered him, justifies his subjugation. He does not have a normal body, he is less than human, and he deserves to be enslaved. Pet's embodiment is different, certainly, but no less monstrous. He looks the part so he must be a monster. But, as we see by the end of the book, he is the hero. The monster's body and our interpretations of it, then, speak to our own fears of difference.

Embodiment in The Tempest

Before Caliban appears on stage, Prospero describes him as inhuman, an animal "littered" by his hideous mother, Sycorax. He is "A freckled whelp, hag-born—not honored with / A human shape" (1.2.283–284). Upon seeing him for the first time, Trinculo describes Caliban as:

> What have we here—a man or a fish? Dead or alive? A fish, he smells like a fish; a very ancient and fishlike smell; a kind of, not-of-the-newest poor-John. A strange fish. (2.2.23–25)

Productions of the play approach Caliban's body differently. The Shakespeare's Globe production in 2013 had a White actor playing him as a creature who mostly walks in a crouch and whose body paint mirrors the island rocks on the stage. In the 2010 film version with Helen Mirren, Caliban is played by Djimon Hounsou, an American actor of Beninese descent. He walks like a human and has a white circle of body paint on his face. Since the textual evidence does not lend itself to a particular embodiment of Caliban, using images from various productions can facilitate a discussion of Caliban's body. How human should he look? How otherworldly? What does each say about why bodies matter?

Embodiment in Pet

Pet's monstrous body is more of a focal point. Before Pet becomes flesh, Jam studies Bitter's painting and describes it as "large and loud in the center of the painting had the hind legs of a goat, fur like grated bone, solid thighs, their surface thrusting toward the ceiling of the studio" (Emezi, 2019, p. 10). As Bitter created Pet's body in her painting, she, too, created a hybrid monster, part human, by putting her own hands on his arms: "Photographs of Bitter's hands were strewn around as studies—she'd painted her own hands into the figure, painted crude stitches that grafted her wrists to its feathered arms" (Emezi, 2019, p. 24). Pet's body is imposing and seems to be what many would expect a monster to look like. Later, Jam asks Pet if he has a heart and blood. He tells her: "My body isn't from this world. I am made of things you have no names for" (Emezi, 2019, p. 108). Pet's body is able to do things the humans cannot, and Jam learns that his body is not monstrous; it actually can soothe her, combat evil, and protect her and others. Jam rejects her society's belief that monsters embody danger and destruction.

Embodiment Activity—Six-Word Body Memoir

Students could summarize why Caliban's and Pet's bodies mean by producing a six-word Body Memoir. They may benefit from an example for Slender Man: "Faceless Monster: Our Hidden, Secret Selves." Students might also create a Body Map/Body Biography. Usually this activity traces the entire body, but a scaled-down version could be contained on a regular sheet of paper. The outline of the body could be filled with cultural representations that dictate how students feel about their bodies. Another variation would be a page with two body outlines. One would be how the world sees their bodies and the other would be how they would like their bodies reimagined.

Difference

Why do the monster's differences matter? Monsters are not created ex nihilo; they are representations of the cultures from which they come. Fragments of that culture, especially fragments of marginalized groups within that culture, are remixed, reconstituted (Cohen, 1996, p. 11), yet, monsters reveal our fears and trauma (Boyer, 2013, p. 256). Whereas embodiment was about how the monster looks, difference is about the monster's thoughts and actions. These actions often serve as mirrors of our own. Who monsters? Why? When we consider Caliban and Pet's actions within the context of their worlds, how do their behaviors, supposedly different from our own, actually tell us more about our own?

Difference in The Tempest

Caliban, as the only character native to the island, acts in ways that are contrary to what the Western characters believe are right or appropriate. This highlights a significant aspect of *monster theory*: the need for the outsider. Caliban is made the outsider because of his thoughts and actions. Early in the play, Miranda confronts Caliban about his attempted assault on her, saying that it was made more horrible because she pitied him,

Took pains to make thee speak, taught thee each hour
One thing or another. When thous didst not, savage,
Know thine own meaning, but would gabble like
A thing most brutish, I endowed thy purposes
With words that made them known. (1.1.353–358)

The meaning is quite clear: Caliban was a savage and only her language would give him purpose. Words made him more human. Caliban responds: "You taught me language, and my profit on't / Is, I know how to curse. The red plague rid you / For learning me your language!" (1.1.363–365). This retort speaks not only to Caliban's situation on the island, but it has also been used to raise concerns about how conquerors and governments suppressed the language of so-called inferior people (Brady & James, 2015, p. 30). This emphasizes a major way native peoples were made to feel like the outsider: they lacked the civilized language that makes one acceptable. By learning Miranda and Prospero's language, Caliban now has a way to protest his position as a monster. Caliban's speech should function as a means of exploring Miranda's own oppressive beliefs. Caliban also holds a mirror up to Prospero when he claims ownership of the island. In his famous speech (1.2.331–346), performed brilliantly by Hervé Goffings, Caliban claims the island for himself, protesting that he is imprisoned on just part of it. Prospero has invaded the island and implemented his rules and used his magic to control Caliban. This relates to the "social hierarchy" that was "firmly fixed in the European mind" (Brady & James, 2015, p. 154). Caliban's use of language and love for the island—different from the European beliefs of the time—can serve as entrance points to critique human behavior.

Difference in Pet

In Lucille, monsters were banished, so when Pet appears, his words and actions cause dissonance for Jam and her parents. It would be easy to dismiss Pet as the monster; after all, his appearance and words are monstrous. However, he is a monster hunting a monster; and the monster is actually someone they called an angel. When Pet discovers who he is, he will hunt the angel-turned-monster and "do what you cannot do" (Emezi, 2019, p. 73). The implied violence is disconcerting for Jam because she does not know what the evil people actually did before the utopian Lucille was created. Later, she and her best friend research topics kept from them. They find pamphlets, for example, of parental neglect. Jam is disturbed, wondering how mothers and fathers could treat their children this way.

Pet's violent goal, to kill this new monster, may seem monstrous, and clearly different than the so-called civilized angels of Lucille, but what is worse: killing this child abuser or allowing him to continue? At the end of the novel, Jam discusses this paradox with her mother, wondering if Pet was not a monster but an angel. Her mother agrees, saying, "I know what you mean, child. Angels could look like many things." Jam agrees but adds, "So can monsters" (200–201).

Pet's thoughts and actions force Jam and the others in Lucille to evaluate what they thought was true; this is why Pet the monster matters; without him, would change have occurred?

Difference Activity—Four Perspectives

Caliban and Pet's thoughts and actions hold up a mirror to other characters, and, as a result, can help students question whose behavior is unjust. This pairs nicely with "Four Perspectives," a teaching strategy from Teaching Tolerance. Students "respond to and pose questions from the four anti-bias domains: identity, diversity, justice, and action." Focusing on The Tempest and Pet, or any of the before-reading examples, organize the class into four groups. Each group formulates text-based questions from one of the domains and then presents them for a whole group discussion. Relevant examples are as follows:

• In what ways does Caliban's identity come from the island?
• In what ways does Caliban's identity come from the people on the island?
• How do the historical contexts of *The Tempest* affect the behavior of the characters?
• How does the angel-turned-monster in *Pet* use his power and privilege to justify his actions?
• How will the trial of the angel-turned-monster in *Pet* help others stand up to injustice?

AFTER READING

The final concept, dependency, could be addressed after reading both texts. It is complex and can be best unpacked after thoroughly investigating the crossroads, embodiments, and differences apparent in the texts.

Dependency

Why do we need monsters? Cohen (1996) suggests that monsters are not from the unknown; they are, instead, from our own psyches and bear "self-knowledge, human knowledge" (Cohen, 1996, p. 20). When we apply *monster theory*, we may begin to understand the cultures from which they come, certainly, but we really come to understand our desire and need for monsters. One way to read this need is through the terms "codependency" or "interdependency."

Dependency in The Tempest

The Tempest explores Caliban's codependency on Prospero and then Stephano and Trinculo. Even before Caliban appears on the stage, Prospero tells Miranda: "But as 'tis / We cannot miss him. He does make our fire, /

Fetch our wood, and serves in offices / That profit us" (1.2.311–314). Caliban is enslaved and needed for their comfort; they depend on him. When Caliban sees Prospero and Miranda, he curses them, and Prospero threatens him with cramps and side-stitches that will take away his breath. When Caliban complains, Prospero tells him that he once treated him well, but then Caliban "did seek to violate / The honour of my child" (1.2.348–349). This attempted rape is horrific, yet Prospero refuses to punish Caliban more seriously; after all, what would they do without him? Given this relationship, and the hatred Caliban has toward Prospero, students may wonder why Caliban trades one master for two others. Why not escape to live freely?

Upon seeing Caliban, Trinculo's first thought is that Caliban could bring him a piece of silver in England. Strange beasts are curiosities, and during Shakespeare's time, explorers brought people of the new world back to be used as sideshow attractions. These "Indians" were cruelly treated for financial gain (Brady & James, 2015). When Stephano joins them, he forces Caliban to drink alcohol, telling him that it will give him "language" (2.2.3). Thinking that Trinculo and Stephano are fine things, perhaps gods, Caliban kneels to them and agrees to their ridiculous plans in hopes they will kill Prospero and free him. Caliban kisses Stephano's foot and blindly follows both of them. Of course, once Prospero catches the three of them and the other members of the Naples court identify Stephano as the drunken butler and Trinculo as the court jester, Caliban tells Prospero that he will be wise hereafter, for he was a "thrice-double ass" to mistake Stephano for a god (5.1.292–294). Just before this declaration, Prospero acknowledges Caliban as his thing of darkness, stating that the two of them are linked, master and slave, and that cannot be undone by Caliban's dreams of another life. This relationship is codependent and was built on manipulation and control (Clark, 2020).

Dependency in Pet

Pet and Jam's relationship is far different. By the end of the novel, they become interdependent and have a relationship where the emotional bond is valued and allows those in the relationship to find meaning within it without compromising themselves or their values (Clarke, 2020). This is seen at the end of the novel when Jam sees Pet for the last time (p. 201).

As Pet fades away, Jam reminds the reader of his message: Do not be afraid. This relationship's emotional bond is far different than Caliban had with Prospero. Monsters can make us better; we can depend on them.

Dependency Activity—Two-Voiced Poem

Students can discuss the importance of people's dependency on monsters by creating a Two-voiced Poem. Students write a poem focusing on two different characters (e.g., Caliban and Prospero) and their dependency on one another. The process works like this:

• Left side of the paper: Words/actions related to the Monster
• Right side of the paper: Words/actions related to the Human
• Middle: Words/actions they share

These should emphasize the codependency or interdependency of the relationship. If students worked in pairs, they could read their poems aloud, each doing the voice of one character. Those verses in common, the chorus, could be read together.

EXTENSION ACTIVITIES

Unfortunately, examples of monstering others are apparent in the twenty-first-century U.S. landscape: high murder rates of trans and queer people, police shootings of Black and Brown people, children in cages on the U.S. border, and treatment of Asian Americans during the COVID-19 pandemic. Students can research these examples with special emphasis on action. Students can use a four-prong approach to the topics (adapted from K-20 Learning):

• What? (Summary)
• So what? (Implications)
• Now what? (Actions Taken)
• What can I do? (Action Plan for Self)

   Students could also benefit from an example based on another contemporary issue: racial profiling and unconscious bias. Show students a short CBS Morning News video about Nextdoor, a popular social media site, and its approach to curtailing racially charged posts.

• Summary: The crime and safety section of Nextdoor allowed users to post comments like "a dark skin man was breaking into a car."
• Implications: Nirav Tolia, cofounder and CEO of Nextdoor, felt these perpetuated stereotypes.
• Actions Taken: Tolia and his team reworked Nextdoor and put in place multiple steps required to report a crime or safety issue. These curtailed the use of generic reports based on skin color alone.
• Personal Action Plan: When I see this happening on my social media, I will report it and ask the social media site to find ways to stop this kind of racial bias.

After students research an example of someone being treated like a monster, they can present their findings publicly during a poster session. NYU's Library website describes academic research posters as artifacts that "summarize information or research concisely and attractively to help publicize it and generate discussion." Examples of well-designed and poorly designed posters are on that website, and NYU offers suggestions for open source software to produce posters. Once they are done, students can post them around the room, and others can comment and question their findings.

Theoretical Connections

Some students may be interested in reading Cohen's chapter on *monster theory* in its entirety, or perhaps they may be interested in how others have applied Cohen's work. For example, Boyer's (2013) article "The Anatomy of a Monster: The Case of Slender Man" applies several aspects of *monster theory* and is relatively accessible for secondary students. Cohen's work intersects with other theories, especially postcolonialism, which discusses, among other things, The Other and Othering. The Other

> represents a group of people who are intentionally culturally divided from the Oppressor group. This is accomplished through *Othering*, a term that refers to the social and psychological methods that exclude, marginalize, subjugate, and/or oppress a group of people. (Malo-Juvera, 2017, p. 42)

These two concepts are apparent in Marcos Gonsalez's 2019 essay "Caliban Never Belonged to Shakespeare," a visceral rumination on how the author himself embodies Caliban and Prospero *simultaneously*. After reading this essay and finding instances of both The Other and Othering, students could discuss the article in a Socratic Seminar. Students can spend time preparing their own questions for the activity, and these could help start the process:

- Why do we Other?
- In what ways do people oppress others? Themselves?
- What are the effects of othering or oppression?

CONCLUSION

Monsters indeed matter. Whether they are like Caliban—human-like made into a monster—or like Pet—a monster made more human, they hold a mirror up to our culture, our bodies, and our behaviors. We continually create them because we depend on them to complete ourselves. Using *monster theory* to reimagine the monstrous Caliban allows students to see how events informed his and others' behaviors. In contrast, the benevolent Pet shows how monsters can help humans. Students need to reimagine literature and dig deeper; *monster theory* is one way to engage them in ways that help them understand themselves and others.

REFERENCES

Boyer, T. M. (2013). The anatomy of a monster: The case of Slender Man. *Preternature: Critical and Historical Studies on the Preternatural, 2*(2), 240–261.

Brady, L., & James, D. (Eds.). (2015). *Cambridge school Shakespeare: The tempest.* Cambridge, UK: Cambridge University Press.

Bruce, D. L. (2012). Learning video grammar: A multimodal approach to reading and writing video texts. In S. M. Miller & M. B. McVee (Eds.), *Multimodal composing in classrooms: Learning and teaching for the digital world* (pp. 32–43). New York, NY: Routledge.

CBS This Morning. (2016, September 8). Nextdoor CEO on changes after racial profiling criticism [Video]. *YouTube.* https://www.google.com/search?q=cbs+news +nextdoor+app&oq=cbs+news+nextdoor+app&aqs=chrome..69i57j33.6799j0j4 &sourceid=chrome&ie=UTF-8.

Clark, C. (n.d.). 40 frightening monsters from around the world. *Daily Infographic.* http://www.dreams.co.uk/sleep-matters-club/40-monsters-and-where-to-find-th em/.

Clarke, J. (2020, February 2). How to build a relationship based on interdependence. *Verywellmind.com.*

Cohen, J. J. (1996). Monster culture (seven theses). In J. J. Cohen (Ed.), *Monster theory* (pp. 3–25). Minneapolis, MN: University of Minnesota Press.

Dewey, C. (2016, July 27). The complete history of 'Slender Man,' the meme that Compelled two girls to stab a friend. *Washington Post.* https://www.washingtonpos t.com/news/the-intersect/wp/2014/06/03/the-complete-terrifying-history-of-slende r-man-the-internet-meme-that-compelled-two-12-year-olds-to-stab-their-friend/.

Eilish, B. (2019). Bury a friend. Genius.com. https://genius.com/Billie-eilish-bury -a-friend-lyrics.

Emezi, A. (2019). *Pet.* New York, NY: Make Me a World.

Gonsalez, M. (2019, July 26). Caliban never belonged to Shakespeare. *Lit Hub.* https ://lithub.com/caliban-never-belonged-to-shakespeare/.

Gonzalez, J. (2015, October 15). The big list of class discussion strategies. *Cult of Pedagogy.* https://www.cultofpedagogy.com/speaking-listening-techniques/.

Hetfield, J., Ulrich, L., & Hammett, K. (1991). Enter Sandman. *Metallica.com.* https ://www.metallica.com/songs/song-25920.html.

John, J., & Shea, B. (2016). *Quit calling me a monster.* New York, NY: Random House.

K20 Learn. (2020). Strategies. The University of Oklahoma. https://learn.k20center
.ou.edu/strategies.

Malo-Juvera, V. (2017). A postcolonial primer with multicultural YA literature.
English Journal, 107(1), 41–47.

Neuman, S. (2017, December 22). Teen gets 25 years in mental hospital in
Wisconsin's 'Slender Man' stabbing. *National Public Radio.* https://www.npr.org/
sections/thetwo-way/2017/12/22/572803757/teen-gets-25-years-in-mental-hospi
tal-in-wisconsins-slender-man-stabbing.

NYU Libraries. (2020, May 6). How to create a research poster: Poster basics. New
York University. https://guides.nyu.edu/posters.

The Other Solos, Shakespeare. (2017, August 23). *The Tempest*, Act I, Scene II,
Caliban, by Hervé Goffings [Video file]. Retrieved from https://www.youtube.com
/watch?v=Ld-BbStaPcQ.

Revolver Staff. (2018, July 30). 5 things you didn't know about Metallica's "Enter
Sandman." *Revolver.* https://www.revolvermag.com/music/5-things-you-didnt-kn
ow-about-.

Shakespeare, W. (2015). *Cambridge school Shakespeare: The Tempest.* L. Brady &
D. James (Eds.). Cambridge, UK: Cambridge University Press.

Teaching Tolerance. (n.d.). Four perspectives. Retrieved May 9, 2020 from https://
www.tolerance.org/classroom-resources/teaching-strategies/community-inquiry/f
our-perspectives.

Weiner, J. (2019, February 22). Billie Eilish's teenage truths. *Rolling Stone.* https:/
/www.rollingstone.com/music/music-features/billie-eilish-album-songs-interview
-tour-tickets-797040/.

Chapter 9

Shakespeare versus the Homosapien Agenda

Exploring Gender in A Midsummer Night's Dream *and* Simon vs. The Homosapien Agenda

Pauline Skowron Schmidt and
Matthew Kruger-Ross

When the word "they" was honored as the "Word of the Year" by *Merriam-Webster* (Harmon, 2019), we began to fully appreciate that our understanding of gender and sexuality was shifting and that most teachers may want to address this phenomenon, but may not even know where to begin. At no other time, other than possibly the 1960s, has gender been at the forefront of the U.S. cultural context. Even in our home state of Pennsylvania, it was just announced that we will have a third option on our drivers' licenses for Pennsylvanians who identify as nonbinary. We know that it can be challenging to discuss difficult topics such as gender identity in classrooms, but we also know that fiction can help with tackling this task.

Specifically, pairing Shakespeare's *A Midsummer Night's Dream* and Becky Albertalli's *Simon vs. The Homosapien Agenda* (2015) works well to examine the themes of gender identity, sexuality, and love/relationships. These works, though distinct in their own way, contain a play within a play and have happy endings, making them lighthearted enough with content to handle some heavy discussions and activities in classrooms. They also discuss crucial issues related to sexual identity in a subtle and accessible way that honors the cultural context at present. In this chapter, we provide activities and strategies that address the theme of gender by drawing inspiration from the pairing of these texts. Since this unit can be perceived as quite personal, we advise that it takes place after a safe community is established in the classroom, or, implemented in the second half of the school year if possible.

A Midsummer Night's Dream by William Shakespeare

Shakespeare's *A Midsummer Night's Dream* is categorized as a comedy and one of very few of his plays to include elements of fantasy. There are two main locations for the action of this play: Athens and the forest, just outside of Athens. While the play begins and ends in Athens, the majority of the story takes place under the influence and manipulation of the fairies in the forest.

There are several plotlines for students to consider: First, there is the impending wedding of Theseus and Hippolyta, centered around a power couple; then, there are the young lovers Hermia, Helena, Demetrius, and Lysander where the women seem to be interchangeable; then, there are is a small group of actors who will be performing the tragic-comedy *Pyramus and Thisbe* at the wedding celebration; and finally, there is Oberon and Titania, essentially king and queen of the fairies. *Midsummer* explores romantic desire and mistaken identity, while also playing with ambiguous and/or androgynous characters in the fantasy realm.

Simon vs. The Homosapiens Agenda by Becky Albertalli

Simon vs. The Homosapiens Agenda by Becky Albertalli is set in a present-day suburban high school just outside of Atlanta, Georgia. The story begins with the protagonist, Simon, who is blackmailed when someone learns that he is secretly gay. Even though Simon feels safe at home and in his school community to a certain extent, he is choosing to be tentative about this important revelation about himself. He has been emailing a character the reader knows as "Blue" and Simon is trying to both protect Blue and figure out Blue's identity as the story progresses. Things are complicated by the use of technology in the story, particularly a site called "Creek Secrets." It leads characters to present one version of themself online and present an entirely different version of themself in real life.

Throughout this story, as Simon attends typical high school events—soccer games, parties, musical practice—he is on the lookout for clues to reveal Blue's identity. There are mistaken identities, a love triangle, and all the usual teenage drama you'd expect from a YA novel. Simon's ongoing negotiation of his sexual identity, as it relates to his gender identity, provides us with a useful storyline to help explore how all students (and us) engage in a similar negotiation.

BEFORE READING

Before discussing the content and theme of either text in greater detail, teachers should begin by exploring some fundamental and basic vocabulary with their students. Issues of gender identity and sexual orientation are important generally, and, more specifically, have taken on greater importance within current popular culture. Consider, for example, the impact that the #MeToo movement has had on conversations about sexual violence and inappropriate comments and behavior. This cultural movement has rippled out and touched all aspects of life from popular music and politics, to workplaces and class-rooms. English teachers are role models for their students and modeling the importance of vocabulary to begin gender and sexual orientation conversations with students should be seen as critical.

Solid Footing: Getting Clear on Vocabulary

Issues surrounding gender and sexuality are complicated and secondary students may not even know where to begin. Many students and teachers, however, still may mistake biological sex for gender identity, or collapse the meaning of gender and sexual orientation. A helpful activity to begin with would be to generate a list of key terms with students relevant to gender and sexual identity (see figure 9.1). The aim of the activity is to make sure that all students are working from the same understanding. Because gender and sexual orientation are so impactful in the ways students move through their worlds, it is important to point out and make visible the importance of the terms and how they are related as well as how they mean very different things.

For a class that possesses a strong culture of discussion, having students call out words and phrases relevant to gender and identity as a teacher writes them on the board might be the best way to start. With a class of students who tend to need to think and reflect before transitioning into larger, whole class discussion, large pieces of paper could be placed around the room with terms already listed. Students in this scenario spend time reflecting while moving around the room and offering their thoughts in written or drawing formats about the terms on the pieces of paper. After this timed activity, the teacher would gather everyone together to start discussion as a whole group about the terms, their meanings, and any confusions or misconceptions that may have been uncovered.

Given the importance of the terms and their intersection with students' everyday lives, a teacher must mentally prepare and come to lead this discussion attuned to the possible pitfalls that could occur. Whether beginning with a preset list or having encouraged students to develop their own, teachers will eventually reach a point where boundaries must be set and foundational definitions must be made. This portion of the activity could happen on the board with the teacher (or another student) as notetaker, or with the use of a laptop and projector with the teacher (or other students) serving as the transcriber. Prior to the activity, teachers should consult a resource to make sure they, too,

Identity, Vocabulary term	Definitions
Gender	A set of cultural identities, expressions and roles — codified as feminine or masculine — that are assigned to people, based upon the interpretation of their bodies, and more specifically, their sexual and reproductive anatomy.***
Cisgender	A term that describes a person whose gender identity aligns with the sex assigned to them at birth.**
Gender identity	The psychological sense of self. Who a person is (within themselves) based on how much they align (or don't align) with what they understand to be the options for gender.*
Gender expression	The outward expression of "traditional" socially obstructed and situated gender roles. Gender expression may not align with other parts of identity, such as gender identity or biological sex.*
Gender Neutral	A description for a gender identity that does not align with either female or male, but neutral. Some persons in this space prefer they/them pronouns.
Nonbinary	Associated with people whose gender identity exists outside of the traditional binary of male/female.
Two Spirit	An umbrella term and identity within many first nations communities both historically and presently that describes people who live within a spectrum of genders, sexual identities, gender expressions and gender roles.**
Transgender	An umbrella term for people whose gender identity and/or expression is different from cultural expectations based on the sex they were assigned at birth. Being transgender does not imply any specific sexual orientation.**
MtF/FtM	Acronym some (but not all) transgender people use to identify and describe themselves: Male-to-Female, Female-to-Male.
Biological sex	The physical sex characteristics a person is born with and develops, including genitalia, body shape, voice pitch, body hair, hormones, chromosomes.*
Intersex	A term for someone born with biological sex characteristics that aren't traditionally associated with male or female bodies. Intersexuality does not refer to sexual orientation or gender identity. (NYT)
Sexual orientation/attraction	A descriptor for physical attraction that exists on a spectrum from same sex to opposite sex attraction. Lesbian, gay, bisexual, intersex, or asexual are a few identities generally understood to be sexual orientations.
Feminine/Female-ness	Relevant to gender, identity, biological sex, attraction, and expression - but ultimately socially constructed, characteristics typically (but not always) associated with the terms woman, female, femininity, or femme.*
Masculine/Male-ness	Relevant to gender, identity, biological sex, attraction, and expression - but ultimately socially constructed, characteristics typically (but not always) associated with the terms man, male, masculinity, or butch.*
LGBTQIA	An acronym that stands for a variety of identities. This has changed over time, this current iteration stands for: lesbian, gay, bisexual, transgender, queer or questioning, intersex, asexual or ally.
QTPOC	An acronym that acknowledges the intersectionality of identities and stands for Queer, Trans, People of Color.**

Figure 9.1   Definitions of terms relevant to gender and sexual identity, adapted from Genderbread*, Welcoming Schools**, GLSEN***. *Author created—adapted from Genderbread*, Welcoming Schools**, GLSEN***.*

are fully aware of all the key terms and definitions. An excellent resource for these definitions is website The Genderbread Person, which includes posters, PDFs, and other useful guides for teachers and students.

To bring the vocabulary activity to a close, students could be put into teams to evaluate and further edit and finalize the drafted definitions. Once the individual teams have finished their review, the entire list could be regenerated and evaluated by the class. To conclude this activity, the finalized list of defined terms should be made available publicly within the classroom space.

For example, a copy of the definitions could be printed onto large paper and posted on the classroom wall or the finalized document could be uploaded and linked within the class learning management system (LMS). Ready access to these definitions and terms will be helpful as students continue in their study of the books and engaging with other activities.

Both *Midsummer* and *Simon* provide opportunities for students and teachers to engage with complex issues surrounding gender and sexual identities. Being clear about what is being talked about is the first step to encouraging fruitful and meaningful discussions when teaching these texts.

Gender and Sexual Identity Today: Recent U.S. Supreme Court Cases

In order to demonstrate that concerns around gender and sexual identity are by no means settled, teachers can point to recent and ongoing legal conversations where these matters are continuously being contested and reinterpreted. One possibility might include examining recent decisions of the U.S. Supreme Court to situate how the larger cultural context seemingly creates a space that might seem safe, open, and supportive for lesbian, gay, bisexual, transgender, queer/questioning, intersex, asexual, pansexual (LGBTQ+) people. Court cases, specifically U.S. Supreme Court cases, can be reframed and introduced to students as legal conversations. These conversations live in the written briefs submitted to the court, the public arguments made by lawyers to the justices, and culminating in the written opinions made by the justices themselves. Students could be divided into teams and assigned a court case to study. The culmination of their work would be an in-class presentation sharing what they have learned and how the case has impacted understandings related to gender and sexual orientation within the cultural milieu. This activity could follow the introductory vocabulary discussion as a further example of how even adults continue to struggle in their understanding of identities.

Two cases to highlight and focus on are *Obergefell v. Hodges* (2015) and *Bostock v. Clayton County* (2019). The *Obergefell v. Hodges* (2015) decision declared same-sex marriage constitutional, and *Bostock v. Clayton County* (2019) offered gay, lesbian, and transgender employees protection from employment discrimination based on sex. Before moving further into the activity, the teacher could open a whole-class discussion about how aware students are of the impact of large court cases on their lives. What gets reported in news headlines and summary articles covers and hides the complicated legal (and conceptual, interpretive) questions being worked out. Brief summary articles from popular news sources could be provided to the whole class, either projected on the screen or printed and shared hard copies. After students have had a chance to read the news articles, the teacher could begin a whole-class discussion. Suggested questions for whole-class discussion include the following:

- What in the course case shocked or surprised you?
- Why did this issue arrive at the Supreme Court?
- In the context of the court case, what were the fundamental arguments made for and against?
- What was not mentioned, shared, or named in the summaries provided about the cases in the articles?

Following the discussion, students should be given time to work in their teams to further research the individual court cases. Because government documents are not protected by copyright law, all of the opinions, briefs, and much of the supporting documentation are publicly available. Some resources that students could be directed to include the U.S. Supreme Court official website and other supporting organizations such as Oyez to gather data and further contextual information about their assigned case. A suggested set of team instructions might include the following:

1. Begin by finding the court cases' website on both the U.S. Supreme Court website and the Oyez website.
2. Within each team, assign students into four focus sub-teams:
   a. Majority opinion(s) (Justices and the written opinions, questions during oral arguments)
   b. Minority/Dissenting opinion(s) (Justices and the written opinions, questions during oral arguments)
   c. Advocates for (Persons and supporting documents)
   d. Advocates against (Persons and supporting documents)
3. In the smaller sub-teams, students should read, listen, and view in order to understand the background context of the case. The ultimate aim in this endeavor is to review the information through the lens of gender and sexual orientation as negotiated and social situated.
4. At the end of one or two class periods (suggested amount of time needed to complete this activity), the four sub-teams should gather to share their findings with the larger team.
5. A culminating whole-class presentation from each of the eight sub-teams would conclude the activity.

While these cases no doubt demonstrate an advancement in the rights and privileges of LGBTQ+ individuals, they do not tell the entire story about cultural and local acceptance. As an extension of the vocabulary activity, the goal of this activity is to demonstrate how the vocabulary work does not end in the classroom. It continues even at the highest levels of law and government. The two court cases presented above offer examples and windows into this space for students. The ultimate aim, however, is to prepare students to be ready to engage with *Midsummer* and *Simon*, two texts that also engage in critical conversations about gender and sexual identity.

DURING READING

While *Simon* might be left to students' independent reading time, teachers should consider that experiencing Shakespeare's work needs more scaffolding and support for students to truly appreciate the work. The Folger Shakespeare Library provides resources both online and in a traditional text; the *Shakespeare Set Free* series offers solid lesson plans for each play. Teachers beginning work with *A Midsummer Night's Dream* should focus on helping students see themselves as actors, comparing film versions, and then analyzing the play within a play.

Digital Resources to Acquaint Students with Shakespeare

In addition to unpacking terminology around gender, students will also benefit from a bit of orienteering in relation to one of Shakespeare's most intriguing and whimsical plays. A few additional resources that can help students get an overview of *Midsummer* as they read it are Nick Newlin's *30 minute Shakespeare*, *MyShakespeare*, Video SparkNotes, and Greg Edwards's *Thug Notes*. Each of these online resources presents an abbreviated version of *Midsummer* in unique and engaging ways. Newlin (2010) has condensed scripts to cover the basic outline of the story for students. His compact volumes include a list of characters, several short scenes, and a list of props. The idea is that students will "act out" the play, but it will be a considerably shorter version of the play in its entirety, giving them an overview and summary. Following this activity will give students a sense of the plot line so they won't get lost in the language.

The online tool MyShakespeare.com is also a valuable resource for students. The web-based application contains the entire text, along with annotations, explanations, video and audio clips and then analysis. Students can also create a (free) login and annotate for themselves and their work remains in the notebook on the site. Shakespeare's plays were intended to be performed and this interactive, multimodal platform gives them small samples of the play being performed in a variety of ways. They can check their comprehension as they are reading different scenes.

Although it does not have students out of their seats, both Video SparkNotes and *Thug Notes* will certainly have students engaged and possibly laughing. Both present the overall plot of the story through YouTube videos in under ten minutes; SparkNotes with animated slides and *Thug Notes* with images and captions. Be warned, however, that *Thug Notes* video uses some irreverent language. Both also integrate visual images and character names to help make the complex plotlines more concrete for students. Again, this will remind students about the general plot and character elements, should they be confused during the reading.

Gender in the *Midsummer* and *Simon*

Mapping the Characters

To focus and highlight the importance of representation, begin with the characters. Within *Midsummer* this means a focus on casting choices and with *Simon* the development of the main character through his identity negotiation and use this initial analysis to serve as a springboard for future study. One of the strategies for during reading will be to encourage students to focus on the characters of both texts. Within *Midsummer* this will include, of course, having students read aloud and act out—literally embodying—the characters. In the negotiation of which students will adopt which role, it may seem easier for teachers to just say that Shakespeare's roles are universal. But casting and performance choices need to be made explicit in order for the teacher to signal that discussions about difference "are not separate from the practice of Shakespeare" (Thompson & Turchi, 2016, p. 79).

Teachers could have students consider the characters as they read and then "map" them onto the scales established at the beginning of the unit. Consider how a character is described, what they say, what they do, and then how others interact with them. Then, teachers can have students use text-based evidence to plot them on various continuums (see figure 9.2).

Mapping the characters can be implemented in the classroom in a variety of ways. Teachers could begin the activity during the reading of the texts but also continue this activity after reading to determine if revisions should be made. The teacher could begin by taking a particular character, Puck in *Midsummer*, for example, and complete the activity together as a whole class. Students could also be placed into teams to produce graphical representations of character continuums that could be hung around the room. In addition, students should always be using evidence from the texts and the language/vocabulary from the earlier pre-reading activities to bolster and argue for their analysis of the characters.

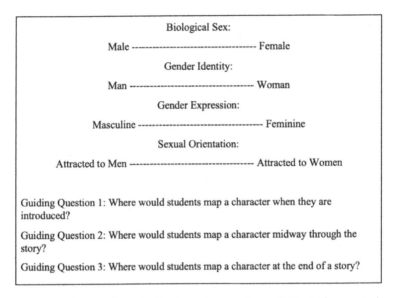

Figure 9.2   **Continuum of gender for character mapping activity.** *Author created.*

Gender and Identity

The intersection of these two texts while reading is considered next. While both texts offer several themes and topics to examine and drive instruction, the focus here is gender and identity. To prepare teachers to guide students through a close reading, and to support the character mapping activity, figure 9.3 offers some specific references to gender and suggested questions for discussion.

Gender on the Silver Screen: Analyzing Gender in Film Adaptations

An effective strategy for teaching complex texts is to share short film clips during the unit plan. Teachers can sustain the conversation about casting and students can continue to question and analyze the impact of characterization as they read. One approach to propel this conversation is to consider film versions during reading. Peggy O'Brien (1993) suggested that teachers "show two film versions of the same scene and ask them [students] to observe how the actors in each production speak, interpret, and move to the language" (p. 59). This could be as simple as aligning particular passages within each text to the corollary scenes in the film adaptations.

Kerr's 2016 BBC production of *A Midsummer Night's Dream* presents Theseus as a tyrant in a version of Athens with red flags adorning all major

Simon vs. The Homosapien Agenda	*Guiding Questions for Discussion*
P. 31 "I haven't heard anything about him being gay, but there's this kind of vibe I get, maybe." P. 55 "The weirdest part is how they made it feel like this big coming out moment. Which can't be normal. As far as I know, coming out isn't something that straight kids worry about." P. 63 "Wednesday is Gender Bender Day, which basically amounts to southern straight people cross-dressing. It's definitely not my favorite." P. 129 "Once you come out, you can't really go back in."	• Look at how the language is being used - what do you notice? • In what ways are "gender bender" days problematic? • How would you describe/define what 'coming out' means?
A Midsummer Night's Dream	*Guiding Questions for Discussion*
Act I, Scene I: The King declares that Hermia is her father's property and that he can dispose of her as he sees fit. Act I, Scene II: Negotiating dramatic roles and Flute does not want to play Thisbe. Act II, Scene I: The conflict between Oberon and Titania, as gendered, sets the stage for the entirety of the narrative in the forest. Act II, Scene II: Lysander wants to sleep next to Hermia but she insists that they sleep apart in order to preserve her modesty until they're married. Act III, Scene II: Oberon, in an effort to assert dominance, allows his wife to fall in love with an ass-headed man.	• Consider "traditional" gender roles. In what ways do they still exist today? • Find the connection to today's society. • How do you interpret the gendered characters? • Given the historical context of young men playing females, how does that impact your reading of these particular scenes?

Figure 9.3   **Analyzing gender in both texts.** *Author created.*

venues. The opening scene shows him on a pedestal in a red uniform, echoing President Snow in *Hunger Games*, or if one really wants to stretch, Hitler in Germany. There is a scene toward the end where characters rip the red flags, echoing Captain Von Trapp in *The Sound of Music*. While this is visually stark, it is effective in setting the stage and his character. The viewer is led to believe that despite the allegiance to the original language of the play, they are in a modern-day setting as there is technology like television screens and even hand-held tablets. As the characters enter, the viewer immediately notices that Oberon, Demetrius, Hippolyta, Puck, and Helena are all performers of color, making two of the main couples Demetrius/Helena and Hermia/Lysander multiracial representations.

A scene worthy of analysis is the "mechanicals" assigning parts for the "play within a play" *Pyramus and Thisbe* (11:30m) with Quince, the character in charge actually played by a female. She is directing this performance full of men, and as she doles out the parts, there is a moment when she assigns

Thisbe to Francis Flute. This is Act 1, Scene 2, Lines 43–48, as they appear in the original text:

Quince: Flute, you must take Thisbe on you.
Flute: What is Thisbe—a wand'ring knight?
Quince: It is the lady that Pyramus must love.
Flute: Nay, faith, let not me play a woman. I have a beard coming.
Quince: That's all one. You shall play it in a mask, and you may speak as small as you will.

However, in this film version, Flute does not mention his beard; instead, he quotes Polonius in *Hamlet* and says, "To thine own self, be true" with a flourish and a bit of a curtsy. It's subtle, but that male actor is embracing the fact that he has been cast as Thisbe. Historically, men always played the female roles, but this directorial choice creates a tension for further study: *what if the producers didn't avoid it, but embraced it?*

A teaching strategy that would keep students focused on the characters and their gender identities is Body Biographies. Students choose one character from *Midsummer* and then using the clips they've watched, create a representation of the character. Templates are available or students could be really creative and generate their own outlines. They must refer back to the text (the film in this case) and their representation should consider the words, actions, and portrayal of the character as seen in this film adaptation. Further, students can write a short reflection to explain and justify their choices.

Finally, in *Bring on the Bard* (2019), Long and Christel encourage teachers to consider that "Shakespeare can be as vital, relevant, and engaging as we want, and that depends on how we frame a particular play within a unit by selecting carefully orchestrated reading, speaking, composing, and viewing activities" (p. 175). The strategies illustrated above demonstrate just how relevant Shakespeare remains today.

In the film *Love, Simon*, the viewer is faced with the characters' confusion about love. Martin is in love with Abby, one of Simon's newer friends and that is the bargaining chip for the blackmail. Nick also has feelings for Abby, but because he fears being outed, Simon lies to Nick and tells him that Abby already has a boyfriend. Leah shares that she is falling in love with someone and Simon thinks it's Nick, but it's really Simon himself. Just as in *Midsummer*, all of this drama resolves itself with Abby and Nick ending up together, Leah and Simon having a heart to heart about how she fell in love with him not knowing he was gay, and Simon eventually figuring out that Bram was "Blue." The book focuses on how Simon is trying to figure out the identity of Blue and that incorporates some of the literary theory from earlier in the chapter. The film can help students connect to the performative aspect of the play and the casting activity. Some specific scenes in the film where gender is a focus occur at the following time stamps: 0:00–2:45, 45:00–47:30, 1:21:00–1:24:30, 1:28:00–1:30:00, 1:32:30–1:34:00, 1:35:00–1:37:30, 1:39:00–1:43:25. As students watch these scenes, some prompts that a teacher could pose for reflection include the following:

• Describe a "normal" teenager's existence. What does it include/exclude? What is important to the average teenager?
• How would you react if you saw two teenagers ridiculing LGBTQ students at your school? Would you speak out? Would you tell someone in authority (i.e., a teacher) or would you stand by, quietly?
• Reflect on these final two clips. What are your thoughts on these significant moments of Simon's life?

These activities go beyond simple comparison between traditional text and movies. Teachers should consider the power of multimodal texts, including films, to not only engage their students but also expand their literacies.

AFTER READING

The activities teachers could engage in with students after reading the two texts focus on two types of literacies: visual and aural. The first focuses on all the ways that images and graphics can be understood and "read" as texts. The latter considers literacies connected to oral/aural engagement with texts including, for example, audiobooks and podcasts. By adopting these alternative perspectives toward literacy, the predominance of the traditional text-based approach can be challenged.

Responding to Texts Using Visual Literacy

One post-reading activity includes the use of a popular new media format that students and teachers will be familiar with: the Netflix landing page. Many are probably familiar with the image and layout of the Netflix landing page for a TV series but have not considered how it might be integrated into the classroom. After reading the texts, students could be placed into teams and tasked with planning, mapping out, and creating the Netflix landing page for the entirety of the text or a smaller portion, depending on time and resources. For example, while *Simon* has already been adapted for film, how would students approach the telling of the story from the perspective of a ten episode, roughly ten hour, Netflix series? Or, what would *Midsummer* look like as a multi-series production for Netflix? As students create their landing pages, have them consider the following as a guide:

- How could *Simon* be adapted from the book and film production into a ten-episode Netflix series?
- How might *Midsummer* be crafted as a multi-series production for Netflix? What would the landing pages look like then?
- What genres should be associated with each Netflix series?
- What would the related films/shows be for each landing page?

See figure 9.4 for an example of a Netflix landing page for *Aristotle and Dante*.

The Netflix landing page activity not only allows students the opportunity to translate the traditional text into a visual representation. Mirroring the student casting discussion from before and during reading, students could translate and update this same activity to the Netflix landing page. *How would Puck be cast in a modern-day adaptation of Midsummer? What sorts of images would be chosen to exemplify key plot points? How would gender and identity inform these decisions?* Even with the recent film adaptation of *Simon*, this activity could still be utilized. The activity could represent how the students would cast characters (versus how they were actually cast in the existing film) with *Simon* as a Netflix landing page or series.

Responding to Texts Using Aural Literacy

Teachers should also seriously consider using the overlooked skills involved in hearing and listening as after-reading activities. At the most basic level and

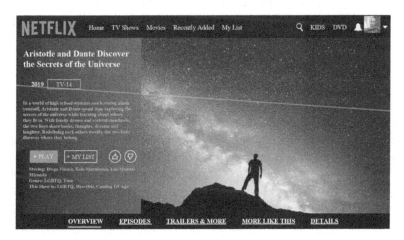

Figure 9.4 Netflix Landing Page. *Author created.*

for example, teachers could support recorded conversations with students to process *Simon* after reading to consider the reality of Simon's experience. They could interview one another and discuss social media, school culture, and so on. This discussion could connect to the pre-reading activity where students analyzed the fundamental vocabulary necessary for understanding and discussing gender and sexual identity.

Podcasts

For teachers ready to explore the next level, they could introduce students to the world of podcasts and podcasting. Instead of simply recording conversations and discussions between/with students, teachers could teach a brief introductory lesson on podcasts and podcasting that could be utilized to frame a deeper analysis of the texts. Podcasts are best approached as a series of episodes rather than stand-alone units of sound. Therefore, having students work in teams to record and produce a number of podcast episodes would be ideal. With very simple technology, even just a single laptop or smartphone, an entire podcast series could be produced and shared with the world. Anchor is a good application for teachers to consider using with their students, or if Apple platforms are readily available, Garageband can be used.

The possibilities of podcasting are truly endless. Teachers could "host" the podcast and interview students about their thoughts on gender and *Midsummer*. Students could be encouraged to, in teams, provide "tips, tricks, and tools" on the complexities of love and sexual identity in *Simon* for future students. Individual students could work on podcast episodes reviewing particular scenes from *Simon* or *Midsummer* and how gender impacts the reading. This individually focused activity could begin with teamwork during reading and be extended after reading by individual students. These can range from very formal and polished to informal and uploaded to Flipgrid.

Student-Created Audio Versions of Scenes

In the same way that casting decisions were central to pre-reading and during reading for *Midsummer*, teachers could also have students record audio versions of particular scenes and require students to explore how gender is performed *aurally* through narration. *How might narration decisions be made that reflect (or challenge) gendered stereotypes related to speech and gender/sexuality?* To raise the profile, students could be challenged to submit their work to LibraVox to allow others the opportunity to hear and enjoy the play. They could also compare their recordings to the other recordings posted to compare and contrast the impact and influence gender has on their comprehension of the text when heard.

Storytelling

Another way for students to respond to these texts is through good, old-fashioned storytelling. Human beings are hardwired to tell stories and at their very basic, these two texts are love stories. This activity can take any of the previously mentioned formats of podcast, visual representation, or even a multimodal video. This can be a literal story or a story crafted with similes and metaphors. Leave that open to the students' interpretations and provide them with the choices. This can be anything and everything from acting out, writing scripts to puppet theater or paper masks. The key is to relegate the choices to the students, centering them in the learning and meaning-making.

EXTENSION ACTIVITIES

To take this work to the next level includes engaging in critical conversations surrounding gender and sexual identity at the local level as well as broader, national levels. In this final section, strategies are shared that can extend and build on the work started in this chapter.

One option in furthering discussions after reading *Simon* might be a meta-reflection about the current context and climate within a school or school district in relation to sexual identity and orientation. As a hook, teachers might provocatively ask whether or not students in a same-sex relationship could hold hands while walking around school campus. If this is too provocative, additional questions that could guide a whole class discussion include the following:

• How has our community (town, neighborhood, city, etc.) historically handled conversations around LGBTQ+ people and issues?
• How is our school situated within the larger community in its relationship to supporting LGBTQ+ students and staff?
• What organizations exist within the community to support and provide outreach for the LGBTQ+ community?
• In what ways do students see LGBTQ+ and their life experiences represented in school curriculum and within school activities?

Teachers could also have students draft responses to these questions in written form either in journals or in another anonymous manner. Once the conversation transitions to the entire class, a workshop approach or Socratic circles that centers the students in the discussion and does not focus on the teacher being an expert in this area would be most appropriate.

If students are unable to fully grasp the discussion questions and specific organizations, teachers can provide national or regional organizations as examples. Teachers interested in this avenue should consult the Gay, Lesbian & Straight Education Network (GLSEN) as a professional resource and venue for connecting with like-minded educators. While it would be ideal that every school and district create and support organizations that ensure the safety and well-being of LGBTQ+ students and staff, this may not be appropriate in some contexts and locales. Teachers and allies will have to use their best judgment in navigating what can be a tricky space in some parts of the United States.

CONCLUSION

In the same way that we would challenge the dominant narrative around all students being digital natives, we would caution against assuming that all students are ready and equipped with the skills necessary to engage in critical conversations surrounding gender. Even though we live and teach in a time that is seeing a flourishing of identity expression and fluidity beyond what we have seen in modern times, we cannot assume that all students are ready and know how to engage meaningfully and purposefully (with care and tact and compassion and empathy) in issues of gender and sexual identity. However, literature, from Shakespeare to modern YA novels, theatrical performances to films, can provide avenues to support students in this way. In this chapter, we have explored how *Midsummer* and *Simon* can support this conversation and work.

REFERENCES

Albertalli, B. (2015). *Simon vs. the homosapiens agenda.* New York, NY: Balzer + Bray.
Berlanti, G. (Director). (2018). *Love, Simon* [Film]. Fox 2000 Pictures.
Edwards, G. (2015, June 23). *A midsummer night's dream (Shakespeare) – thug notes summary & analysis* [Video]. YouTube. https://youtu.be/CpLqTC2-HuA.
Folger Shakespeare Library. (2020). *Folger Shakespeare Library.* https://www.folger.edu.
Genderbread Person. (2017). *The genderbread person.* https://www.genderbread.org.
GLSEN. (2020). *GLSEN.* http://live-glsen-website.pantheonsite.io.
Harmon, A. (2019, December 10). *"They" is the word of the year, Merriam-Webster says, noting its singular rise.* The New York Times. https://www.nytimes.com

/2019/12/10/us/merriam-webster-they-wordyear.html#:~:text=Merriam%2DWebster%20announced%20the%20pronoun,whose%20gender%20identity%20is%20nonbinary.

Kerr, D. (Director). (2016). *A midsummer night's dream* [Film]. BBC.

Newlin, N. (2010). *The 30-minute Shakespeare: A midsummer night's dream.* Brandywine, MD: Nicolo Whimsey Press.

Paradigm Education. (2020). *MyShakespeare.* https://myshakespeare.com.

Shakespeare, W. (1993). *A midsummer night's dream (Folger edition).* New York, NY: Washington Square Press.

VideoSparkNotes. (2010, October 29). *Video SparkNotes: Shakespeare's A Midsummer Night's Dream summary* [Video]. YouTube. https://youtu.be/M1wMfOwlAZ8.

Welcoming Schools. (2020). *Creating safe and welcoming schools.* Retrieved on July 28, 2020 from https://www.welcomingschools.org/.

Chapter 10

Secrets and Spies

E. Lockhart's The Disreputable History of Frankie Landau-Banks *and* Shakespeare's Much Ado about Nothing

Megan Lynn Isaac

Technological innovations have transformed the quantity of information available about each of us, and we are both the objects of surveillance and practitioners of surveillance in more ways than anyone could have imagined only a few years ago. What would once have been considered snooping is now just a normal internet search. At the same time, few things are as provocative as a secret, as tantalizing as an overheard conversation, or as seductive as the opportunity to spy a few moments on a person with romantic appeal. The perception that these opportunities will bring new information and expanded prospects often makes them too attractive to turn down. This temptation to gather information covertly has a long history. Shakespeare's England and the contemporary United States are both cultures that employ an unusually high level of surveillance. For example, Queen Elizabeth maintained an elaborate spy network tasked with protecting the country from religious and political attacks. In her court genuine concerns as well as wild rumors about spies, codes, and secret strategies for passing information were rampant. In this chapter, ideas about surveillance through a study of E. Lockhart's *The Disreputable History of Frankie Landau-Banks* and Shakespeare's *Much Ado about Nothing* are explored. More specifically, this pairing of novel and play forefront different historical forms of surveillance, coded language, and secret societies to help students frame questions about the relationship between knowledge and power as well as exclusivity and inequity.

The Disreputable History of Frankie Landau-Banks by E. Lockhart

During the summer between her freshman and sophomore year of high school, Frankie develops some new curves and realizes everyone looks at her differently—both on family vacations and when she returns to her elite boarding school in the fall. Sometimes being the object of everyone's attention is frustrating, but to her delight, Matthew, a popular senior initiates a romance with her. Dating Matthew draws Frankie's attention to a male secret society with a long history of planning parties and pulling pranks. Frankie longs to join them, but her attempts to cajole information from Matthew and his friends all fail.

Determined to demonstrate she is at least as clever as her male peers, Frankie spies on and then infiltrates the secret society. Under her leadership, the group enjoys a resurgent popularity, but Frankie grows more frustrated. Alpha, the boy whose identity she has stolen, takes credit for her ingenuity, and none of the other boys, even her boyfriend Matthew, suspect her participation, no matter how many clues she drops. When the headmaster eventually pins blame for a prank on Alpha, only Frankie's confession saves him from expulsion, but her unmasking infuriates Matthew. Ostracized by the boys she has most hoped to impress, Frankie reconsiders her strategies and alliances.

Much Ado about Nothing by William Shakespeare

Following a successful military adventure, a prince named Don Pedro and his retinue arrive to rest and celebrate at the home of Leonato. Almost immediately romantic sparks begin to fly between men in the retinue and women in the household. The prince's young friend, Claudio, has his heart set on Leonato's daughter Hero. The prince's older friend, Benedict, admires the looks of Leonato's niece, Beatrice, but the two practice exchanging insults rather than compliments. Determined to see his men happy, Don Pedro devises plans to bring both couples together. Unbeknownst to Don Pedro, however, his jealous brother Don John designs his own plots to foil the romantic pairings.

Soon nearly all of the characters in the play are busy eavesdropping on each other and planting false rumors—some intended to foster romance and some intended to frustrate it. Dogberry, the head of the watch, is particularly inept at understanding what he hears or communicating what he has learned, which further tangles the flow of information. When one false rumor leads Claudio to abandon Hero at the altar, all the relationships appear to shatter. Beatrice is particularly infuriated that her gender prevents her from challenging the men who have betrayed Hero. A new series of tricks and a few convenient discoveries soon lead to the truth, however, and love triumphs.

BEFORE READING

Three Stages of Surveillance

Spy Networks

During the late 1500s, Queen Elizabeth sought to protect England from religious foes who wished to influence the official religion of the country and from political foes who aimed to conquer or at least diminish England's power. She employed men to write codes and to break them; she hired agents to forge documents and others to intercept and read letters sent to rivals (Alford, 2012, p. 19). Most of the records from the masterminds of these espionage offices are long gone, but it is no surprise that historians have discovered some links between spies and actors. The work of each profession overlaps; not only did people in these two professions travel and mingle more broadly than most people in the era but spies and actors are called upon to manage disguises and create convincing alternative personas. Christopher Marlowe, Shakespeare's chief rival in the theatre, is often purported to have been a spy as well as a playwright. Though the evidence for Marlowe's employment in the Elizabethan secret service is limited, there is no doubt that he kept company with other men who were spies, including Robert Poley, who was present during the bar brawl that resulted in Marlowe's early death (Alford, 2012). Shakespeare as well, although frequently the subject of all sorts of unsupported conspiracy theories, certainly associated with spies. One of Queen Elizabeth's spies, Anthony Monday, went on to become a playwright hailed for his plots and a collaborator with Shakespeare on the play *The Book of Sir Thomas More* (Alford, 2012, p. 316). The eavesdropping, rumor planting, and general air of plotting that saturate the atmosphere of *Much Ado* is an aspect of the culture in which Shakespeare wrote it.

Students can prepare for thinking about the history of spying, especially as related to Shakespeare's England in three ways. The instructor can assign just one of these tasks or ask different teams of students to take on different tasks and report back to the whole class.

1. Students prepare short oral reports (two to three minutes) on three Elizabethan figures associated with spying: Christopher Marlowe, William Cecil, and Frances Walsingham. A short, reliable web source for each is suggested below:

- Overview of Marlowe and his connections to spying—*The Irish Times*
- Overview of William Cecil, Lord Burghley—History Learning Site
- Overview of Francis Walsingham—British Heritage Travel

2. Watch one or more episodes of the PBS three-episode mini-series *Queen Elizabeth's Secret Agents* (2017).
3. Brainstorm all the ways theater compares to spying. Consider how actors prepare for their roles, the ways cast and crew work to perform a play, and the role of the audience. After pairs or teams of students fill out a graphic organizer (see figure 10.1), the entire class shares examples.

The Panopticon

Two hundred years after Queen Elizabeth's reign, the English philosopher Jeremy Bentham transformed the idea of surveillance through his invention of the panopticon. Bentham's panopticon was an architectural plan for a new sort of prison. Instead of the rows of windowless cells typical in a dungeon, he imagined a circular building shaped like a donut. Each prison cell in the round building would have a large window facing the center of the donut. A single guard in a tower in the middle of the building would be able to watch every cell and every prisoner at once. Even more importantly, Bentham hypothesized that if the guard tower had blinds or one-way windows, then the prisoners would never know whether there was a guard on duty observing them or not. Therefore, they would always

SPYING AND OBSERVATION IN THE THEATRE	Before writing, or performing, or attending a play	During the production	After the production
The playwright	--Watch people to see how they interact as models for characters		
The actors			-Remove costume and make-up
The technical crew		--Use lighting to obscure things the audience shouldn't see --Wear all black to hide from audience	
The audience	--Read the program to figure out the real identities of the actors		

Figure 10.1 Sample graphic organizer with a few answers provided as examples. *Author created.*

need to behave as if they were under surveillance. Instead of having privacy most of the time with occasional intervals of surveillance, those incarcerated in the panopticon would live as if they were watched most of the time and only rarely experience moments of privacy. By the mid-1970s, the French philosopher Michel Foucault argued that the adoption of aspects of the panopticon into the design of schools and hospitals as well as prisons had transformed society from a place where being spied on was an extraordinary condition to a normative one with significant conse-quences on the psychology and behavior of everyone. In *The Disreputable History*, Frankie realizes how deeply she has been impacted by panoptic habits when she stands on the widow's walk of the Founder's House with Alpha discussing the illusion of rebellion students feel when they stray off the sidewalks in violation of the "keep off the grass" signs while uncon-sciously following the more important rules of campus without even being reminded about them (pp. 206–209).

In order to better understand the ways panoptic architecture and surveil-lance systems impact behavior, instructors should first introduce the concept of the panopticon to students through a quick lecture and then ask them to analyze the physical design of their own school. Students might analyze the school building as a whole or look at smaller spaces in the school—the design of the entrance way, the library, the cafeteria, outdoor seating areas, or any other student-space specific to their school. To further emphasize the effect of panoptic surveillance, have students experiment with different seating arrangements. Begin class with desks or tables organized in rows with the instructor limited to a static position at the front of the room and point out the fact that not all students are equally surveilled. Part way through class, have students rearrange the classroom furniture so desks or tables face inward and the teacher works from the center (a panoptic arrangement that still gives students a lot of power as they can see each other). For the final section of class, have students reverse their seats so that their backs are to the teacher, who remains in the center of the room able to turn and watch any student without anyone knowing who is being surveilled (a reasonable facsimile of Bentham's panopticon). In this position, have students write reflections about how their experience of being monitored by the instructor changed with each seating arrangement and how each arrangement impacts their classroom behavior and experience.

Technology, Social Media, and the Twenty-First Century

Surveillance has again been revolutionized in the twenty-first century with the advent of social media and the technological tools that enable it. Many types of information that previously required significant effort to acquire are now available in seconds. Only a few years ago, a private detective might have needed several days to gather the names of a target's family members, investigate their employment history, discover details about their home, and collect a list of known associates. Now thirty minutes spent browsing a person's name on LinkedIn, perusing their friends on Facebook, zooming in on their home via Google Earth, and following them on Instagram or Twitter will reveal vast quantities of personal information at no cost.

Both governments and corporations employ sophisticated technologies to gather data about individuals via tracking devices built into cell phones and by following a person's web searches and purchasing patterns. Even more often, however, users of technology simply hand over the details of their lives in exchange for access to a special app, better deals on a retail site, or to participate in an amusing game. During Shakespeare's era, personal information was largely private and discovering details about another individual required a good deal of physical work following a target and asking questions, whereas today personal information is largely public and sustaining privacy requires going to significant lengths to protect confidential details and relying on old fashioned technologies, like paper records, that are difficult to hack. The power that comes from keeping secrets or exploiting them has remained important over the centuries, but the ways we do it has changed.

Today, some scholars refer to the information we leave behind us via technological tools as a digital footprint. A good detective can formulate a surprising number of inferences about an individual based on their ordinary physical footprint—the depth of the print can indicate a person's weight, the size can indicate gender, the style of shoe can indicate income level, unequal distribution of pressure in the print can indicate the speed of movement or even health conditions, bits of debris can suggest where the person traveled previously. Similarly, a digital footprint is the information left behind on technological devices or platforms—sometimes intentionally and sometimes through collection practices. To get a sense of how extensive individual digital footprints are today, students working in small teams or alone should fill out the Digital Footprint Questionnaire for one system of surveillance (see figure 10.2). Students might consider what information the school collects about them each day (include attendance tracking, ID cards, cafeteria payment systems, and surveillance cameras, among other strategies) or they could consider different functions that collect information on their phone, car, or personal computer. Comparing the work of each student or small group will reveal how thoroughly each person's activities during the course of a day can be tracked by anyone with access to each step in their digital footprint.

MAPPING A DIGITAL FOOTPRINT

System: School Cafeteria Payment Card

1. **What kind of information does this system collect (photos, text, videos, etc.)?** Lunch items purchased and their cost, for example: Pizza slice: $1.75, Carrots and hummus: $1.50, Orange juice: $1.00
2. **How often does this system get data about me?** Every school day
3. **Who contributes data about me (only me, my friends, family, authorities)?** Only me
4. **How long is this data stored?** To my surprise when I looked it up, I found it goes as far back as the account goes. So, for me, all the way back to 6th grade.
5. **Who has access to the stored data?** School officials, me, and my parents.
6. **Does the data reveal information about my health?** Yes. Looking at it closely, the nutritional quality of my diet is suggested, and it is easy to tell when I made a change two months ago and stopped eating pizza two-three times a week (which was because I started work outs for my spring sport).
7. **Does the data reveal information about my location?** Yes, it serves as a kind of attendance record and shows I was in the cafeteria eating lunch most days.
8. **Does the data reveal information about my appearance?** No, not directly.
9. **Does the data reveal information about who I am with?** I think it probably does. An administrator looking at all of the data in the system in the order it is recorded could tell that I come through the lunch line with the same set of people every day and could make reasonable assumptions about who my friends are.
10. **Does the data capture my conversations?** No.
11. **How can I limit or control what data is collected?** I can bring my lunch instead of buying it. I could use cash instead of the prepaid lunch account.
12. **How might the data collected be wrong or misleading?** About twice a month I buy something for a friend (or a friend buys my lunch).
13. **How might this data be employed to evaluate or make judgments about the user in ways the user never intended or did not overtly agree to?** Someone could look for patterns indicating eating disorders, nutritional problems, or unhealthy eating that might lead to diabetes or other health problems. If this information were made available to health insurers, it could affect my ability to get health insurance when I'm older. Coaches could use the information to see if I am following the healthy diets we've been told to eat during our season. My parents could tell that I buy fruit and vegetables a lot less often than I lead them to believe.
14. **Does this system invade the user's privacy?** Now, I think it does. I don't know how long the data is being saved or if it is protected, so even though someone knowing what I eat for lunch each day seems unimportant, I don't like the idea that there is a long term record that I cannot control.

Figure 10.2 **Sample digital footprint questionnaire with answers.** *Author created.*

DURING READING

Mapping Characters and Connections

Untangling the relationships among characters in a play is key to understanding Shakespeare. Creating maps that show familial and social links both helps acquaint students with the names of characters and helps them understand the motivations of their actions. As the class begins reading *Much Ado*, the instructor can direct students to the dramatis personae, or list of characters, and as a class create two quick maps: a map showing relationships among the characters in Leonato's household and the watch, and a map showing the relationships among the men in Don Pedro's party. While some relationships will be clear—Leonato's status should be higher than that of his brother Anthony, for example, other relationships might inspire discussion. Where should the Friar be placed? How does his kind of religious authority stand in comparison to that of the other characters in the household?

Much Ado, however, calls for an additional set of overlays to these maps, overlays that illustrate which characters spy on or provide misinformation to other characters. For example, in Act 1, a surveillance map might indicate who is involved in: Don Pedro's plan to present himself as Claudio and propose marriage to Hero (1.1), the conversation between Don Pedro and Claudio that is overheard by Anthony's servant (1.2), or Borachio's decision to eavesdrop on the conversation between Don Pedro and Claudio (1.3).

As the play unfolds, the list of characters engaged in spying, eavesdropping, or planting rumors will grow, and the connections among the plots will begin to tangle. What begins as a friendly information campaign waged between Don Pedro's retinue and Leonato's household soon splinters. Developing a graphic representation of the actions the characters take helps students track how the eavesdropping and espionage so rampant in the play gradually shifts alliances among the characters from the household to gender-based groupings, and eventually to romantically paired couples.

Charting Surveillance and Observation

Set in the fall of 2007, *The Disreputable History* does not include quite so much technologically based surveillance as current students might experience, but Frankie's course in Cities, Art, and Protest introduces her to new ideas about the ways planned environments, including her own high school campus, generate a panoptic effect (p. 54). For Frankie, the intriguing aspect of surveillance is not so much the kinds of data that Alabaster collects about her as it is the different ways she feels watched due to the range and variety of people who observe her. As the novel progresses, students can develop a chart of the people who are watching Frankie and what they are seeing or ignoring as well as what she observes about them (see figure 10.3). Analyzing the chart as it develops over time builds an understanding of the surveillance footprint (a less technological form of the digital footprint) Frankie leaves and the ways she interprets other people's footprints. As the book grows more complex, the chart may work best as a class or group project with each student assigned to follow and add details about one character.

One major difference between Lockhart's novel and Shakespeare's play is the way a reader's attention is focused through the limited, third-person omniscient narration of the novel and fractured by the lack of a consistent

Character and relationship to Frankie	What they notice about Frankie	What they overlook about Frankie	What Frankie notices about them	What Frankie overlooks about them	Where Frankie's information comes from
Ruth, mother	growing physical beauty (p. 12)	intellectual competence (p. 11)			visual observation
Franklin (or Senior), father	Gender (p. 18)	aspirations			listening to her parents in the car (p. 21)
Porter Welsch, former boyfriend	her eyes (p. 31); her interest in the Spy Club (p. 29)	her gawky appearance (p. 31)	his love of reading (p. 29-30)	his revulsion for his father (p. 31)	School functions, reading about his family in the newspaper (p. 30)

Figure 10.3 Sample chart for three characters from the opening chapters of the novel.
Author created.

viewpoint in the play. So, while one chart is adequate to understand how surveillance and observation is working in Lockhart's novel, Shakespeare's play needs to be charted through many characters to generate a complete picture. A deeper understanding of who is watching or watched by Hero, Beatrice, Claudio, Benedict, Don John, Don Pedro, Leonato, Borachio, Margaret, and Dogberry can be developed through constructing parallel charts. Working alone or in teams, students can be assigned to fill out a surveillance and observation chart of a single character for each Act (see figure 10.4). Class discussion of the charts will help everyone understand the complexities and competing interpretations that arise in the play from the many different perspectives and experiences of the various characters. Instructors can also ask students who have charted a female versus a male or a high-ranking character versus a low-ranking one to compare their work to enable better insights about the kinds of information and misinformation that circulate among gendered groups and class-based groups in the play.

Language and Codes

Both *Much Ado* and *The Disreputable History* feature characters who manipulate language to comic effect, but who can also be interpreted as playing with the social codes embedded in language. In Act 3 of *Much Ado*, audiences are introduced to Dogberry, the head of the watch. His job places him among the ordinary folk of Messina, but his elaborate diction and aspirational vocabulary reach toward the language used by aristocratic characters in the play. At the same time, Dogberry's insistence on performing his job in the most

CHARACTER: HERO	ACT 1.1	ACT 1.2	ACT 1.3
Who does this character spy on?	Hero has no lines; all she does is watch others.	She is not in this scene.	She is not in this scene.
What does this character learn from spying	No real spying.	She is not in this scene.	She is not in this scene.
What misinformation does this character gather through spying?	No real spying. She does observe others as they talk about Claudio and celebrate his successes in the recent war.	She is not in this scene.	She is not in this scene.
Who spies on this character?	Many people in Leonato's household watch Hero when news of Claudio's arrival is announced (lines 7-20)	Leonato and Anthony talk about Hero (lines 6-20,) but she is not present.	Borachio spies for Don John on people who talk about Hero.
What do they learn through spying	This depends on how the role is performed; they might learn she is excited that Claudio is coming, but it has to be performed wordlessly.	Claudio and Don Pedro are talking about marriage plans (lines 6-13)	Borachio reports to Don John that Don Pedro is arranging a marriage for Hero to Claudio (lines 49-52). Don John calls Hero a "March-chick" (lines 37-40).
What misinformation do they gather about this character thorough spying	They might think she doesn't like Claudio if she doesn't react much. Again, it depends on performance choices.	Leonato and Anthony think Don Pedro wants to marry Hero, but it is really Claudio who hopes to do so.	None. Borachio and Don Jon get accurate information.

Figure 10.4   Sample Surveillance Chart for Hero in Act 1. *Author created.*

literal way possible means he also mistakes the purpose of his assignments. Consequently, neither his own men nor those he reports to are ever exactly sure what he is trying to say or accomplish. These linguistic quirks lead to a kind of coded language that mystifies the other members of the watch and insults Leonato. A prime example of Dogberry's coded language and his failure to communicate important information occurs in 3.5 when he visits Leonato to report the men of the watch have overheard a plot aimed at Hero and captured some of the scoundrels involved in it. Frustrated by Dogberry's malapropisms, real words employed inappropriately, and rambling attempts at courtesy and self-promotion, Leonato sends him off to make his report elsewhere. The tension generated between Dogberry and his audiences highlights the way language use includes codes for class and social standing.

In order to clarify the difference between Dogberry's and Leonato's understanding of the scene, ask students working in small teams to rewrite the fifty-five lines of dialogue in 3.5. Some teams should rewrite it from Dogberry's point of view and others should be assigned to rewrite from Leonato's perspective. As an example, 3.5.8–11 appears below first as Shakespeare wrote it, and then as Dogberry perceives himself, and finally, as he is perceived by Leonato:

> **Original:** Dogberry: Good man Verges, sir, speaks a little off the matter. An old man, sir, and his wits are not so blunt as God help, I would desire they were. But, in faith, honest as the skin between his brows.

> **As Dogberry perceives himself:** Dogberry: Please excuse, Verges, sir. He doesn't know what he's saying. He's an old man and ignorant now that his mind is going. I wish he were sharp as a tack, like you and I are. I pray to God he were, because I'm a respectable and devout man, just like you are. But, he's an honest idiot, as you can tell by his face; I wouldn't keep him around otherwise. I'm sure you can see I'm as upstanding and reliable as you yourself.

> **As Leonato perceives Dogberry:** Dogberry: Please don't pay attention to the babbling old man. It's my turn to babble now. I'm the one who can tell you exactly what's happening. I'm in charge here! He isn't a helpful fellow, and since he isn't, direct your attention to me. He's as honest as a fool can be, but I'm the one with something to say worth listening to.

After students have finished rewriting the scene, have them perform their new versions—the one that "translates" Dogberry's coded language (i.e., Dogberry's perception of the exchange) and the one that showcases the way the coded language miscommunicates (i.e., Leonato's perception of the exchange).

Frankie also regularly employs coded language, though unlike Dogberry her wordplay is intentional. Throughout the book Frankie peppers her dialogue with neologisms, words she has invented herself. The first two examples of Frankie's verbal gymnastics occur in her opening letter to the headmaster, when she employs "pugn" and "dulge" (pp. 2–3). Frankie's theory of language, explained in the chapter "The Neglected Positive," plays with root words and prefixes to build three categories of new (or rarely used) words: neglected positives, imaginary neglected positives, and false neglected positives (pp. 107–115). Careful attention to Frankie's sentences demonstrates what she means, though, as with Dogberry, what is most important about her wordplay is how other people react to it.

After discussing the grammar rules Frankie explores and plays with in "The Neglected Positive" chapter, ask students to consider the following questions:

- How does Matthew react to Frankie's wordplay?
- What does Matthew's reaction reveal about him?

- How does Zada react to Frankie's wordplay (consider pp. 128–129)?
- How does Trish react to Frankie's wordplay (consider pp. 154–155)?
- Although the first chapter of the novel opens with Frankie's letter to the headmaster, it is actually one of the last statements she makes in the book. Why does she employ wordplay in the letter? What does it tell readers about Frankie and her future?
- What other examples of coded language do you see in the book? (Students might discuss the way the boys refer to Alpha's girlfriend as "the she-wolf" on pp. 72–73; refer to Starr as a DOD in the discussion on pp. 89–93, or call each other "dog" throughout the novel but especially on p. 339.) Why do the male characters have so many code words, but the only female character who uses language experimentally is Frankie?

The idea of a secret code hiding the meaning of a message from the uninitiated is a familiar concept, but what Dogberry and Frankie both highlight is the way violations of expected or regular language systems reveal hidden social codes. No matter how sophisticated his vocabulary may be, Dogberry will never be recognized as an equal by Leonato, and no matter how clever Frankie's word games might be, Matthew dismisses them in favor of correct usage. Leonato and Matthew enjoy the status quo because both are granted privilege—in one case due to class standing and in the other due to gender. Neither character sees a benefit in changing any of the rules—linguistic or social. Teaching students to read the subtle codes of each character's language and the sometimes even more subtle social codes revealed when conflicts over language use arise uncovers new meaning in both the play and the novel.

AFTER READING

Rivalry and Spying

The parallels between *Much Ado* and *The Disreputable History* include a pair of male characters who struggle to balance friendship and competition—Don Pedro and Don John in Shakespeare along with Matthew and Alpha in Lockhart. How does spying and dissimulation impact each relationship? To answer this question, divide the class into four teams—one for Don Pedro, Don John, Matthew, and Alpha. Ask each team to discuss and make notes that answer the following questions:

- How much spying does this character do?
- If they spy, who do they spy on?

- Which character in each pairing (Matthew/Alpha and Don Pedro/Don John) is more powerful? Why?
- How does the more powerful character use his power?
- How does the less powerful character struggle to gain power?
- How do the characters use or manipulate other people as part of their power struggle?
- How does your character betray his friend or brother?
- How does your character perceive himself to be betrayed?
- What information do they withhold from their best friend/brother?
- Does being a spy or being spied upon change your character by the end of the literary work?

After each team has spent about twenty minutes making notes on their character, including finding references to specific pages or lines in the novel or play, return to full class discussion so the groups can report out to each other and draw some conclusions about how spying and rivalry feed off of each other in these two works.

Investigations into Performance

Shakespeare's plays were obviously intended to be performed rather than read, and both the audio and visual components of each actor's performance communicates important elements of the story. Many instructors have discovered the value in employing drama-based pedagogies like those described by Banks (2013) to enhance student agency in creating textual meaning. For most modern students, however, formal education has emphasized reading literature rather than experiencing it as a kind of performance, but recently the surge in popularity of audiobooks and podcasts has made listening to stories newly appealing. Consequently, *The Disreputable History* and *Much Ado* can both be explored through performance—scenes from Shakespeare can be acted and scenes from Lockhart can be turned into a podcast. Putting the two pieces of literature into conversation with each other, however, invites students to wed interpretation and performance in a way that expands both experiences.

One activity for achieving this goal is to assign students to cast a production of *Much Ado* using the characters from *Disreputable History*. Students can discuss who each character in *The Disreputable History* would want to play. For example, would Frankie prefer the role of a strong woman who also achieves romantic success, like Beatrice, or would she prefer to be the one plotting romantic entanglements as Don Pedro does? Would Alpha be more likely to enjoy the comic limelight of Dogberry or the aggressive flirtation required of Borachio? Students can explain their choices verbally, in a written assignment, or even as imitation program notes. Additional products to augment this activity might include a poster advertising the production or a set design using Alabaster and its environs as the location for this modern-dress production.

Alternatively, students working alone or with partners can choose a pair of characters from these two works who share an issue or concern and write a dialogue between them about the issue. *What points would each one want to share? How might they sympathize, influence, or argue with each other?* Options could include discrimination against women as experienced by Beatrice and Frankie, disgruntled younger brothers as exemplified by Don John and Porter, patriarchal expectations as voiced by Leonato and Franklin, rejected girlfriends like Star and Hero, ambitious wingmen like Benedict and Alpha, romantic traditionalists like Claudio and Matthew, to name a few of the possibilities. Together each pair of students film, perform, or make an audio recording of their dialogue.

EXTENSION ACTIVITIES

Secret Societies and Secrets about Society

Beatrice and Frankie both find themselves frustrated by the loyalty their male counterparts express for a small group of men above all else. In Shakespeare's play, the loyalty among the men is justified as the camaraderie shared by a band of recently returned warriors. In Lockhart's novel, the members of the Loyal Order of the Basset Hounds see themselves as carrying on a long-standing school tradition shaped by a silly initiation ritual, a nearly uninterpretable oath, and an aspiration to sustain the legend of their presence on campus. Each group is deeply exclusive.

While the idea of powerful secret societies might seem more the stuff of conspiracy theories than a feature of the modern education system, following World War II they were considered a menace in many American high schools. School administrations worried that membership in an "oath-bound secret society" would prevent students from functioning as loyal or devoted members of the student body (Graeber, 1987, p. 415) and instead segregate them into class, racial, ethnic, or religious-based factions (p. 430). The problem was so endemic that by the early 1950s twenty-five states had laws regulating secret societies in public high schools (p. 413). Indeed, in *The Disreputable History*, after Frankie's activities expose the Basset Hounds, the more democratic Geek Club Conglomerate and the student government become "interested in discussing strategies for social change" at the school (p. 335).

At Alabaster, being male-identified is the primary qualification for membership in the Basset Hounds, but Lockhart hints occasionally at the ways Alpha's limited financial resources imperil his position in the group, and, unlike the rest of the boys, his real name, Alessandro Tesorieri, suggests his parents may have immigrated to the United States more recently than the rest of the boys in the society. And while Frankie's primary disqualification from consideration as a Basset is her gender, she is also aware that her Jewish heritage is uncommon at Alabaster and sometimes rubs up uncomfortably with its religious trappings, like mandatory meetings in the Chapel.

Today, overt laws against secret high school societies are uncommon, but the problems they were intended to address may or may not still exist. Instructors may begin applying the insights about exclusive societies garnered from *Much Ado* and *The Disreputable History* by asking students to evaluate how both school-sponsored programs and extra-curricular activities function in their experience. Students should begin by brainstorming a list of the organizations available at their school. These might include an honor society, a national afterschool organization like Key Club or Future Farmers of America (FFA), and organizations specific to their high school like a film club or group dedicated to fundraising for a local charity. Once a list has been developed, students should develop a list of questions that can be asked of each organization to better understand how it attracts or selects members. Students should be prompted to consider overt and covert barriers to entry as they formulate their questions. After a class-wide list of shared questions has been developed, students should be divided into groups, and each group should be assigned (or choose) one school organization to research. In order to make the assignment productive for the school, the instructor should emphasize the outcome of the project will be a small report that will be turned in to the teacher and shared with the faculty sponsor or student leaders of the organization in the hope of celebrating the inclusive practices organizations already have in place and encouraging more inclusive practices where they are absent.

Once each team in the class has an organization to research, they can proceed with the assignment below:

ASSIGNMENT: In small teams, research the membership opportunities of one school organization.

GOAL: Develop a deeper understanding of how organizations in the high school can work to welcome or exclude potential members.

PRODUCT: Produce a written report (approximately two to three pages) that includes six sections:
- official membership policies of the organization
- recent data about membership in the organization

- anecdotal evidence about finding and joining or being unable to join the organization
- a list of overt and covert barriers to membership
- acknowledgment of inclusive membership policies or practices
- recommendations to bring the membership policies and practices of the organization into better alignment with the mission of the school and promote greater inclusivity

AUDIENCE: Class members and the leaders of the teams being analyzed.

Suggested tasks for research teams:

- Request the formal membership policies of the organization being explored. These may be available online or through the organization's faculty sponsor or student leaders.
- Request data about the number of members in the organization over the past three years. If possible, sort the members into categories that seem important. These might be gender categories, age categories, bus rider versus private transportation students, racial categories, or others.
- Interview a faculty sponsor or school administrator about their perceptions and experiences with organization membership, outreach, and limitations.
- Interview student members of the organization about their perceptions and experiences with membership, outreach, and limitations.
- Gather to discuss the data collected and make decisions about what to include in the report.
- Assign each group member one or more sections of the report to write.
- Meet to assemble and revise the entire report as a group.
- Present the report to the class and send a copy to the organization's faculty sponsor or student leaders.

Film Adaptation and the Eye of the Camera

There are two dynamic film adaptations of *Much Ado about Nothing*. Branagh's 1993 adaptation of Shakespeare's play features lush Tuscan sets and period costumes along with a variety of young actors who went on to greater stardom, including Keanu Reeves, Denzel Washington, Emma Thompson, and Kate Beckinsale. Shakespearean film critic Sam Crowl lauds the "lushly cinematic" handling of this adaptation as well as the largely "sure and intelligent translation of Shakespeare's comic energies into film images and rhythms" (2007, p. 235). Joss Whedon offers a very different interpretation in his 2013 noir version shot in black and white amid the arrow hallways and tight enclosures of his own home. Dark and tense, film critic

Sheila O'Malley describes it as "one of the best films of the year" (2013). Choose one of these productions and analyze how the setting and camera work emphasize the theme of spying. Consider who is included in frames, who is excluded, and whose point of view a scene is shot from. Apply the ideas about panopticism explored in Lockhart's novel to reveal how the architecture of a building or garden is used to create or destroy privacy in each scene. If both film productions are available, choose one scene and compare the decisions each director makes as he adapts the play for film. One scene that works particularly well for this comparison is Claudio's "discovery" of Hero's infidelity (3.2.67–115).

Personal Rights and Modern Surveillance

Surveillance scholars are often critical of the way surveillance technologies are implemented without the full knowledge and consent of those being surveilled. They also argue that the way to prevent inappropriate surveillance is to put regulatory practices governing surveillance into place before new technologies are implemented. Given recent concerns about health due to the COVID-19 virus, it is easy to imagine new surveillance policies unlike anything we have ever seen before springing up. Already, some businesses and agencies both in the United States and abroad are experimenting with tracking apps on phones to make contact tracing fast and thorough, requesting customers provide a phone number so they can be reached immediately if it is discovered they have been exposed to the virus, taking the temperature of every client entering a business, and demanding employees be tested for antibodies or active infections before they return to work even if they seem healthy. The range of surveillance practices is sure to expand as scientists discover which are more effective in different situations and with different populations and with different cost parameters. Consequently, there is no better time than now to define what kinds of medical surveillance are acceptable—including in the high school.

In order to empower students to see themselves as members of a community who exert control over surveillance practices rather than members of a community who are merely objects of surveillance without agency or authority, challenge the class to coauthor a student bill of rights that outlines what expectations of privacy students can expect in their school, what kinds of data can be collected, what forms of data collection can be employed, who the data collected can be shared with, when the data must be expunged, and how students will have a voice or representation in the forums where decisions about school surveillance are made. Make a plan as a class to share this draft bill with other students, student government, the school administration, or even the local school board.

CONCLUSION

Systems of surveillance, forms of spying, and a wide variety of secrets are at play in both *Much Ado* and *The Disreputable History*. Some of the rumors and pranks that shape the texts are lighthearted or humorous, but others are more serious and exposing them reveals inequities and injustices. The first mention of secrets in *The Disreputable History* appears when Frankie recalls all the dinners she and her sister have sat through while her father and his friends reminisced about their exploits as Basset Hounds in high school but refused to answer any of the girls' questions. Yet, when Frankie suggests their secret society cannot be all that clandestine since the men so enjoy dropping hints about it, one of them explains to her, "Secrets are more powerful when people know you've got them . . . . You show them the tiniest edge of your secret, but the rest you keep under wraps" (p. 63). To put it another way, for these men, knowledge is power.

Yet, this formula, so inspiring to Frankie, turns out to be incomplete. Knowledge alone is not enough to win entry into exclusive circles—whether those circles are bounded by age, race, religion, or, in the case of Shakespeare and Lockhart's tales, gender. Just as Frankie is crushed by the discovery that learning even more about the history and traditions of the Bassets than the boys do themselves still fails to win her acceptance among them, Beatrice rages that her knowledge of the truth about Hero is meaningless since no one will listen. Claudio, she complains, is seen by all the world as valiant because he "tells a lie and swears it" but because she isn't a man, her words to the contrary carry no weight (4.1.315). As both these texts show, power is leveraged not just by collecting knowledge or deploying misinformation but also through the covert codes of language use and via traditions that privilege the status quo while throwing up barriers against the curious and the ambitious. Yet, while Frankie is never invited to become a Basset and Beatrice compromises her commitment to independence both, like many of the other characters in the two works who expose secret plots or disclose secret deeds, are rewarded not so much with power themselves but with a better understanding of the channels through which power flows. Students who follow the characters through these journeys—eavesdropping on the conversations among them and spying on their dreams—find secrets about their own world revealed as well.

REFERENCES

Alford, S. (2012). *The watchers: A secret history of the reign of Elizabeth I*. London: Allen Lane.

Banks, F. (2013). *Creative Shakespeare: The globe education guide to practical Shakespeare.* London: Bloomsbury.

Branagh, K. (Producer & Director). (1993). *Much ado about nothing* [Motion Picture]. BBC Films.

Crowl, S. (2007). The flamboyant realist: Kenneth Branagh. In Russell Jackson (Ed.), *The Cambridge companion to Shakespeare on film* (pp. 226–242). Cambridge: UP.

Durlacher, C., & Jones, J. (2017). *Elizabeth I's secret agents.* 72 Films.

Flanagan, V. (2014). *Technology and identity in young adult fiction: The posthuman subject.* London: Palgrave Macmillan.

Flynn, D. (2016, June 6). Christopher Marlowe: The Elizabeth James Bond. *The Irish Times.* https://www.irishtimes.com/culture/books/christopher-marlowe-the-eliza bethan-james-bond-1.2674323.

Freer, A. (2020, May 26). What you need to know about Francis Walsingham, Elizabethan spymaster. *British Heritage.* https://britishheritage.com/history/francis -walsingham-elizabethan-spymaster.

Graebner, W. (1987). Outlawing teenage populism: The campaign against secret societies in the American high school, 1900–1960. *The Journal of American History, 74*(2), 411–435.

Isaac, M. L. (2018). Surveillance as a topic of study in the work of E. Lockhart and Cory Doctorow. *Children's Literature in Education, 51*, 228–244.

Lockhart, E. (2008). *The disreputable history of Frankie Lockhart.* New York, NY: Hyperion Books.

Mallan, K. (2014). Everything you do: Young adult fiction and surveillance in an age of security. *International Research in Children's Literature, 7*(1), 1–17.

O'Malley, S. (2013, June 21). Much ado about nothing movie review (2013): Roger Ebert. Retrieved March 3, 2020, from https://www.rogerebert.com/reviews/much-ado-about-nothing-2013.

Shakespeare, W. (2018). *Much ado about nothing.* In S. Greenblatt (Ed.), *The Norton Shakespeare: Essential plays and sonnets* (3rd ed., pp. 337–404). New York, NY: W.W Norton & Company.

Trueman, C. N. (2015, March 17). William Cecil, Lord Burghley. The history learn ing site. https://www.historylearningsite.co.uk/tudor-england/william-cecil-lord -burghley/.

Whedon, J., K. Cole (Producers), & Whedon, J. (Director). (2013). *Much ado about nothing* [Motion Picture]. Bellwether Pictures.

Chapter 11

To Write or Not to Write—
That's the Question

Bryan Ripley Crandall

This chapter begins with the following assumptions: (1) readers are vaga-bonds in search of ideas to use in their own classrooms, (2) pairing young adult literature with William Shakespeare to reach desired written outcomes is an effective strategy, (3) stealing like an artist (Kleon, 2012) is not a crime, and (4) the best writing instruction recognizes youth literacies and community engagement as powerful (Haddix & Mardhani-Bayn, 2016). In short, good writing instruction improves student writing (Applebee & Langer, 2013) and should include an inquiry-stance, writers' notebooks, teacher mentorship, the use of effective models, peer collaboration, and proactive conferencing, especially when teaching in diverse, inclusive settings (Chandler-Olcott, 2019). Good writing teachers recognize that a majority of students are aware of social issues and arrive at our classrooms ready and able to communicate with multiple audiences. According to Sandra Murphy and Mary Ann Smith (2020), "It's not easy to grow up in their world, but it is a world made for doing" (p. 132) and writing helps them to accomplish this. To write is to be active, to be thought-provoking, to be explorative, and to be informative. For these reasons, it is important to teach students to have a writer's mindset as they read, and to offer writing assignments that are purposeful and authentic (Crandall, 2016).

The following suggestions are not exhaustive, but a taste of what is possible when instructors intentionally pair and teach Shakespearean texts with young adult literature to inspire written outcomes. These suggestions are written with core principles promoted by the National Writing Project (Eidmann-Aadahl, 2019; NWP & Nagin, 2013), especially that writing can and should be taught, not just assigned. Section one pairs *The Tragedy of Hamlet, Prince of Denmark* with Jason Reynold's *Long Way Down* (2017) as students write Op-Eds. The second section brings *As You Like It* in conversation with Nic

Stone's *Dear Martin* (2017) and Walter Dean Myer's "Tags" to encourage monologues and script writing. The third, and final section, shares ways poetry might be taught while Shakespeare's *The Tragedy of Romeo & Juliet* has an opportunity to dance with Kwame Alexander and Mary Rand Hess's *Solo* (2017).

WHAT DO THEY STAND FOR?

Writing Op-Ed with *The Tragedy of Hamlet, Prince of Denmark*, Jason Reynolds, and *Long Way Down*

This section promotes writing argumentatively with students as they read William Shakespeare's *Hamlet*, and uses the writing of Jason Reynolds to initiate conversations about taking a stance. Shakespeare's plays are full of characters who make choices and every choice has a consequence. Hamlet, however, offers a location where one's inability to act has consequences, too. Pairing and teaching *Hamlet* with Jason Reynold's *Long Way Down* (2017), as well as a commencement speech Reynolds delivered at Lesley University in 2018, offers a writing opportunity for young people to explore opinions, rhetorical skills, and logic, especially through modeling Op-Eds as a real-world writing genre.

Taking Arms against a Sea of Trouble

In 2012, the musical group *FUN* debuted the song "Some Nights," in which they sing, "But I still wake up, I still see your ghost. Oh Lord, I'm still not sure, what I stand for . . . What do I stand for? . . . Most nights, I don't know anymore" (Ruess, Dost, Antonoff, & Basker, 2012, Track 2). Standing up for one's convictions is at the heart of writing argumentatively. Hamlet's inability to act, though, is the crux of his character's flaws, faith, and mortality. In a soliloquy, the Prince of Denmark deliberates,

Ham. To be, or not to be, that is the question:
Whether 'tis nobler in the mind to suffer
The slings and arrows of outrageous fortune,
Or take arms against a sea of troubles,
And by opposing, end them. To die, to sleep—
No more, and by a sleep to say we end
The heart-ache and the thousand natural shocks
That flesh is heir to; 'tis a consummation
Devoutly to be wish'd. To die, to sleep—
To sleep, perchance to dream—ay, there's the rub,

For in that sleep of death what dreams may come,
When we have shuffled off this mortal coil,
Must give us pause; there's the respect
That makes calamity of so long life. (*Hamlet*, III.i.55)

In a search for what he stands for, Hamlet wrestles with life's meaning, his role in it, and whether or not existence is worth it at all. He is indecisive about a vengeance against King Claudius, his uncle who killed Hamlet's father and who married his mother. Hamlet's cynicism and apathy, "the earth a sterile promontory" (*Hamlet*, II.ii.299), keeps him from revenging his father's death. Why would he take arms against a sea of trouble?

For educators, putting decision-making onto students to act or not to act can be fruitful, especially when teaching effective argumentation in real-world forms such as speech-making and/or Op-Eds. Inspired by reading *Hamlet*, a teacher can ask students,

- Is Hamlet's quandary believable? What does life mean to you?
- Do you believe in an eye for an eye, and a tooth for a tooth? Why or why not?
- Could you take the life of another human being? In what circumstance?
- Are you an individual who acts on convictions? How do you make decisions?
- What is it you stand for? How do you know that you're right?

A next step is to find models of effective speeches and/or Op-Eds to use with students. Several newspapers have Op-Eds online (i.e., *New York Times*, *Washington Post*) and offer easy-to-navigate search bars so teachers can find timely, relevant opinion pieces to use as mentor texts. Many newspapers offer student opinion pieces, as well. As they read Op-Ed examples, students can be asked, "What is the purpose and intent of the writing? How does the writer make their argument? How do they defend their points?" Answers to these questions can help young writers to craft an Op-Ed of their own.

Jason Reynolds—A Commencement Speech and *Long Way Down*

On May 19, 2018, Jason Reynolds addressed a graduating class at Lesley University with a commencement speech worthy of classroom discussion. The ten-minute speech is entertaining, concise, and inspiring. In the tradition of the commencement-speech genre, too, he makes the argument, "Let's get to work." The fish tale he shares does something larger, though. He asks the graduating audience to be on the lookout for those "could use a feather or two" as he recollects Mr. Williams, a Global Studies teacher, who mandated one rule for their senior class pet, "We could not, under any circumstance, touch the fish." If disobeyed, students would be suspended. Students fed the fish regularly, until the day Mr. Williams grabbed it from its bowl and threw it to the floor. Their class fish flipped, flopped, and agonized to stay alive.

Reynolds's classmates, two girls, however, grabbed the fish and returned it to the bowl. They were sent out of the room and the class grew furious. As they departed, Mr. Williams announced, "Pick your heads up. You have no reason to hang them because you, in fact, did the right thing. But sometimes doing the right thing has consequences." In retrospect, Reynolds added, "As for the rest of us, we then had to sit through the remainder of the class, wallowing in our guilt, in our fear, shifting uncomfortably in our skin."

Similar to Hamlet, students in Mr. Williams's class faced an ethical location to act or not to act. The girls acted while the others, including Reynolds, did not. Years later, Jason Reynolds turned an inability to do what was right into a commencement speech—one speech that makes the argument to be on the lookout for anyone seeking an opportunity in this world.

A Long Way Down—Decisions Need to Be Made

Reynolds's young adult novels often depict characters who wrestle with ethical decisions. Similar to Shakespeare, Reynolds writes stories where characters make choices to act one way or the other, only to experience the consequences that come with such decisions. In *Long Way Down*, for instance, Reynolds poetically brings readers down seven floors on an elevator with William Holloman as he contemplates morality, vengeance, and history. Will must decide whether or not to seek repayment for his brother's death. Buck, Dani, Uncle Mark, Pop, Frick and Shawn, all ghosts who greet him, wonder if he will go through with it. Reynolds writes, "I stood alone / in the empty box, / face tight from dried tears / jeans soggy, / a loaded gun / still tucked in my waistband" (pp. 305–306). The ghosts call to William, wondering if he will join them. William Holloman needs to decide. Will he murder like they did? Will he repeat a similar history? Will he make some other choice?

Flooding the Room with Op-Eds

Long Way Down, the commencement speech, and *Hamlet* prompt the question teachers can ask students, "What do you stand for?" While exploring ethical and moral decisions with students as inspired by Hamlet, a commencement speech, and William Holloman, educators can also tap resources from local, national, and international newspapers and model how civic-minded individuals act upon their convictions. As noted, the *New York Times* makes numerous Op-Eds available for readers. These opinion pieces cover a vast number of controversies, topics, orientations, and arguments. In the student section online, educators can find opinion pieces on racial profiling, standardized tests, inspirational books, and even high school rituals such as proms—subjects relevant to the lives of young people.

Choosing good models. In collaboration with reading *Hamlet* and *Long Way Down*, teachers can introduce Op-Eds to students and work with them on characteristics of the genre. If the intention of an Op-Ed is to offer one's opinion logically in a short, concise piece for publication, then a teacher might opt for models most relevant to classroom discussions. If there is a debate to be had in the world—an ethical decision to be made—there is an Op-Ed written about it. For example, a quick search on the topic "guns" wielded over twenty-five Op-Eds in a three-month period. Similarly, a search for "vegetarianism" offered eight Op-Eds (including one written by Jonathan Safran Foer highlighted below).

Teachers should provide models for students to explore and guide them to name characteristics and styles each writer uses. After discussing, a teacher should note Op-Eds have,

- a title that lures readers in (e.g., The End of Meat Is Here),
- a tag-line offsetting the title (e.g., *If you care about the working poor, about racial justice, and about climate change, you have to stop eating animals*),
- a date (May 21, 2020),
- a rhetorical question or two (e.g., Is any relief more primitive than the one provided by comfort food?),
- ten to thirty paragraphs arguing an opinion—most paragraphs are short,
- researched arguments, facts, histories, and personal anecdotes,
- use of graphs, visuals, and statistics when appropriate, and
- an awareness of how others may think differently (with a brief address to them).

Reading several Op-Eds with students, and guiding them to name the parts, should prepare them to think about writing their opinion pieces.

Taking a Stance with Op-Eds. Arguments are ubiquitous and even this chapter makes one: pairing and teaching YA literature with Shakespeare can spur desirable written outcomes, especially when teachers provide models and allow choice for what students write. Scholars have long made the case for argumentation (Lunsford, Ruszkiewicz, & Walters, 2007), and Op-Eds move in a similar direction. They require opinion to be backed with logic, research, and reason.

Teachers can ask students: *What topics are important for you, your friends, and/or your family to discuss? What controversies do you witness in the world around you today? Which ones catch your attention? Why? What are your passions? Are their debates there? Do others feel the same way?* Students should choose a topic that is important to them (e.g., *gaming, school shootings, homelessness, animal rights, sports, part-time jobs, dating, fashion, heroism, movies, military*).

Assigning Op-Eds asks young people to make decisions on what they stand for. Hamlet needed to stand for vengeance or not to stand for vengeance. Reynolds and his classmates needed to stand for saving a fish or not saving a fish. William Holloman needed to decide to go with the ghosts or to stay behind. Op-Eds require young people to take a side on an issue important to them and, through writing, make an argument that defends what they stand for.

SCRIPT WRITING

As You Like It, *Dear Martin*, **and Walter Dean Myers's "Tags"**

This section promotes writing monologue and dialogue with students. For purposes here, *As You Like It* is paired and taught with Nic Stone's *Dear Martin* (2017) and "Tags," a script by Walter Dean Myers published in *Fresh Ink* (2018), an anthology of #WeNeedDiverseBooks writers. Critically analyzing mentor texts, reading as a writer, and stealing like an artist (Kleon, 2012) are ways to help students compose monologues and/or create short scripts.

Pairing Shakespearean Monologues

Although there are many monologues throughout Shakespeare's Folio, Jaques's words in *As You Like It* are highlighted for purposes of reading and writing monologues with students.

All the world's a stage,
And all the men and women merely players;
They have their exits and their entrances,
And one man in his time plays many parts,
His acts being seven ages. At first, the infant,
Mewling and puking in the nurse's arms.
Then the whining schoolboy, with his satchel
And shining morning face, creeping like snail
Unwillingly to school. And then the lover,
Sighing like furnace, with a woeful ballad

Made to his mistress' eyebrow. Then a soldier,
Full of strange oaths and bearded like the pard,
Jealous in honor, sudden and quick in quarrel,
Seeking the bubble reputation
Even in the cannon's mouth. And then the justice,
In fair round belly with good capon lined,
With eyes severe and beard of formal cut,
Full of wise saws and modern instances;
And so he plays his part. The sixth age shifts
Into the lean and slippered pantaloon,
With spectacles on nose and pouch on side;
His youthful hose, well saved, a world too wide
For his shrunk shank, and his big manly voice,
Turning again toward childish treble, pipes
And whistles in his sound. Last scene of all,
That ends this strange eventful history,
Is second childishness and mere oblivion,
Sans teeth, sans eyes, sans taste, sans everything. (*As You Like It*, II.vii.139–166)

The stage, like a classroom, is a metaphor for life. Young people arrive and depart with personalities and lived experiences full of dialogue, actions, internal monologues, and story lines. Jaques, however, captures the septennial essence of life in this monologue, including an infant's "mewling and puking" (p. 144), a schoolboy's "whining" (p. 145), a lover's "sighing" (p. 148), a "quick in quarrel" soldier (p. 149), a justice with "eyes severe" (p. 153), the pantaloon "turning again towards childish treble" (p. 163), and the old when they are young again, "Sans teeth, sans eyes, sans taste, sans everything" (p. 166). An initial question to ask of students is, "Do you agree with Jaques'? Are there more than the stages he names? less?" A follow-up question to ask is, "What makes humans human? Why do playwrights write?" Theater, after all, captures humanity at its best.

A monologue is a speech offered by a single character to express a collection of ideas or thoughts aloud to an audience. Sometimes a monologue is a soliloquy, which does not involve others, but is spoken as if a character is thinking out loud while alone. Teachers should begin by reading Jaques's monologue analytically with students, while asking

- What is the purpose of Jaques's speech?
- What are his seven stages of life?
- Why does Jaques speak such words to the Duke?
- What commentary does the monologue make on life?
- What humanity does the monologue present?

Modeling Monologue with Myers and Stone

Educators who pair and teach William Shakespeare with YA literature can ask students: *Where do we hear monologues in the real world? What do monologues accomplish? When do you talk to yourself the most? About what? What do you, or others, talk excessively about?*

Such questions prompt young people to think about monologues in their own lives. If harnessed intentionally, such talk can be a catalyst for great writing.

Walter Dean Myers's "Tags" (2018) is a short script that captures four young males spray-painting names onto buildings, marking themselves into the world, while they wrestle with their personal legacies. Each, however, is a ghost of who they once were. In one moment of the script D'Mario, explains his back story through a monologue to the other characters. "I was with my cousin Pedro and his little sister on his stoop," he explains. "We were just chilling. We were talking about this and that, you know, light stuff. Then a car pulls up" (p. 81). His internal thinking is explained externally as he contemplates the moment he lost his life. A guy jumps out of the car, pulls a hat over his face, and begins firing. D'Mario's monologue recollects this story while they are *tagging* their lives across the city landscape.

Similarly, in Nic Stone's *Dear Martin*, Justyce writes journal entries to Martin Luther King, Jr. that, when read out loud, serve as models of internal monologues. For example, in Justyce's January 19 entry, he writes, "You know. I don't get how you did it. Just being straight up. Every day I walk through the halls of that elitist-ass school. I feel like I don't belong there, and every time Jared or one of them opens their damn mouth, I'm reminded they agree" (p. 95). Justyce explains his frustrations with racial inequities in the United States. Letters like this in *Dear Justyce*, D'Mario's out-loud thinking with peers in "Tags," and Jaques's philosophy in *As You Like It* provide examples for how characters expand original thinking in monologue form. Reading the three together provides an opportunity to assign writing monologues to students.

Writing Monologues. Students should be given space to write, explore language, and imagine a world from their experiences, histories, and curiosities. To prompt this, ask students,

• Who is a character you know, and why might they talk at length?
• How do they talk? How do they act when speaking?
• What do they think about? Who do they speak to?
• What emotion do they express?
• What's a monologue you can write?

The intent is not only to read Shakespeare in relation to young adult novels, but to interrogate how language is used by both writers and within the numerous communities they inhabit. They should have opportunities to be writers, too.

Pairing and Teaching Dialogue. In *As You Like It*, Rosalind contemplates her admiration of Orlando with Celia, and discusses how she tricked her banished father, the Duke, when dressed as Ganymede. This scene, fifty-five lines long, is a good location to prompt students to discuss how dialogue works in plays.

Ros. Never talk to me, I will weep.
Cel. Do, I prithee, but yet have the grace to consider that tears do not become a
   man.
Ros. But have I not cause to weep?
Cel. As good cause as one would desire, therefore weep.
Ros. His very hair is of the dissembling color.
Cel. Something browner than Judas's. Marry, his kisses are Judas's own children.
Ros. I' faith, his hair is of good color.
Cel. An excellent color. Your chestnut was ever the only color.
Ros. And his kissing is a full of sanctity as the touch of holy bread. (III, iv, 1–14)

A teacher can ask: *What are the two young women talking about? Why? How does their exchange add to what we know about them? To the larger story? How do such conversations move a scene along?* The scene is a quick location to analyze how dialogue works with students and to get them thinking about writing their own scripts.

Modeling Dialogue in Myers and Stone. A script, in contrast to a monologue, is the dialogic interaction between two or more inventive characters that captures one moment in time (very much like the exchange between Rosalind and Celia). Ten-minute scripts, discussed here, are quick, deliberate stories delivered through conversation and human interaction (Dixon, 2001). Assigning students to write ten-minutes scripts during a Shakespeare unit is logical, as it helps them to read like playwrights, and to write like them, too.

While teaching script writing to students, have them pay attention to language use all around them—the styles, tones, purposes, pace, and theatrics—and to read plays with their own conversations in mind. For example, in *Dear Martin*, Chapter 3, Doc supervises Justyce, Manny, Jared, SJ, and others in a debate about the equality of all men—a scene very familiar to most classroom debates when students get heated. Manny wants to know why he's always getting pulled into racialized conversations and Jared responds, "Obviously because you're black, bro" (p. 28). The students argue from their varying viewpoints while the teacher, Doc, moderates so they don't get too out of hand. The conversation, written in script form in *Dear Martin*, is a vehicle for Nic Stone to develop characters, establish narrative pace, and to capture individual voices. Dialogue in Walter Dean Myers's "Tags" moves the story along in a similar way. Eddie asks, "First wall. Hey, man, you scared?" and Willie responds, "No, I ain't scared. You know some dudes just give up, but I ain't stopping, man. I got to hold on. How about you?" (p. 74). The boys recall advice they've heard from others about tagging. They want to be remembered.

Teachers can prompt students to think strategically about such dialogue as they read with students. Some questions for thinking strategically about dialogue that a teacher can pose are as follows:

• What are the characters speaking about?
• Where does the scene take place?
• How does what each character says help you to understand more about who they are?
• What stage directions, clues are given by the author, but also in what characters say?
• How do characters respond to what is being said?
• How does the dialogue create pace, and a sense of time?
• How does the dialogue of a particular scene add to the larger theme(s) of the story?

Indeed, if the world's a stage, then students in every school are players with their own experiences, storylines, and casts of character. Their worlds can become settings for them to craft monologues and ten-minutes scripts similar to the prose of the pro's.

Writing Scripts. After students look deeply at scenes from Shakespeare, *Dear Martin*, and "Tags" they can be assigned to write scripts themselves. Some play script writer advice includes the following:

• Focus on a snapshot—a moment in time.
• Have characters wrestle/maneuver with this moment (conflict).
• Draws on real language—people you hear every day.
• Ask "what if?" (use your imagination to explore options).
• Make a comment about life.
• Upset the balance in the moment—shake up the universe.
• Provide stage direction(s) when necessary.
• Have friends perform what is written (and edit accordingly).

The writing task requires students to see themselves as playwrights and novelists who capture dialogue in a scene of their own choosing. Such script writing, too, can be adapted to performance in real time and in digital spaces.

STUDENTS AS POETS

Going *Solo* with Kwame Alexander and Mary Rand Hess While Teaching *The Tragedy of Romeo & Juliet*

This last section is written to highlight a tradition with Shakespearean Sonnets and to model how a teacher can pair and teach young adult literature with *Romeo & Juliet* to assist students to compose poems on their own. Kwame Alexander and Mary Rand Hess's *Solo* (2017) is highlighted here, as it tells the story of Blade Morrison, a graduating senior, who sets out in search of the man he's supposed to be. On the way, he walks in the shadows of a rock star father, alongside a girlfriend who guides his way, and toward a mother he has never met. Teaching students to read like poets and to study poetic craft helps them to develop voice and creativity for themselves. Pairing *Solo* with *Romeo & Juliet* assists a teacher to offer a variety of poetic styles with discussion of language and style. Sonnets, conversational (two-voice) poems, "Title" poems, and "Track" poems are discussed with this pairing.

Pairing Shakespearean Sonnets

There are 154 sonnets in *The Riverside Shakespeare*, including #103:

Alack, what poverty my Muse brings forth,
That having such a scope to show her pride,
The argument all bare is of more worth
Than when it hath my added praise beside.
O, blame me not if I no more can write!
Look in your glass, and there appears a face
That overgoes my blunt invention quite,
Dulling my lines, and doing me disgrace.
Were it not sinful then, striving to mend,
To mar the subject that before was well?
For to no other pass my verses tend
Than of your graces and your gifts to tell;
And more, much more than in my verse can sit,
Your own glass shows you, when you look in it. (1768)

When students are introduced to traditional forms of poetry (Dacey & Jauss, 1986), it requires a teacher to introduce detective work. #103 is a melodious example of a poet's writer's block composed in true sonnet form: fourteen lines of iambic pentameter following a structured rhyme scheme that adheres to tight, thematic organization. Shakespeare's #103 demonstrates ten heartbeats true to form, and follows the abab/cdcd/efef/gg rules. At the same time, #103 exemplifies a poet's contemplation, if not frustration, for the writing process.

Poetry is often associated as an intimate and personal style of writing. Throughout history, individuals have been drawn to the genre in an attempt to capture the extremes of human emotions and the soul. This is true for "a pair of star-crossed lovers" (I, i, 6) in the opening sonnet of *The Tragedy of Romeo & Juliet*, as well as the flirtatious exchange between Romeo and Juliet when they first meet:

Rom. [To Juliet.] If I profane with my unworthiest hand
This holy shrine, the gentle sin is this.
My lips, two blushing pilgrims, ready stand
To sooth that rough touch with a tender kiss.
Jul. Good pilgrim, you do wrong your hand too much,
Which mannerly devotion shows in this.
For saints have hands that pilgrims' hands do touch,
and palm to palm is holy palmers' kiss.
Rom. Have not saints lips, and holy palmers, too?
Jul. Ay, pilgrim, lips that they must use in pray'r.
Rom. O, then, dear saint, let lips do what hands do,
They pray—grant thou, lest faith turn to despair.
Jul. Saints do not move, though grant for prayers' sake.
Rom. Then move not while my prayer's effect I take.
Jul. Then have my lips the sin that they have took.
Rom. Sin from my lips? O trespass sweetly urg'd. (I,v, 93–109).

Unique to the form here is the dialogic exchange between Romeo and Juliet. The abab/cdcd/efef/ gg rhythm flows between them in conversational form.

There are several steps a teacher should take during a Shakespearean unit, especially to have students write poetically themselves:

Step 1. Assign a sonnet.
Step 2. Have students deconstruct the sonnet for its form, its rhyme scheme, beats per line, and meaning. Discuss.
Step 3. Assign two or three more sonnets.
Step 4. Repeat Step 2.
Step 5. Have students write their own, but *don't stop there*. Explore a variety of poetic forms, and bring in many models, including those from young adult texts.
Step 6. Center language use, vocabulary, word choices, and style in the unit.

It is equally important for young people to read great literature in our classrooms and to be composers of great work for themselves, too. A Shakespeare unit can be an invitation for students to explore and write a wide variety of poetry, especially when paired and taught with novels written in verse such as Kwame Alexander and Mary Rand Hess's *Solo*.

Going *Solo* with Student Poets

Assigning young people to write poetry during an instructional unit assists them in seeing the richness, complexity, beauty, and magic of language. Introducing sonnet forms and following with an assignment for students to write their own is common practice. Beyond this first step, though, a teacher can tap the poetic talents of their students by finding other poetic models to share. There are an infinite number of poems and poetic novels to choose from. Here, however, three poetic styles are drawn from Alexander and Hess's *Solo* to highlight how educators can pair and teach YA literature in collaboration with Shakespeare plays.

Conversational (Two-Voice) Poems. One style of poetry found throughout *Solo* are the conversational, two-voice poems. Alexander and Hess use italics and non-italics to distinguish speakers who are in dialogue with one another, as with Blade and his tattoo artist. The conversation begins, *"Where do you want it? /* Right here, on my bicep" (p. 184), and the poem continues with the two of them discussing the font Blade wants for his girlfriend's name to be tattooed on his arm. The tattoo artist declares, *"Buck up, kid, it may sting a bit"* (p. 184). Such dialogic style (similar to Romeo and Juliet's sonnet) is a way Alexander and Hess move the narration in *Solo* along. As Blade prepares for an overseas trip to Africa in search of his biological mother, he reconciles his relationship with Chapel, the high school girlfriend, by having her name permanently marked on his skin. Teachers can find many of these poems throughout *Solo* that represent verbal exchanges between adolescents and their peers, and adolescents and the adults in their lives. Such talk works well with scenes throughout *The Tragedy of Romeo and Juliet* to discuss, as well as assign, poetic language.

Track Poems. Alexander and Hess also provide thirteen "Track poems" in *Solo* (2017), a style unique to them, where a particular song important to Blade's character is named, and then described in relation to his life. For example, "Track 11: With or Without You" introduces U2's album *The Joshua Tree*, including the label, the recording date, and the studio where it was made, before Blade reflects on the song and its meaning to his life. Blade writes, "A haunting, aching song / about the complex / tangle vines / that leave you / feeling twisted / and crazy" (p. 351). He uses the track as a metaphor between his father and him—a knotted relationship with Rutherford he fears will never loosen up. It is a clever style.

Students can be assigned to find a song they enjoy, to research where it was recorded, and to poetically express what the song means to them (perhaps a song Romeo and Juliet would dance to if they were teenagers today). Teachers should ask students, "What does the song mean? What does it mean to you? How might you use lyrics in a poetic fashion to offer commentary on your own life? How about writing like Alexander and Hess?"

Title Poems. A third style of poetry used in *Solo* (2017) are "Title" poems (pp. 10, 21, 23, 34, 43, 45, 56, 57, 59, etc.). In these, the title of the poem is also its first line. For example, when Blade sees his biological mother for the first time, Alexander and Hess write, "**My mother /** walks like / an angel, / literally" (p. 408). The poem continues with a description of the young girls who walk beside Blade's mom, the way Blade's mom is dressed, and how Blade's mom responds when she finally sees her son. "Title" poems are thin, offering a few words on each line. These define an item, a person, or a theme, and the title is always the introduction to the poem. Within the burglary of reading as writers, students can write "Title poems" on their own, as well. They simply need to choose a subject that matters to them, to use it as the title, and to make that title the first line of the poem.

Sonnets written by Shakespeare are an initial way to explore poetry. Pairing and teaching them with YA literature such as *Solo*, though, adds additional ways for young people to play with forms and language. Modeling a variety of styles helps young people to find a poetic voice of their own.

EXEUNT

Kara Peters, an English teacher and actress in Greenwich, Connecticut, says "Shakespeare unlocks the use of imagination, intellect, empathy and courage, and through language, students' ideas, responses, and feelings can be expressed and communicated, which carries the potential to challenge, to question, and to bring about positive change." Teachers who strategically pair Shakespeare's plays with young adult texts—themes, writing styles, and language—can help students to read as writers and steal like artists (Kleon, 2012) before they pick up the quill for themselves. A great way to create tomorrow's playwrights, poets, journalists, politicians, activists, scholars, and novelists is to unlock the imaginations of young writers through mentor texts and prose.

REFERENCES

Applebee, A. N., & Langer, J. (2013). *Writing instruction that works: Proven methods for middle and high school classrooms.* New York: Teachers College Press.

Chandler-Olcott, K. (2019). *A good fit for all kids: Collaborating to teaching writing in diverse, inclusive settings*. Boston: Harvard Education Press.

Crandall, B. R. (2016). Teaching as a writer - Assigning as a reader. In K. A. Munger (Ed.), *Steps to success: Crossing the bridge between literacy research and practice* (pp. 153–166). New York: OPEN SUNY Textbooks.

Dacey, P., & Jauss, D. (1986). *Strong measures: Contemporary American poetry in traditional form* (1st ed.). White Plains, NY: Pearson.

Dixon, M. B. (2001). *30 ten-minute plays from actors theatre of Louisville for 2 actors* (Vol. 1). Hanover, NH: Smith & Kraus.

Eidman-Aadahl, E. (2019). Getting better at getting better: Lessons from the National Writing Project. *Journal of Adolescent & Adult Literacy, 63*(3), 342–346.

Freire, P. (2005). *Teachers as cultural workers: Letters to those who dare to teach*. Cambridge, MA: Westview Press.

Haddix, M., & Mardhani-Bayn, A. (2016). The power of youth literacies and community engagement. In S. Greene, K. J. Burke, & M. K. McKenna (Eds.), *Youth voices, public spaces, and civic engagement*. New York, NY: Routledge.

Kleon, A. (2012). *Steal like an artist: 10 things nobody told you about being creative*. New York, NY: Workman Publishing Company.

Lunsford, A. A., Ruszkiewicz, J. J., & Walters, K. (2007). *Everything's an argument* (4th ed.). New York, NY: Bedford/St. Martin's Press.

Murphy, S., & Smith, M. A. (2020). *Writing to make and impact: Expanding the vision of writing in the secondary classroom*. New York: Teachers College Press & National Writing Project.

National Writing Project & Nagin, C. (2013). *Because writing matters; Improving student writing in our schools*. San Francisco, CA: Jossey-Bass.

The Riverside Shakespeare. (1974). New York, NY: Houghton-Mifflin Company.

Ruess, N., Dost, A., Antonoff, J., & Basker, J. (2012). Some nights. On *Some Nights*. CD. New York: Fueled by Ramen, Warner Music Group.

Index of Shakespeare and Young Adult Literature

Subject Index

OpEds, xii

panopticon, 156–57
podcasts, 146, 148, 165
poetry, xii, 14, 45, 63–64, 83, 100, 174,
    183–86
power, x, 2, 9–10, 15, 17, 21–32, 36–41,
    73, 77–78, 93–96, 116, 128, 153,
    155, 158, 165, 170
prison, 17, 65, 156–57

race, 7, 16–17, 57, 63–64, 70, 90–91,
    96–97, 100, 113, 170
revenge, x, 43–58, 61, 70, 77, 78, 108
rhetorical device, 23–24, 29–30, 34

script, 61–62, 65, 69–70, 141, 149, 178,
    180–82; script writing, 174, 178,
    180–82

secret society, 154, 166, 170
sexual identity, 136–41, 148–50
social justice, 88
speeches, 22–23, 34, 37–38, 40, 111, 175
spying, xi, 155–56, 160, 164–65,
    169–70
suicide prevention, 47
surveillance, xi, 153–62, 169–70

tragedy, 47, 52–53, 61, 71, 73, 104, 110,
    173–74, 183–85
trust, 68, 81

urban legends, xi, 121

war, 21, 25, 27, 28
writing, xii, 13, 30, 47–49, 53, 61–71,
    81, 90, 98, 107, 110, 113, 122, 149,
    163, 173–86

About the Editors

Victor Malo-Juvera is a former middle school teacher and is currently an associate professor of English education at the University of North Carolina Wilmington, where he teaches young adult literature and multicultural young adult literature, among other courses. He has coedited several books such as *Breaking the Taboo with Young Adult Literature, Critical Explorations of Young Adult Literature: Identifying and Critiquing the Canon*, and *Critical Approaches to Teaching the High School Novel: Reinterpreting Canonical Literature*. His scholarship has been published in journals such as *Research in the Teaching of English, Teachers College Record, English Journal, Teaching and Teacher Education, The ALAN Review, Journal of Language and Literacy Education*, and *Study and Scrutiny: Research on Young Adult Literature*. Victor is the chair of the NCTE English Language Arts Educators Commission on the Study and Teaching of Adolescent Literature and is on the board of the directors of the Assembly on Literature for Adolescents of NCTE as well as being on the editorial boards of *English Journal* and *Study and Scrutiny: Research on Young Adult Literature*. Furthermore, he has appeared on *NPR* and in the *New York Times*, discussing his research and teaching of the young adult novel *Speak* in relation to sexual assault and the #MeToo movement.

Paula Greathouse is an associate professor of secondary English education at Tennessee Tech University. She has coedited several books, including *Adolescent Literature as a Complement to the Content Areas* book series and *Queer Adolescent Literature as a Complement to the English Language Arts Curriculum*. Her research on adolescent literacy and young adult literature have been published in books and top-tier journals such as *Educational Action Research, Study and Scrutiny: Research on Young Adult Literature*,

The Clearing House, and *English Journal*. She was a secondary ELA and reading educator for sixteen years. She has received several teaching awards, including the National Council of Teachers of English (NCTE) Teacher of Excellence. She is an active member of the National Council of Teachers of English, International Literacy Association (ILA), and Association of Middle Level Education (AMLE), and is a state representative for the Assembly of Literature for Adolescents of NCTE (ALAN).

Brooke Eisenbach is an associate professor of middle and secondary education at Lesley University. She has coedited several books, including *Queer Adolescent Literature as a Complement to the English Language Arts Curriculum* and *The Online Classroom: Resources for Effective Middle Level Virtual Education*. Her research on middle-level education, virtual education, and young adult literature have been published in books and top-tier journals such as *Voices from the Middle, Research in Middle Level Education Online, The Clearing House*, and *English Journal*. She is a former middle-level English and YA literature teacher and virtual school teacher with over ten years of experience. She has received several teaching awards, including the National Council of Teachers of English (NCTE) Outstanding Middle Level Educator Award.

About the Contributors

Amy Connelly Banks taught junior high and high school English for five years and was a Gallo Grant recipient to attend the ALAN Convention as a young educator. She then pursued a master's degree in English from Brigham Young University (BYU) and studied Early Modern literature. Her thesis is entitled "Shakespeare's Leading Franciscan Friars: Contrasting Approaches to Pastoral Power." A recent graduate, she teaches ACT Preparation Courses for BYU, and she is writing a young adult novel adaptation of *Much Ado about Nothing.*

Laura Bolf-Beliveau, PhD, is a professor of English at the University of Central Oklahoma, where she teaches classes in Shakespeare, secondary methods, young adult literature, and first-year composition. She is a former high school teacher with over fifteen years of experience in urban, rural, and suburban districts. Her research focuses on diverse topics, including feminist readings of Stephen King's *IT*, emotions in education, post-structural analysis of young adult horror, and educational reforms critiqued in HBO's *The Wire.*

Sarah K. Burriss is a doctoral student in the Department of Teaching and Learning at Vanderbilt University in Nashville, Tennessee. Her research focuses on digital literacies, young adult literature, and teaching and learning about ethics and advanced computational technologies like artificial intelligence. Sarah is a former public librarian who worked in young adult services and popular materials in Charleston, South Carolina.

Bryan Ripley Crandall, PhD, is the director of the Connecticut Writing Project and an associate professor in the Graduate School of Education and Allied Professions at Fairfield University. He taught English in Louisville,

Kentucky, and now publishes on inclusive writing communities, young adult literature, and K–12 professional development. His work received a 2019 award from the Coalition of Community Writing, a 2018 Divergent Award for Excellence in 21st Century Literacies, and a 2017 Elizabeth M. Pfriem Civic Leadership Award. He serves on the board of directors of Hoops4Hope, an international nonprofit committed to improving the lives of youth through sports.

Chris Crowe, PhD, is a former high school English teacher and current professor of English at Brigham Young University, where he teaches courses in young adult literature, English education, and creative writing. A long-time member of ALAN, he has also served on its board of directors and as its president in 2001–2002. He has published books and articles about young adult literature, including *Presenting Mildred D. Taylor*, and has published fiction and nonfiction for young adult readers, including the novel *Mississippi Trial, 1955* and the nonfiction book *Getting Away with Murder: The True Story of the Emmett Till Case.*

Jennifer S. Dail, PhD, is a professor of English education at Kennesaw State University, where she works with graduate students in secondary English education and directs the Kennesaw Mountain Writing Project. Dail has published multiple articles and book chapters on young adult literature and technology. She also coedited *Toward a More Visual Literacy: Shifting the Paradigm with Digital Tools and Young Adult Literature* (Rowman & Littlefield, 2018) and *Young Adult Literature and the Digital World: Textual Engagement through Visual Literacy* (Rowman & Littlefield, 2018), both with Shelbie Witte and Steven Bickmore. Her most recent books, *Playing with Teaching: Considerations for Implementing Gaming Literacies in the Classroom* and *Studying Gaming Literacies: Theories to Inform Classroom Practice* (Brill Sense, 2020), were both coedited with Antero Garcia and Shelbie Witte.

Michelle B. Goodsite, MED, is a senior lecturer of English education at Kennesaw State University, where she works with undergraduate students in the secondary English education program. She also serves as the clinical practice coordinator and as the NCTE student affiliate adviser at the university.

Susan Groenke, PhD, is a professor of English education at the University of Tennessee, where she directs the English education master's program and the children's and young adult literature PhD program. Dr. Groenke also directs the Center for Children's and Young Adult Literature on the university campus. Dr. Groenke also serves as a senior editor of *The ALAN Review.*

Dr. Groenke's research interests center on adolescent reading motivation/ engagement and young adult literature. Dr. Groenke has published in *Review of Research in Education, English Education, English Journal,* and *Journal of Adolescent and Adult Literacy.*

Joseph P. Haughey, PhD, is an associate professor of English education at Northwest Missouri State University, where he teaches classes in literature and pedagogy, including courses in Shakespeare and young adult literature. His research interests include the historical analysis of Shakespeare's evolving role in American education, the use of graphic adaptations in the teaching of challenging and canonical texts, and general issues more broadly in critical literacy and rural education. He first read *Forgive Me, Leonard Peacock* shortly after its initial publication upon the recommendation of a student, loved it, and since has taught it in several of his classes.

Melanie Hundley, PhD, is a professor in the practice of English education at Vanderbilt University's Peabody College; her research examines how digital and multimodal composition informs the development of preservice teachers' writing pedagogy. Additionally, she explores the use of digital and social media in young adult literature. She teaches writing methods courses that focus on digital and multimodal composition and young adult literature courses that explore race, class, gender, and sexual identity in young adult texts. She has taught both middle and high school English language arts. She is currently the director of Undergraduate Studies for the Department of Teaching and Learning.

Megan Lynn Isaac, PhD, is a professor at Elon University, where she teaches classes in young adult literature, Shakespeare, surveillance in literature, and writing. Despite her professional interests, she almost never worries about other people's grammar nor spies on them. She does have a bad habit of hoarding university library books. She is currently balancing her new work on surveillance in young adult literature with her old habits of procrastination.

Matthew Kruger-Ross, PhD, is an assistant professor of educational technology in the Department of Educational Foundations and Policy Studies at WCUPA. He teaches undergraduate and graduate courses for in-service and preservice teachers on effectively integrating technologies into the classroom. Dr. Kruger-Ross's research interests include the philosophy of technology and its impact on educational practice, curriculum theory as it relates to teaching and being a teacher, and the intersection of philosophy of education and technology.

Jen McConnel, PhD, is an assistant professor of English education at Longwood University in Virginia. She is a former ELA teacher, and her research interests include academic writing, children's and young adult literature, and teacher professional development.

Lisa Scherff, PhD, teaches English and AP research at the Community School of Naples. She has published more than twenty-five peer-reviewed articles and coauthored/coedited seven books. An award-winning educator, she received the UA College of Education's Faculty Excellence Award (2008) and the American Library Association's Intellectual Freedom Award (2008), and was selected as Lee County Schools' Secondary English Teacher of the Year (2016).

Pauline Schmidt, PhD, is an associate professor of English education in the Department of English at WCUPA. She is also the director of the Pennsylvania Writing & Literature Project (PAWLP). Dr. Schmidt's teaching and research interests include the infusion of the arts in English education, diversifying the canon of literature for children and young adults, and the impact of new literacies on curriculum and teacher preparation. In 2020, Dr. Schmidt was awarded the Lindback Distinguished Teaching Award from WCUPA, recognizing her contributions to her students and the profession of teaching.

Made in the USA
Las Vegas, NV
08 April 2022

47085019R10118